Mason's hunger for Faith became all-encompassing when her eyes finally met his.

Faith stepped closer and, reaching out with a shaky hand, tentatively brushed his mouth with her fingers.

The effect, for Mason, was immediate. Every warring part of himself congealed with desire for her, pushing the urge to possess her, wrap himself in her, take from her all that she had to give.

Faith made no sound as she ran the tip of her finger across the points of his fangs. Tapping that fingertip, she winced. Then she held the finger up, at eye level, for him to see the drop of bright red blood pooling on it.

Mason's thirst engaged. Every one of her rasped breaths became his as he stared at the blood. He barred himself from reaching out to take what he wanted, shaking with restraint.

"Is this what you want?" she asked.

Books by Linda Thomas-Sundstrom

Harlequin Nocturne

Red Wolf #81
Wolf Trap #83
‡*Golden Vampire* #110
‡*Guardian of the Night* #137

*Wolf Moons
‡Vampire Moons

LINDA THOMAS-SUNDSTROM

author of contemporary and historical paranormal romance novels, writes for Harlequin Nocturne. She lives in the west, juggling teaching, writing, spending time with her family and caring for a big stretch of land. She swears she has a resident muse who sings so loudly she virtually funds the Post-it company. Eventually Linda hopes to get to all those ideas.

Visit Linda at her website, www.lindathomas-sundstrom.com, and the Nocturne Authors' website, www.nocturneauthors.com.

GUARDIAN
OF THE NIGHT

LINDA THOMAS-SUNDSTROM

TORONTO NEW YORK LONDON
AMSTERDAM PARIS SYDNEY HAMBURG
STOCKHOLM ATHENS TOKYO MILAN MADRID
PRAGUE WARSAW BUDAPEST AUCKLAND

Recycling programs
for this product may
not exist in your area.

ISBN-13: 978-0-373-88585-5

GUARDIAN OF THE NIGHT

Printed in U.S.A.

Dear Reader,

Vampires. Tall, dangerous, gloriously sexy immortals with enough worldly and otherworldly experience to knock your socks off. What's not to love?

To those of us addicted to that little kick of adrenaline a gorgeous immortal can provide I dedicate my Vampire Moons series. It includes an international quad of atypical vamps—who are loyal to a cause and to the women they desire.

When those qualities are mixed with the words *sexy* and *forever*...well, I'm hooked. Hopefully, you will be, too.

Vampire Moons, the series, goes like this: *Vampire Lover*—a Nocturne Bites ebook novella. *Golden Vampire*—dark full-book fare. *Night Born*—a Nocturne Bites ebook novella. *Guardian of the Night*—dark full-book fare.

And yes, I'm also a werewolf lover. So my sexy wolves always make unscheduled appearances.

Linda

www.lindathomas-sundstrom.com

To my family, those here and those gone,
who always believed I had a story to tell.

Chapter 1

Faith James wanted to fight what was happening. She wanted to shout expletives and punch somebody, but no one was in the car with her, and there was no time to stop and think about alternatives. She was a surgeon in a Miami hospital of merit, yet here in a remote corner of southern France she was out of her element, and feeling anxious.

Something felt *off*. And it wasn't just because she had left the last town of any notable size behind more than an hour ago. Her heart had been pounding for the past six miles of dusty one-lane roads. She had always been sensitive to feelings; almost supernaturally aware of things other people didn't perceive or care to acknowledge if they did. This gift was a boon in her work. A James family trait.

But jet lag tended to scramble everything up. Fear

didn't help any, either, or the fact that bad feelings didn't come with a guidebook.

More to the point, it had become quite evident that some James females didn't cope well with the supersize sensitivity of others. Her sister, Hope, for instance, instigator of this last-minute, nerve-racking trip to France.

"What the hell, Hope?" Faith muttered, driving too fast in the dark, taking an impossibly tight curve in a slide of gravel. "What made you leave that tour? What were you thinking?"

It was too dark to see the slip of paper lying on the passenger seat, but that was okay. She had memorized the name of the person the French police liaison recommended to help her find her sister. Mason LanVal lived out here, in the middle of nowhere, a recluse no doubt as crusty as this bumpy road.

It may have been well past the civilized hour for a house call to a person who didn't even have the courtesy to own a phone, but she couldn't have waited until morning to find LanVal. Her sister had been missing for seven days now. Way too long. She didn't want to imagine what that might mean, and kept her mind from going there by getting angry.

"Damn it, Hope. Where the hell are you?"

She swiped at the prickling sensation on the back of her neck, a subtle warning that at this time of night, in pitch-dark, with the forest canopy blocking out everything but the blue sweep of her headlights, she shouldn't have come here alone. Even for such a dire cause.

Her body was telling her this.

Vibrations surfed the bare, bronzed skin of her forearms. She wasn't breathing properly, couldn't get enough air. It was as if the trees used up all the oxygen they produced with none to spare, and every now and then she got a noseful of damp, alien greenery that nearly made her choke. Her knuckles ached from her tight grip on the steering wheel.

This place was everything Miami wasn't. Dark. Remote. Unfamiliar. Underpopulated. *Hell, that was an understatement,* she thought, since the area didn't seem to be populated at all.

"And it's too damned quiet!"

Other things lived here, of course, if people didn't. Not the kind of animals found on bustling Miami boulevards in fancy cars, but real animals. Furry creatures that kept darting out of the way of her tires, causing her heart to lurch. She felt that spike in her heart rate again now as her tires hit another pothole. Cursing, she glanced up and caught a glimpse of something large in the headlights that she had to pull the wheel hard to avoid.

The car swerved, missed traction, spun. Darkness swirled in a vortex of flashing lights, followed by a terrible screeching sound. Heat slammed into her. She missed a breath.

Reeling, Faith wrenched the door open and was out of the car and running, without regard for the steaming rental, its hood tight up against a tree, its lights flickering as if they barely had any life left. She ran blind, into the dark forest, her mind grappling with what she'd seen in the headlights.

Her sister.

She'd seen her. For real, this time, not just wishful thinking about a face in a crowd. Hope's face had flashed in the light in this godforsaken place. Dark hair. White features. It seemed impossible, absurd, a miracle. Everyone in this part of France was looking for Hope James, and Faith had just stumbled on her by accident?

What were the odds of that happening? Still, she knew every expression on Hope's young face. She had seen them all as she watched her little sister grow up. It was a shame her own promise to look out for her rebellious sibling hadn't turned out to be so easy. But right now, nothing else mattered except finding Hope and making sure she was safe.

"Stop!" Faith shouted through air that seemed thinner off the road where the surrounding blackness greedily enveloped her.

Maybe she was hyperventilating.

Gritting her teeth, she took in sharp, earthy smells, part vegetation, part animal, that ripped her further from her comfort zone. It was a damned forest, for God's sake, the type of place she'd spent a lifetime avoiding.

Raw nerves were overheating and starting to burn as her legs churned. She tripped, righted herself and sprinted on. The word *flashlight* came and went, unhelpful since she hadn't thought to pack one and probably wouldn't have remembered to grab it if she had.

White face. Dark hair...

Hope?

What was her sister doing here, anyway, so far from anything, and even farther from home? Why would Hope be out at night in a place like this, whatever the reason for her disappearance?

"Hope!" she shouted again, ignoring the sting of barreling through low-hanging branches, and the ache in her left hip where she had rammed up against the steering wheel upon impact. Adrenaline was fueling her run, a jolt better than ten cups of caffeine, a rush she needed to get this far.

But questions continued to plague her as her fear escalated to near scream level, like why her sister hadn't stopped when she'd shouted her name. Hope would have recognized the voice of the sister who had raised her, even if she hadn't liked her much lately.

None of this made sense. But then, very little about her sister's life had made much sense lately.

Faith pressed on, her eyes slowly adjusting to the dark, her mind looping back to the glimpse of impossibly white skin against a swirl of glossy black hair, attributes so opposite from her own blond, tanned appearance that their mother had once described the James sisters as "Night and Day." Different from the beginning.

Hope had once clung to her big sister for support and direction, Faith remembered longingly, until teenage rebellion and hanging with the wrong crowd had severed that bond. For some time now, Hope had resented her older sister's accomplishments. The fact that Faith had been so busy with medical school had made matters worse.

Night and Day.

"Damn it! Where are you?" Faith called, her muscles twitching with uncertainty, her fear of densely wooded places pummeling at her with an intensity only those kinds of innate fears had.

There! A flare of white on black ahead.

Another wave of nerve burn hit Faith dead on, tightening her jaw to the point of real strain. The burn, the fear and the impulse to scream were all physical warnings, big red flags. That white patch ahead seemed an unnatural glow under the trees, and nothing like the illumination of a moonbeam or a lantern. The light ahead didn't feel light at all. It felt oppressive.

Chills overcame the heat flushing Faith's skin, leaving her icy. As she backed off her pace, the trees seemed to press closer, squeezing the rest of the air out of her. On legs like lead, she slowed to a walk, concentrated harder.

Warnings. Red flags.

Had something been wrong with that image of her sister?

Two more steps…

Utter freaking silence.

Then, without warning, pain came crashing in. Vicious, searing, blinding pain that was acute, unimaginable, unbearable.

Faith cried out as she collapsed in distress. An ominous vertigo caught her up in a tailspin as she hit the ground with ringing sounds in both ears.

Jesus. Had she been shot?

The pain was…

Thoughts fled, overpowered by a sudden odor of blood drifting upward. Acrid, metallic, cloying.

No mistake. She smelled this same thing every day at the hospital. Only this was her blood.

God. Hang on. Think!

Panic never helped anyone.

Her leg. The pain was radiating upward from her right leg. Reaching out with shaky fingers, Faith found a thick band of steel cutting into her, several inches above her ankle, slicing all the way to the bone. She hadn't been shot. She'd stumbled into some kind of old, rusty trap, the kind hunters set out for wolves and bears.

Hell, did they even have bears in France?

The scent of blood grew stronger by the second,

flowing from a wound impossible to see clearly. The trap was like a vise, tearing into her with each frantic move she made to free herself. She'd been caught in a corroded, torturous device that civilized people in this day and age would protest as obscene cruelty to animals. Had someone forgotten about it? Left it here for years?

Desperate to stanch the flow of blood, Faith tore off her blouse. With the last of her frantic energy, she wrapped the silky fabric around her leg, as low down as she could reach, and tied the sleeves together to form a makeshift bandage. After that, even the horrors of how terrible this injury actually might be began to distance themselves. The act of breathing became a chore. Hissing at the thought of defeat with a flare of fiery anger, Faith looked up through eyes refusing to focus…to see someone standing over her.

Real person? Hallucination, due to blood loss?

"One too damned many," a deep, almost growling voice declared as Faith fought, with no luck, for the ability to ask this stranger for help.

Mason had scented the blood easily, as others soon would. Particles of it wafted in the close summer air, a heady draw to an unmistakable spot, no GPS tomfoolery necessary.

One of the traps set by the bloodsuckers had been tripped, and they were bound to know about it.

Inhaling deeply as he walked, processing the scent, Mason picked up his pace, determined to get there first, knowing this particular catch would send the monsters into a frenzy. Female blood was a vampire delicacy. This catch was young, her fragrance more like the first blush of a fine burgundy wine than the usual saturation of copper and aluminum. The brightness of her scent caused his muscles to ripple with apprehension and his legs to carry him faster along the darkened path.

There was something else, he decided as he walked. Her scent had an unusual component he identified as *similarity*. He had come into contact with a related scent recently, in the blood of another female caught out here too close to this night to be coincidence. But that other female had been human. This one wasn't. *Not quite.*

This female's flavor held an undercurrent that seasoned the air with the taste of pepper. Humans didn't have anything in them to resemble that, which meant that his nasty neighbors would have a field day if they were to get their hands on such a unique specimen. There was no doubt about what they would do to her, beyond the torture of catching her in their filthy trap in the first place.

A strange female.

She was alive, Mason knew. Though badly injured, he sensed a spark of life curling within her. He imagined he heard her heart's fluttering beat. It wasn't surprising for him to sense a flickering life force. Immortality equipped him with highly sensitive internal modifications. He perceived every animal and beast within a quarter-mile radius, every living thing with blood in their veins.

He had freed so many creatures, both two-legged and four, from the traps lately, making sure to complete his rounds each night. Too many people had disappeared from the area since his ghastly neighbors had taken up residence in the abandoned chateau next to his own estate. People in the towns were starting to notice. Soon the authorities would be nosing around.

This female was icing on the bloody cake. Missing women tended to whip the public into hysterics. Two missing tourists in a row, and…

Mason frowned, cutting the thought short.

The female's scent intensified suddenly, balling into a solid wall of gut-wrenching awareness that brought him to a halt. His skin blazed with a telling lick of fire that heralded the rise of a long tamped down thirst. His fangs extended with a sound like a sigh, as if the woman in the trap was an open invitation, and so much more than a task.

But he wasn't like *them*. He was no bloodthirsty monster, the bane of present-day civilization. He hadn't acted upon his cravings in all these centuries gone by, not since drinking his maker's blood in order to become what he was.

Guardian.

Temptation had no part in the boundaries that defined him. Blood-celibacy set him apart, and kept him apart. Yet…his fangs suddenly ached for a dip into dewy feminine flesh. For a sip of that fragrant blood-wine. Other body parts of him were rising to the wrong occasion, as well, excited, urging him to get to this woman, or whatever the hell she might be, with haste. His very soul seemed to react to the narcotic femininity perfuming the air.

Swallowing back his baser instincts, linking them to the crass reminder of how low his monstrous cousins, the blood spin-offs called *vampires,* had sunk, Mason started out again, way too attuned to what lay waiting.

All that blood in the air…close enough now to reach out and touch.

He found her just yards away, in a blood-drenched clearing. She was sitting down, rocking back and forth, doubled over at the waist with her hands scratching at the iron contraption holding her. There was blood on the trap and pooled on the ground. The great iron jaws had snapped her right shinbone, below the knee.

He felt her pain, hot and terrible and pulsing outward from her in waves. The atmosphere was thick with the stink of trauma. Yet this female didn't cry out.

Mason settled his gaze on her with interest, able to see details clearly in the dark, eyeing the massive trap and its destruction with the knowledge that any decent hunter stumbling upon this kind of damage would have put the injured animal down.

This was, of course, no animal.

"One too damned many," he said.

Too many casualties.

She didn't appear to have heard him. She was shaking violently with her head thrown back and her eyes half-closed with pain. Her frantic hands moved over the bands, searching for a release trigger, finding none. The trap was so heavy it couldn't have been dragged an inch, even if she hadn't been injured so badly. But she hadn't given up. Not yet.

She was a small specimen, slender, fair haired, golden skinned. She was missing her shirt. Her toned torso was bare, except for a band of blue lace spattered with crimson covering her breasts. Her wounded leg, also bare beneath her skirt, had been bloodied to the deep purple color signaling a serious wound.

Mason's chest began to thud as he stared at all that naked skin. Breathing in the humid air carrying the smell of her injury, he dug his teeth into his lower lip and kept them there, despite the razor-sharp points. Several more seconds flew by while an army of inner cautions sped along his nerve endings. But he knew he had to get this female away quickly, and that time was of the essence. She wouldn't last much longer.

Perhaps, though, he wanted to touch her too badly? Maybe the wish to find out whether or not her golden skin would be as silky as her hair was nothing more than a trap set for *him,* with the intent of his downfall. Already, staring at the female, his heart beat furiously. Thirst beckoned at the back of his throat.

"Did they send you?" he whispered to her.

If put here by the vampires as bait to catch a bigger creature, the lure had worked. This golden female with her strange scent was temptation itself. A grade-A test of his will.

Did he dare touch her? She was badly hurt, perhaps mortally injured, yet whatever else she might be, or whoever had trapped her here, at that moment she looked fragile, human and helpless. She looked up at him with green, pleading eyes. Her lips parted wordlessly, riveting his attention.

Mason dropped onto one knee beside her to search her ashen face. "If the monsters sent you, it's likely you didn't know about it," he said. "It's entirely possible you are innocent of their crimes. However, the danger remains grave."

The urge to rest his lips on hers and to soak up her feverish breaths came as a surprise. His fangs, fully stretched, ached damnably to find the source of her unusual perfume.

What was it about her that he found so enticing?

Dismissing forbidden impulses with a sharp head shake, Mason laid his hands on the iron bands cutting into her leg, silently cursing her, and himself, for wanting so badly, so suddenly and completely, something he hadn't cared about in decades.

*   *   *

Faith's insides heaved. Her stomach turned over. She was shaking convulsively and couldn't stop. The doctor had exchanged places with the patient in a fight with death, in a world blackened by pain.

She felt the heaviness of shock moving in, but sensed that the stranger, so far only an outlined, insubstantial shape, was going to help her. She felt the weight of his hands on the cruel metal and bit back a cry as the pressure tripled her agony.

"Your leg is broken," he said, his voice low and steady. "You have to be moved. When I open the trap, you're going to scream, because the pain will be nasty. Much greater than it already is."

Faith knew this and nodded. She also knew it was a miracle she hadn't screamed already.

"If you cry out, the things who set the trap will come all the quicker. They're already on their way," he warned.

Things? On their way?

Faith nodded again, realizing that her blood pressure had dropped to critical levels. She was losing too much blood, and understood that she didn't stand any chance at all if she stayed where she was.

"I'm going to give you something to bite on," he said. "So that you don't shriek."

Faith struggled to look up, thought she saw him removing his shirt. He dropped back down, pressed a wad of cloth to her lips and said, "Chew on this."

She obeyed without hesitation, opening her mouth, accepting the cloth, feeling that scream crawl its way up her windpipe.

"Are you ready?" he asked.

Nodding, Faith closed her eyes.

"How human are you, I wonder?" he said. "Bite. Now."

She bit down on the cloth and heard the screech of iron hinges being strained open. With the sound, a fresh round of pain hit in a relentless, consuming roll of blackness that defied the laws of nature...and spirited her away.

Chapter 2

"Hold on," the voice commanded.

Faith came to with a start, and willed her eyes to open. She was being moved. Each jarring step caused a new agony that kept the blackness hovering.

She was in the stranger's arms, being carried. One of his hands held the pieces of her leg together. She couldn't help his balance by wrapping an arm around his neck, fearing that any move might send her back into the inky blackness of unconsciousness. It was possible she was already inside that limbolike realm. As they left the blood stench behind, she kept hearing this man ask the nonsensical question, *"How human are you?"*

Her head rested against a taut, bare chest, cool against her cheek. Shudders rocked that chest, at odds with her own shudders. Male smells she was too ill to identify permeated the fabric still clenched between her teeth. She couldn't pry her jaws open long enough to ask what the hell was going on, not even to thank whoever this was. The simplest things were beyond her.

When they stopped abruptly, a more lethal version of pain seemed to rain down from the sky. Her head swam in darkness. Her body quaked.

"Damnation!" her rescuer swore.

She would have chosen a curse far more severe had she been able to speak; something to match the degree of suffering roiling through her. If, in fact, there was such a word for this agonizing pain.

The descending black net of haziness nipped her face with a bitter chill, scattering thought. She was cold on the outside, on fire beneath and unable to concentrate or stay in the moment until gasoline and hot metal fumes had the temporary effect of a sniff of smelling salts.

He had taken her back to her car, useless now as a mode of transportation. She was, she knew, royally screwed, if this guy didn't have a car of his own nearby. She needed a hospital, where she'd be given a transfusion to offset the blood loss. She needed drugs to manage the pain. Her heart was beating slower and slower. Her systems were closing down.

"Hospital," she muttered with a failed attempt to see the face above hers.

"Closest one is fifty kilometers," he said. "And it looks like we'd have to walk."

"Can't."

"No," he agreed. "You're in no shape for that."

Another physical spasm rocked him, and the pain accompanying her shift in position was outrageous. Groaning, Faith fought to hold on, stay awake. If she were to die, who would find her sister?

The man holding her spoke again in a strained voice. "They're coming."

He didn't say this like it was a good thing.

Mason tightened his grip on the woman in his arms, though having her pressed against him, skin to skin, was a torture equivalent to being stuck in the trap he'd pulled her from.

Her blood, a spreading wetness on his thigh where her leg had brushed his, was an unanticipated excitement for him, just as it was going to be for *them*. It seeped through his skin, tickling his insides, inciting a perverse kind of sensual riot.

Other things about her tugged at him, myriad sensations all at once. Her hair was as silky as he'd imagined, and draped over his biceps in a yellow cascade. She was beautiful, he saw now, her features elegant, with high cheekbones, a small nose and a full mouth. Her naked skin was sleek, sultry, streamlined. Although she'd been feverish when he lifted her from the dirt, her sun-kissed flesh was already beginning to cool.

She was slipping away.

The woman who had called this thirst into the present, from its long-hidden past, was fading. Her injury was severe, her car was trashed and he hadn't believed in the technology that could have helped them here. He didn't own an automobile or a cell phone. Hadn't felt the need. Nevertheless, he hadn't saved her so that she could be dessert for the creatures now creeping closer like a silent, deadly onslaught of the plague. *Not for them*—the monsters who were a mistake, their birth a slip of a fang from a source he'd long been searching for.

Mason glanced down at the female nestled against

him who by all rights shouldn't exist, either. Like vampires, she was some sort of combination of DNA building blocks never meant to be joined. She looked human, and spoke like one. Her blood was the same color as most of the mortals spread out across the globe. Yet she wasn't like those other mortals. Her scent hinted at Otherness, and that faint undercurrent of difference had drawn him to her.

The little blonde was much more than she seemed. Add half-crazed vampire blood from the monsters next door into whatever mixture ran through her veins, and who knew what might happen or be created in such a fragile golden casing?

All the more reason to get her away from here, Mason reasoned, ignoring his stiffening body parts that suggested he might want to save her for completely selfish reasons having nothing to do with the word *species,* and everything to do with *pleasure.* Her Otherworldly scent had reeled him in, all right, an unexpected circumstance since he hadn't been bothered by temptation for such a long time.

And actually, he hadn't held a female close to his body in all that time, fearing this very reaction.

Immortals weren't supposed to have needs.

As he listened to the rasps of the female's breathing, and the little groans rattling deep in her chest, Mason felt a whole new instinct kindle that went beyond the usual translation of his vow as a protector. He wanted to hold her. Liked holding her. She really was a tough little thing, but in the end, not quite tough enough. She needed looking after.

His stomach clenched with the sexist bend of that last thought. He shook his head, knowing where that sort of thinking could wind up.

"Not going to happen."

Ignoring her partial nakedness and the softness of her bare shoulder pressed against his chest, Mason snapped his fangs together angrily and peered out at the night. There were more important issues at hand than debating the possibilities of an improbable relationship. The approach of the others was like a hundred tiny spear points to his nerves that he couldn't shake off. The ground beneath his boots undulated, as if the soil itself wanted to flee from what was coming.

"We're going to have to run," he said to her.

Her response was one breathy sigh of protest that told him she knew how badly injured she was, and that she wasn't sure if she could make it. And that seemingly insignificant sigh, exhaled through her pale, parted lips, threatened to undo the bindings that kept him tied so tightly to his vow.

What are you? he silently asked, surprised to find his lips touching her hair—another unprecedented moral slippage that forced him to fixate on his dilemma. He couldn't afford to keep her, and he couldn't let her die. Getting her away quickly, and to someone who could help with her injury, was the only way to save her life, and let him get on with his.

There is another way.

He was surprised to have thought it, though. Because this other way meant giving her a drop of his blood, blood he had given up his own life for.

Giving her a single drop, in order to save her, might be condoned by the nature that conditioned him. However, that sort of gift might also mean he could lose everything, starting with the oath he had taken to protect the purity of the ancient blood in his veins…even if it meant another being would live for a while.

But live as what?

And what would he become if he gave that blood to her?

Just like the thing I've sought all this time? A monster maker?

A hideous thought. So, why had he even considered this a dilemma at all—whether to kill his vow, and the reason for his own survival, or kill *her* by allowing fate to take its course?

What was so special about this female, when the world was full of them?

She's not completely human, his conscience reminded him.

As such, what vow would I be breaking if I aided her just enough to give her a chance?

His conscience was at war with itself, delaying escape, while he remained cognizant of what was heading their way. Vampires were on the run. Vampires, a virulent form of hybrid. Creatures whose blood had become increasingly diluted with each generation the monsters themselves created.

Most vampires nowadays were entities that seemed to rejoice in torturing others, though it didn't have to be that way. For some reason, their insides and their minds had been twisted, as if they'd gone over to the dark side as easily as lemmings took to cliffs.

He had hunted many of them down over the centuries, exacting penance for the way they preyed on others, ending many a monstrous existence. This had become his quest, his task, the contemporary morphing of the sole purpose of the vow he had taken. Protecting the blood of the immortals was his reason for walking this earth, and it had become a daunting task by the time of the arrival of the twenty-first century.

He could have these vampires now, if he waited. He could take them down for the atrocities they'd committed upon the innocent people of this quiet countryside. End it.

However, if he took the time to do so now, here, he'd ensure the death of the beautiful creature curled up against him. Also, his presence would be known.

Where did his allegiances lie in this case? To death, or to life?

"Hurt." Only his ears could have picked up her whisper. The sound caressed him as wickedly as a velvet-tipped arrow, wringing from him a surge of empathy, and more than a little guilt.

He looked down warily to meet her glassy-eyed gaze.

"LanVal," she sputtered.

The reaction over hearing her speak his name manifested as a shock wave; a swift buildup of pressure inside his body that felt like he'd swallowed an internal storm system, thunder and all. Streaks of heat tore through him. A hot wind brushed over his soul.

"What is that name to you?" he asked.

"Hope," she said, desperately.

She hoped he'd save her. No, she meant something else. He saw this in her eyes.

Enlightenment struck when he remembered the familiarity of her scent. He glanced at the car, then back to her, realizing she'd come out here to seek his help. What other reason would have brought her so far from the city? How else could she have known his name?

It was a short leap from the acknowledgment of that to a guess as to what she wanted. The girl who had been freed from the traps the week before had to be her relative, as he'd surmised.

Someone else had supplied her with his name, along with directions on how to find him. That same person would know she came out here, and what she came in search of. They'd find her car eventually. If she went missing or turned up dead, these woods would no longer be safe for him. He'd have to move on, his work only partially completed. And the townspeople would pay for his absence with their blood.

The situation would have been laughable if it weren't so appallingly serious. *He* was the reason vampires in these parts hadn't stretched their fangs far enough to make an unmistakable presence on the towns. *He* was watchman, sleuth, judge, executioner, vampire hunter… working underground, with few knowing about it or patting him on the back.

He was one of the Seven, an immortal Blood Knight. He had drunk the blood of his maker, not from her vein, but from the chalice. The most holy Grail. If not exactly the best friend of mortals, he should be, since his quest had evolved into doing his part to keep humanity safe.

Now, it all came down to this. If he didn't handle himself properly in this situation, his own existence in these woods would be questioned. He couldn't afford for the authorities to look at him or the area too closely. He was tired of moving from place to place, from century to century, like a dark avenger.

Nor could he allow these vampires to find him. His existence lay beyond their capability to perceive him, if he so willed it, but he'd grown angry over their ghastly antics, and too long distracted tonight by the female in his arms.

Her scent would be a homing beacon for the bloodsuckers. The forest was already saturated with its ripeness. These neighboring vampires would find her wherever she was, wherever he took her, after this. She stood no chance of eluding them. Once they'd tagged a scent, they took on the aspect of ghoulish bloodhounds on the trail of a kill.

Unless he were to…

Mason glanced up, as if someone had spoken those words aloud. Although he knew they had actually come from some internal glimmer of an idea within himself, they still caught him unaware.

He couldn't go there. He didn't owe this female anything. He didn't know her, or what price saving her might exact. So far, the monsters remained ignorant of his presence, which meant that he could maintain his element of surprise when the time came to put an end to their grisly hunts.

But the idea of helping the female in his arms returned so persistently he couldn't avoid it; just as he couldn't stop himself from looking into her half-open green eyes. If he were to give her his blood, merely one drop, her scent would be masked by the superiority of his own altered genetics.

One drop.

Not nearly enough to influence the rest of what she might be. Possibly having no effect on whatever else swam in her veins, other than to help her make it to safety.

Then you will be out of my hands.

Mason's pulse raced as he watched her eyes drift closed, and as he felt the reluctant slide of her soul into the dark unknown. The pressure of the indecision building inside him beat insistently at his insides.

Did these physical sensations mean he didn't want her out of his hands?

Time was getting away from him while he stood

rooted in place. Danger approached. The fact of the matter was that he couldn't allow this wounded beauty to die, and couldn't let *them* have her. No matter how much he wanted to meet the vampires here in a final showdown for hurting her and others, the way his body, and perhaps even his own soul, responded to this strange woman was winning the day.

This woman, innocent, injured and now limp in his arms, had to live. He had to see that she did.

"You came here to find me, fair one?" he asked, knowing she was beyond hearing. "What a big mistake that turned out to be."

Bristling leaves over his head made Mason look there. The forest's rustling was an oddity since vampires moved as lightly as if their cursed feet never touched the earth.

His neighbors were beings neither in, nor completely removed from the normal scope of reality. They were animated evil, traveling through a phosphorous gray zone that ran between the two layers of existence. Not close with the life forms above them, and not ruled by death, below. True anomalies. Infringers. Trespassers.

Now was not the time to deal with them.

He could not play with this female's life.

"Later," Mason said, choosing the current vernacular for clipping more complex ideas into a single word, and uttering that word with the emphasis of a threat, a promise.

Lifting the wounded female higher, Mason dragged his lips across her cheek, her chin, then hesitated above her slightly open and bloodless mouth. Again, the thought struck that he might want this too much, and therefore might be manipulating his own actions. But he honestly couldn't see any other way out.

As the fires of forgotten lust burned away at him, he whispered to her, "I'm doing this for you."

It wasn't entirely a lie. He wasn't actually breaking his vow. He wasn't passing sacred blood to a human. Not a one hundred percent human, anyway. In any case, not nearly enough to matter much.

When he rested his mouth on hers lightly, his heart hammered. He was stunned to find her ragged breath so sweet.

Lust soared upward with a staggering swiftness, spreading through him with its fiery fingers, causing his muscles to seize. His fangs raked her bottom lip. A bead of her blood filled his mouth. *An accident...*

With a practiced tight hold on himself, Mason bit into his own lower lip, then punctured hers with his blood-tipped fang.

The strike sent him spiraling inward and off balance. The world went red with the rise of his thirst as her sultry sweetness spread through him, enticing, exacting, as if she'd been the donor here. And as if the soft, guttural sound she made in her unconscious state could mimic the effect of a silver chain wrapped around his soul.

It took all of his will and most of his strength to separate himself from her. Without waiting for hell to break loose or the sky to fall, Mason wheeled. Holding his golden-haired bundle close, he headed deeper into the woods, taking a route the bloodsuckers wouldn't dare to use.

There were other grudges against vampires, besides his own. Old grudges. He was counting on help from that arena now. He was going to call in a debt so that *she* might survive. And so that he might untangle himself from the womanlike creature who, in all her innocence, had inexplicably threatened the core principles of his existence.

"Hold on," he whispered with his lips pressed against hers, his speech massaging the puncture he'd made in order to speed the blood's effect.

He willed that drop of blood he'd placed inside of her to obey his command and save her...while the flare of his raging thirst tinted the starless night crimson.

Chapter 3

A lightning strike to the heart yanked Faith upward. She gasped as if she'd been jump-started. Her muscles again convulsed as the sizzling heat of that strike spread through her chest.

Had she made it to a hospital? Was someone using the paddles?

The feeling became one of plunging into an inferno, of being burned alive from the inside out. White light passed behind her eyes, then burst into a flame of brilliant color that further seared the air. It seemed to her as if this last small intake of oxygen might stand between life and oblivion.

But she was able to take another breath—a shuddering, unsubstantial one, like that of a newborn baby's first attempt at breathing through its nose. She continued to shake uncontrollably while her guts writhed.

There was blood in her mouth.

And pain…

Pain that crashed her system and shackled her to its breast. She knew she had to bear this round of pain if she wanted to live. She had to come to her senses. She had to open her eyes.

Attempting a third inhalation, she rocked with a series of internal explosions as her heart struggled desperately to find a rhythm in a world that had otherwise gone quiet. Her awareness prickled, a warning, in spite of her sorry state, of a vibration in the air that made her skin crawl.

Open your eyes. You must open your eyes.

She forced them open.

"Welcome back," said a gritty voice.

Back?

She was moving again. The surroundings flew by in a blur, no longer pitch-black, but bleached to a dim, dull gray. Hazy outlines came and went, nothing clear. She had no sense of her own motion because she was still being carried, smoothly, effortlessly, over the tricky terrain she'd earlier tried to traverse on her own.

She was still in the arms of the stranger.

"They don't often come this way," he said solemnly. "That doesn't mean they won't try."

The word *they* resonated in Faith's psyche like the buzz of a neon sign. Anxiousness returned, revving her fear levels, jangling already overwrought nerves. Bits of memory danced in her mind like dust motes caught in strobe lights.

Night. Car. Running. Blood. Man.

Hurt.

She had been injured, then rescued from certain death. She was alive, but something else was in play.

Were they being chased? Who would be out here in

the middle of nowhere? Who was this man trying to keep her away from?

Frightened, and with her insides churning, Faith dived inward, past the searing heat, to locate the persistent uneasiness in her limbs. Going deeper, thinking harder, she heard the echo of the sound of her bones snapping in the jaws of an iron trap.

"I promise," this stranger said, his voice yet another tendril of the swirling grayness coating everything, his wide chest amplifying the sound, "that you won't die on my watch."

Inside the darkened pit where she wallowed, Faith felt a storm brewing that triggered another spark of discomfort. She rode its current, so like that of wayward electricity, carried along until equally quickly and almost as startling, the pain flattened out. Her inner turmoil quieted.

It was possible that her perceptions had been shaken up by the accident. It was also possible that she wasn't going to die. But none of this seemed real, or right. After an accident like the one she'd had, she shouldn't be able to open her eyes.

She tried to focus on the face above her, thinking she saw a curtain of black hair outlining a stern, chiseled face. She couldn't make out more details in the darkness; she shouldn't have been able to see as much as she did. Was he old? Young? Would the intensity of his tone be mirrored in his eyes? He had to be exceptionally strong in order to carry her like this. He wasn't even breathing hard. Energy radiated from him in a continuous surge.

The displaced air from his pace was a brief comfort on her cheeks. She was so damned hot inside. Burning up. Another bad sign, and the possibility of infection already settling in.

Fearful of closing her eyes, now that she'd gotten them open, Faith knew that was the only way to glean more information. Closing off her sight would open her up to alternate pathways of perception. She needed insight, answers. When even one of the five senses was taken off-line, the others kicked into overdrive. Beyond those five, there were a whole host of others she was familiar with. An inherited gift from her mother. A precious legacy.

Blinking the surroundings out, she floated on the rawness of pure feeling. Another lick of fire flashed over her as her awareness touched the man whose bare skin met with her own.

She felt a charge, the impact of a powerful male vibration that was very complex, with no easy diagnosis. The man's aura was as dark as the night, and silent. Silky, yet substantial. Not exactly wild, but different. Unrecognizable. Like nothing she had ever come across.

Her inability to read him produced a deep-seated frisson of surprise, yet his presence was a cool spot in a world of fire, a quiet place in the tumble of inner and outer chaos. Against her inflamed cheek, the coolness of his bare chest, like the passing breeze, was a blessing.

She curled her awareness around him, seeking firmer hold, finding a gap. He was thinking about her. He was taking stock, assessing, searching. For what? Was he afraid she would die, in spite of his assurances to the contrary? Maybe that trap had been located on his property, and his concern was about in-

surance and lawsuits. If so, where would he take her?
Toward help, or…

Her attention was fractured by something in the distance. Veering toward whatever it was, Faith found another frightening anomaly: an image of the strangely
silent approach of advancing shadows, of things giving
chase that couldn't be shaken off. Shapeless shadows.
Creeping black holes issuing voiceless, ceaseless
shouts. Horrible things with human outlines were on
their trail not far behind.

Something else nagged at her.

Something equally insane.

The air virtually pulsed with *hunger*. The compo-
nents of a deep, greedy appetite spread through the
forest like the wildfire that had already caught her up;
a discovery that affected her like a jab to her stomach,
sickening her further, bringing up bile. Whatever blood
that remained in her body coiled within her as if seeking refuge, as if hiding from whatever these approaching entities might be.

While that same pulsing hunger, she now saw, resonated in the churning limbs of the man in whose arms
she rested.

Hunger. Outrageous, unrelenting, easily contagious, because Faith suddenly hungered for life, and
for the stamina to continue breathing. She longed to
be as strong as the man carrying her so effortlessly.
Through the heat and the pain, and although her own
hunger seemed minuscule compared to this man's, she
felt a vicious need to be running beside him, on her
own two feet, outdistancing the fever so that she could
find her sister.

Another whip of electricity stung her with that
thought of Hope, snapping her head upright. The man

was watching her as he slowed to a walk. There was more to discover in his gaze, but that discovery was camouflaged by a startling sense of connection to him.

With his cool, smooth skin against hers, Faith felt tethered to this stranger, as if bound by an invisible rope. No doubt this sensation was merely the inexplicable bond that sometimes formed between a terribly injured patient and their rescuer. Between a doctor and a pain-threatened patient. What else could it be?

More awareness flooded in, now that the gateway of her senses had opened.

There was no smell of sweat on his naked skin, or slick film of moisture from his exertion. His chest didn't rise and fall in any recognizable pattern. He wasn't winded.

This wasn't normal, her mind warned.

He wasn't normal.

The shadows giving chase aren't, either.

When she cried out, the sound made the man halt. But his muscles continued to rumble and twitch as if the hesitation proved a chore for one who moved so effortlessly.

Leaning his head down, he spoke very close to her ear. "It's best not to think of them, or of what has happened. Close your mind."

Through the haze of grayness, Faith watched his lips form those words and thought she remembered his mouth touching hers. There had been a pinch of pain.

"Tamp the pain down," he directed. "We must move on."

Pain. Yes. He had to know how badly she'd been hurt. He held her broken bones in his hand. And he hadn't actually read her mind, because that was impossible. He had just presumed to know what she might be thinking after such an awful accident, and he happened to be right.

It was probable she was delirious, and that her delusions had invented the longings, desires and whispers related to this man, as well as any thought of his lips on hers. Outside of CPR, there would have been no reason for such a thing.

God. Trepidation riddled her thoughts. *Is there a chance I died, and the strange ideas are my soul's attempt to tie up loose ends?*

Is the electricity in his touch nothing more than my mind's residue sifting through events, striving to make sense of a senseless incident?

But if that were the case, and she had died, or was in the final stages of dying, would she long to run her hands over each expansion of the muscles of this man's broad chest? Long to touch her tongue to those incredibly taut striations? Those longings felt real. *He* felt real, and completely unlike some final random brain malfunction.

Another burst of memory hit her.

A flash of white in the dark.

She had seen her sister in the headlights and had given chase. A stupid action, in hindsight. Nevertheless, she felt in her bones, even now, that her sister was out here somewhere. Hope might also be in danger, hurt, caught in a trap.

Hope. I'm sorry!

"Help…me," she panted, desperate for the man carrying her to understand that if he took her far away, or if she lost her life, her younger sister might be lost, as well.

So, if this man could actually read minds, or see the stress in her face…

If he had any sense at all, special or otherwise…
Surely he'd hear this.
Please help me!
Had he heard? His answer came to her as another whisper of warning, with the inflection of an oath.
"It's too late," he said. "Let her go."

Mason knew he had to set the female down, get her away from him, and quickly.
He knew the exact moment her blood chemistry changed.
The drop of himself he had given her was working its terrible magic, just as he'd willed it to. Because of his actions, every cell in his body surged toward her like stray shards of metal to a magnetic source. His muscles were a rumbling mass of need for her, and worse now that she smelled something like him.
He had never been close to a blooded female. None of the Seven, the original immortals, had breasts. Vampire vixens were a disgusting concoction of diluted viruses that produced a toxic fragrance. Human women had to be shunned because of their innate fragility.
It has been a very long time.
So long, in fact, since he had been attracted to a female and done anything about it, that he hadn't been fully prepared, hadn't foreseen the possibility of the swiftness of this reaction, or that his heart could beat loudly enough for the man in the moon to hear.
Man in the moon, indeed. Seems he wasn't far off the mark there.
The air around Mason stirred uncomfortably, as if something silent had slipped through an invisible door. He looked to the shadows, knowing that he and his precious cargo were no longer alone. The help he'd been

seeking, its form humanlike without the full moon necessary to illicit physical changes, appeared on the path, looking dangerous even without the fur.

"Out for a stroll, LanVal?" the tall, lithe, silver-haired Lycanthrope said in a voice like hammered gravel. "Hell of a night for a blood bath."

"I have a present for you." Mason carefully eyed the Were. Werewolves were longtime enemies of vampires, but this one seemed to know the difference between a true immortal and the bloodsucking masses.

"A present. Is that so?" the Were said. "I thought it was the other way around, and I owed you."

"This one's on me."

The Were cocked his head, as most wolves did when tuning in to a scent. "I can smell her from here."

"So can they," Mason said.

"Will they be as confused as I am?"

"If she's lucky."

The rangy Were stood in a splayed-legged stance with his arms loose at his sides—the epitome of supernatural health. Dressed in jeans and the kind of plaid shirt preferred by the French locals, no one in their right mind could have failed to perceive the threat of the corded musculature beneath that clothing, or the flash of Otherworldliness in the Were's green eyes when he lifted his face, inhaled and said, "They're close."

Mason nodded. "She'd be a treat."

The Were pointed at the female's broken leg. "Another trap?"

"Damn things are set again the minute we take one down."

The Were's shoulder-length hair, much like the color of moonlight itself, fell to cover half of his face, a look exemplifying the term *feral*. Yet werewolves, out of necessity, knew a lot about healing.

"How is the arm?" Mason asked.

The Were opened and closed the fingers of his left hand, as if testing their function. "Good as new," he said.

Mason nodded, waited.

"You want me to take her," the Were guessed.

"She's badly hurt."

"She's also unusual."

"Like I said, a treat."

"So, you'd deliver her to her own kind," the Were noted. "I suppose we'll owe you double for that."

Mason shrugged off the rightness of the Were's suggestion about the female being one of the Were's kind, though it struck him like a slap in the face. This was the source of her uniqueness, then. She had wolf in her somewhere, though she didn't present as anything remotely close to this silver-haired Lycan that he'd once helped out of a jam.

Perhaps the wolf gene was tucked down deep inside her, too deep for the moon to pull free. Not so hidden, though, that one of her own kind couldn't recognize it.

Shocking news.

A personal setback.

"I'll take her." The Were took a step forward.

Mason shook his head. "*I'll* take her. You lead the way."

The Were grinned threateningly, with a show of teeth that Mason had seen tear into vampire flesh with the full moon's blessing. But this Were was also a man most of the time, with a name. Andre.

If this wounded female was part wolf, she would be safe, even with no outward show of Lycan heritage. The night of Andre's curse was a few days away, so Andre would have the time to help her. His pack wouldn't have gathered yet.

This particular silver-pelted werewolf had helped Mason dismantle the traps on numerous occasions, freeing many of Andre's own kind. Pulling Andre himself from a particularly nasty bit of iron had sealed the truce between them. Although Andre wasn't a friend, and never would be, they shared a kind of acceptable mutual respect.

And they both hated vampires.

"Ah. It's like that, is it? You'll take her?" Andre said, eyeing the female before lifting his eyes to meet Mason's. "Perhaps you're not aware of the facts."

"I don't know what you're talking about," Mason said.

"I can see that, though I have to wonder what it is you've done to mask what she is."

"I've done what needed to be done to guarantee she wouldn't fall into the wrong hands."

"At some cost to yourself?"

"Little enough cost, if it works."

The Were nodded his head slowly. "I'm honored by your trust, LanVal. Still, if you take her to where we're going, you'll know how to find her again."

"I'd know anyway." *That drop of my blood in her veins calls and entices. I feel it now.*

"Thought as much." The big Were gave Mason a knowing look before pivoting on his boot heels. "But my pack won't like it, all the same."

Andre took off at a lope, his long, sterling hair and the faint trace of anger trailing after him.

Mason hesitated before following. His blood stirred

restlessly. Glancing down, he found the blood-drenched femme's eyes open and fixed on him.

The streak of excitement stemming from the meeting of their gazes spanned his body in an all-encompassing sweep. Beneath his belt, his groin pulsed. His fangs again extended.

What have I done? he asked himself. *What have I started?*

Her green gaze was steady and lucid, for all the trauma she'd suffered. He'd had a hand in making this so.

But had he imprinted with a Lycan? Accidentally seen to it she was permanently sealed to him by supercharging her dormant wolf blood with the blood of the immortals?

"Andre is the better option," he said to her, careful to hide the fangs. "You'll have to trust me on this."

Not expecting a reply, though her lush, bloodless, lips remained parted, Mason gathered himself.

Then they, too, blended with the night.

Chapter 4

Faith was reborn in light. The flickering, yellowish glow of candles, smelling heavily of beeswax and wicks. She blinked, startled, and searched for the remembered stench of blood without finding it.

"You're safe, for the moment," someone soothed.

Safe? God, where am I?

A phrase of random words appeared in the forefront of her mind as if in answer to her question. *Andre is the better option.*

Better than what? she thought. Dying alone in the dark?

The man who'd just spoken wasn't her dark stranger. This voice was more stone than velvet, and older, carrying in it the hint of a different sort of nature.

Trembling uncontrollably, Faith looked up.

The narrow, lined face leaning in bore a no-nonsense expression and heavily lidded eyes shaded by an uncombed mass of gray hair. Though an interesting face, it wasn't the one she'd expected to see. Disappointed, Faith looked beyond the wide shoulders partially blocking the light, scanning her surroundings for *him,* her rescuer—knowing he was here, feeling his presence in the ongoing electrified thrill of her nerves.

"I've set your leg," the man beside her said, forcing Faith's attention back to him.

"Impossible." Her voice sounded as thin as the atmosphere.

"She speaks," he noted. "I'm taking that as a good sign."

A damned good sign! Faith silently added, wanting to ask where she was, but fearing even the tiniest action of her throat might bring another eruption of pain.

"How long…out? Days? Weeks?" she asked in staccato syllables, panic threatening to return. If she had been out of it for days, where was her sister?

Her heart ramped up its beat as she awaited the answer to her question. Each hard, beating thrum stuck in her throat.

"You've been here for about two hours," the man replied.

"Mistake," Faith stuttered. She couldn't have heard him correctly. Even in a good hospital, with an orthopedic surgeon and an anesthesiologist on call, she would likely have lost her leg, if not her life. She'd been on the managing end of too many injuries like this one in the emergency room to champion the outcome.

She lifted her head to frantically search the length of whatever covered her. It was a blanket, and there were two raised rows beneath it, running outward from her hips. The outline of two legs, with the bumps of two feet beneath that. Both legs were still there!

Light-headed from the strain, she fell back.

"The leg was badly damaged," the man beside her said. "You were lucky he found you."

He. Where was he? Why didn't he speak when she so clearly felt his nearness? What was he waiting for?

"The trap tore you up good. If the wound hadn't finished you off, the iron would have, if you'd been left there for much longer," the man beside her explained.

"Need a tetanus shot," Faith said.

Recognizing the prickling sensation on the back of her neck, and knowing what it meant, she sent her senses toward another more elusive shadow in the corner...and found him.

He was here with his dark and silky vibe.

He was watching.

The knowledge made her shaking intensify.

"Somehow I don't think you'll need that shot," the gray-haired man told her. "If you can ride this out."

He may have been trying to tell her something he didn't come outright and say, but connecting to the other man who had carried her here, wherever *here* was, had become a compulsion from which Faith couldn't detour. She owed that other man, needed to thank him for getting her this far, yet couldn't open her mouth to utter those words because beyond her gratefulness was another layer of need that beat at her awareness with a padded fist. A need that superseded the pain and shock of her injury. So intimate, it registered as heat.

She heard a voice and looked up expectantly. But the sound had come from inside her head. Her mind was replaying parts of a recent conversation.

"Two hours."

And—

"I don't think you'll need that shot."

Those fragments of memory were nonsensical streams of consciousness in need of attention.

Ignoring that warning, Faith again looked to the corner for the man in whose arms she had experienced a feeling curiously similar to safety. Safety, with a nameless, faceless stranger who had cautioned about added pain and about someone coming that might be a further danger to her.

He'd promised she wouldn't die, and now she was being tended by someone hospitable, if not in a hospital. She was thinking rationally just two hours after a life-threatening incident, and experiencing another brief moment of comfort.

Two hours...

Nowhere near being a viable timetable for any sort of healing to take place on a wound as serious as hers had been. Something was definitely wrong, and all part of the alienness she'd discovered the minute she'd hit that gravel road. She couldn't be relatively pain-free, or sitting here, with this sort of injury. Either someone was lying to her, or what? What was the alternative?

Had she been sedated? Given an injection to block the pain? If she'd been sedated, how could she feel *him* watching? Whatever meds they'd given her hadn't stifled her perception of the strength of her rescuer's presence, or how that aura was affecting her. His attention was like the intimate roaming of a lover's hands. The touch of those hands made the pain lessen.

Why don't you speak? she silently asked, afraid he would answer, and afraid he wouldn't. He might think her ungrateful when she came right out and asked for more help. Not for herself this time. For Hope.

I need you!

Would he take that statement the wrong way if he read her thoughts? Had she, in fact, meant it like that? She felt his mind touching hers, and though she couldn't see him, she wanted to close her eyes and allow him access. She wanted to tell him to stop doing whatever he was doing and find her sister. That pain and need were becoming intertwined, mixed up in her addled mind.

Show yourself.

She felt his desire to comply. The air seemed to crackle between them while he considered it. But he didn't show himself. His reply came, not by speech, but in the form of a further mental touch—a cool kiss on her frantic mind.

The shock of it tilted the room. Heat flooded her chest, her neck, her face, mingling with the chills of her illness. Two extremes were engaging in a battle for dominance on the surface of her skin.

An interruption came. An untimely distraction. The man beside her cleared his throat, bringing her back to him again.

"Where am I?" she asked, speaking to both males in the room, her voice steady enough now to complete a sentence and make it heard.

"In a safe place," the closer man replied.

Again, the wrong voice. She didn't want to hear someone else. She expected to communicate with her rescuer, and squeezed her eyes shut to ensure that exchange happened. She had to shrug off the physical sensations he provoked, and get help. He knew where she'd been trapped. He had been in the area, and might have seen Hope. At the very least, he would know where to begin the search for her sister.

But her dark stranger remained silent.

She grew more frightened and tried not to show it.

She'd been trained, as all physicians were, not to give in to emotion, but realized that she was on the verge of hysterics. Giving in to that was not an option. She had to be strong, had to get herself together. The future depended on her actions. Hope's future depended on them.

"It's too late. Let her go." The stranger had spoken those words, and she'd imagined he'd been alluding to Hope. She wondered now if he might have meant something else, if he had been talking to himself about her, instead of her sister. Did he feel this same connection? Feel responsible for her?

Maybe you are afraid to show yourself.

"Are you feeling all right?" The gray-haired man spoke in such a way that she had to answer.

"Safe place," Faith muttered without looking at him. "Safe from what?"

"Those who would harm you."

Reluctantly, Faith turned her attention to her host, nearly stumbling over the penetrating intensity of his sober green eyes. They were slightly disturbing eyes, much the same shape and color of her mother's.

Beyond the odors of ash and scented wax, she perceived an animal scent that burned her throat as she swallowed, but had to let that go for now. Pets didn't concern her.

"I need further assistance," she said, steadying her voice by clearing it. "It's a lot to ask. I'm sorry. This isn't for me. I have to find someone."

"Who are you looking for?"

"Mason LanVal."

"LanVal?" Her host raised an eyebrow. "What would you want with him?"

"Help."

"What a coincidence, then, since it seems that's exactly what you got."

While Faith tried to make sense out of that, the voice she'd been waiting for rang through the small space at last, reaching her like an altogether new vibration. She would have known this voice anywhere. She had been waiting to hear it.

"It's true then," her mysterious rescuer said from the sidelines. "She was related to you."

Faith knew a flush of heat reddened her face, in spite of the blood loss that shouldn't have made that possible. She hadn't dreamed this man up, which meant that some of her perceptions remained in working order.

Looking from the man beside her, who slowly got to his feet, to the unilluminated corner of the room where she had pinpointed *him*—the other—she absorbed an inexplicable trill of pleasure.

"Well, LanVal," the gray-haired man said, following Faith's glance. "I'll leave you two to discuss this, though I won't go far. This one doesn't belong to you."

LanVal? Faith's heart lurched when she heard the name. She looked back and forth between the two male presences. Did her host mean that the man in the corner, the one who had pulled her from the trap, was Mason LanVal?

Yes. She saw this. Felt its rightness.

"Small world," his husky voice suggested, as if he did possess the skill to know what she was thinking. But when he didn't appear, no matter how much she had wished for it, Faith sent more of herself out to meet him in the shadows, even while acknowledging another unforgivable slip in procedure.

She had been so involved with the need to find Mason LanVal, she hadn't taken the time to appreciate the gray-haired man's ministrations. This was another unforgivable faux pas. An unintended slight. Her connection to the person now addressing her had taken precedence over manners, as did awaiting the approach of a stranger who had already done her one great service, and hopefully would do another...

If she truly wasn't imagining all of this in some trauma-induced coma.

Mason cautioned himself against taking a single step toward the bed and the woman on it. He hadn't meant to speak at all, yet somehow she had known he was here, standing guard.

The wolf in her connects us.

My blood in her veins strengthens that bond.

She also seemed to acknowledge this, without explanation. And the wary cast to Andre's eyes, as the Were had departed, warned that the silver wolf would see to it this treasure remained beyond Mason's reach.

Not quite human. Not quite Were. Do you reside in the middle?

If she was a werewolf, he had no business interfering. Immortals and moon-cursed people didn't mix, except superficially, when their paths crossed. And not always then.

Mason stared at her in puzzlement. He would have recognized a full-blooded Lycan, and hadn't immediately pegged her as one. He'd been considering how Andre had so easily known of the similarity between the two of them. Like calling to like, even when calculated in the tiniest particles?

It was possible. He felt the droplet of his ancient blood flowing through her, and knew he could call upon that blood swimming in her baby-blue arteries if he wanted to—in essence, shaping these moments in any way he chose. His blood was so much stronger than hers.

Acknowledging this bond, as well as the possibilities of how he might use his gifts, kept him hard in all the wrong places. His hold on his libido was so tight it became an effort to speak.

"You came here to find me?" he asked, fearing the deeper instincts keeping his fangs at the ready.

"It's not too late. Can't be," she said.

He knew what she alluded to. She was remembering what he'd told her out there.

His body was already leaning toward her, independent of his will. It was physical sacrilege for his own blood to be calling to him so clearly from inside her body. He hadn't meant for this to happen. His reactions to it were unique and unprecedented. His head felt uncommonly light.

Without pretending to misunderstand her meaning, he said, "Who is she?"

"My sister."

Her voice, low-pitched on the sound register and sultry, even in illness, added to his discomfort.

"You think she's here?" he asked.

"I saw her. In the headlights. On the road."

She was breathless, as if each word she spoke was hard-won. Her eyes were bloodshot and open wide. More fascinating for him than the heat in those eyes, or the way her chest rose and fell beneath the blanket covering her, was the way he could trace the path his blood was taking inside her. The droplet had already threaded through the chambers of her heart and had reached the artery that flowed to her hips. Looking there, as if he could see into her despite the blanket, Mason spoke through his tenseness.

"That's why you crashed the car. You thought you saw her."

She nodded and put a hand to her forehead as if just remembering about the crash. Her hand shook.

There was, Mason noted, no gold metal band or whitened spot of skin of her fingers where a ring might recently have been. He saw no evidence of a bond with someone else.

Why he had noted this or felt relief over the outcome was another question best left unanswered.

"What happened?" he pressed, noticing also that her face was opaque with strain, and that her damp, fair hair tended to curl across her forehead.

"My sister jumped off a bus near here and disappeared. You know about this already, don't you? You told me to let her go."

"I know little enough about her," he said.

"Her name is Hope. I saw her just hours ago, if the gray-haired man was truthful about how long I've been here."

Though her eyes had located him in the shadows, Mason had the odd sensation she could see his face, and therefore read the expression of interest on it. His body responded with a second stab of long-withheld hunger that served to highlight the importance of remaining apart from her.

He hungered too much. More than one emotion was running through him, and the onslaught was confusing for a being used to separating himself from the lives speeding past.

This female's hold on him was an enigma.

One step into the light, and he would be at her side.

"Andre told the truth," he said.

Out of sheer desperation, he supposed, her voice rose in volume. "I chased her out there, in the dark!"

"How do you know it was your sister you saw?"

"How did you know I was going after someone?" she countered. "Weren't you speaking about her when you told me to let her go?"

"Yes," he admitted.

"How did you know?"

"Your scent is similar. I believe you wear the same perfume."

Her eyes shone with a fevered brilliance. Despite the pain she was trying to ignore, frustration was her greater foe.

"It's the fragrance our mother wore," she said. "There are probably thousands of women who wear it. My sister and I don't look anything alike, yet you somehow knew what I was after. If you recognized the perfume, you must have been close to her, too."

There was nothing wrong with her reasoning powers, Mason concluded, acknowledging that if she and the other female were sisters, they were completely dissimilar in appearance and temperament. These differences were the reason he couldn't allow a she-wolf, ignorant of her bloodlines, to find her sister. Not until she healed. Not until she could hear and accept the truth of the situation.

The sisters, if that's what they actually were, would now be on different sides of a line drawn in the dirt centuries ago. Werewolf versus vampire. Pitting them face-to-face would be a torture for this one, and upset his plans for upturning the neighboring nest.

He would not tell this wounded woman that her sibling had gone over to the dark side, or that the young woman named Hope had run—not away from the vampires, but toward them, knowingly, willingly, when she'd been released from the trap's firm hold on her boot.

It wasn't his place to be the bearer of bad news.

Yet the pale face across from him was so eager, so hopeful, the things he didn't tell her tore at his heart.

Why the sister, who'd surely have to also possess wolf particles somewhere in her genetic makeup, would open her arms to the enemy, and why she hadn't possessed the same peppery scent, lay heavily on Mason's mind. It was possible, he conceded, that when they had stumbled upon the sister, Andre's presence at the scene had been a distraction, smelling up the place with the Were's own wolfishness.

If that was true, however, his own powers of observation were slipping. Not an altogether impossible glitch, but it would be a first.

No, he tended to think the answer had to lie elsewhere. Maybe her sister wasn't a wolf after all. Maybe this female on Andre's cot wasn't one, either. Reason dictated that if the sisters were Weres, no matter how deep or dormant those tendencies were buried, Andre must have known about the sister, as well. It was Andre who had been closest to her. Andre had pried open the trap a week ago, and set one of the sisters free.

This was an important detail in need of further contemplation. If the freed girl was a werewolf and had gone to the vampires, a vampire-wolf hybrid would be a true abomination, a travesty against the already fraying laws of nature. The bloodlust of the bloodsuckers, combined with the unparalleled instincts of a werewolf…

God above. What would such a creature be like?

It was imperative that he found out.

Looking at the woman on the cot, feeling for her, hungering for her in a way that made every fiber of his unnatural self want to get closer to her, Mason said, "I can't be of further assistance. I'm sorry for what you've been through."

Any further liaison between us is forbidden.

I have to see what's been done. You cannot be involved in that process.

He was refusing her request for added assistance, but his insides writhed with a different truth. There would be a further liaison between them, if only because her lost sister had become a factor further binding them together. Neither he nor Andre could allow the survival of such an abomination as her sister was likely to be by now, if she had been born Were.

He couldn't help this injured female in her quest because he was going to have to work against her by killing the sister she wanted so badly to see, along with the others he was after. This was his task. His quest. A God-given directive.

"Are you sorry?" she said, speaking through trembling lips that continued to hold a fascination for him despite his superior powers of reasoning.

"You'll never know how much," he confessed, planning to leave her, but unable to move. His arms ached to hold her. He drank in her beauty as if she alone could satisfy his insatiable thirst. Although he was a Guardian of souls, he knew that if his vow meant anything, he would have to protect his own soul from the woman openly staring back at him.

"Don't go," she said.

Perhaps the drop of his blood in her veins was what made him uneasy.

"You need rest."

"Do you believe I can rest with my sister out there?"

"No, I don't suppose you can," he conceded. "But I'm needed elsewhere."

She lifted her chin, exposing a sinuous expanse of her graceful, golden neck. Her eyes, though dark-ringed by pain, remained exceedingly bright. "Will you help find my sister if I beg hard enough for long enough?"

"Rest," he repeated, using the force of his will to direct her. And as her gaze slipped from him, Mason tore himself away from her, knowing with all that he was that the woman across from him, if in any way a wolf, would not give up her hunt; just as he knew that if she stayed here long, he'd be unable to keep himself from her.

Andre had been right in his accusations, and long on foresight. Mason LanVal, one of the Seven Holy Knights charged with the task of keeping the blood of the original immortals pure, a defender of the faith who had once been in the presence of the Grail and had sworn his fealty to protect it, irrationally wanted this female in both emotional and carnal ways. Out there, in the woods, in a moment of weakness, he hadn't given a thought to saving her soul for someone else's benefit.

Way too long without closeness, he concluded as he strode toward the door, determined to exit while her eyes were closed. Inexplicably, however, he found himself beside her, instead. His right hand was clutching the edge of her blanket as if he'd tear it away to get at what lay beneath. His fangs were exposed.

Dropping the blanket as if he'd been burned, Mason fled from the room with his fangs sunk deeply into his own bottom lip as both penance for straying from his goal, and as a dire warning to purge himself of the thirst racking his body and his conscience. A thirst that would surely be thwarted by a werewolf pack protecting one if its own.

This woman was a setback he didn't need, one that if pursued just might end up driving a stake through his uneasy truce with the werewolves and send them all back into the grudges of the past.

Therefore, he wasn't surprised to find Andre waiting in the yard to address this issue.

"Will it wear off?" the Were asked, showing a frown that deepened the lines beneath his eyes and made him look as wolfish as a man could get.

"Are you talking about my attraction to her, Andre?"

"A fool could feel it. So, is it the chicken or the egg?" Andre said. "Attraction first, and then the blood gift? Or blood gift, and then the attraction? I haven't known you to stray, LanVal. Either way, are you admitting to a moment of weakness after all this time?"

"Do I look like I've had a moment of weakness?"

"No. You're as formidable as always, and that power reeks. But I perceive something new in the air."

"As do I."

The urge to look over his shoulder at the door, in search of the cause of his current anxiousness, jolted Mason into taking a step.

"She doesn't know what she is," Andre said.

"Why is that? Isn't she past the age of her coming-out party? Wouldn't her parents have told her about her bloodlines?"

He didn't give Andre the opportunity to reply. He had so many questions in need of answers.

"She was bitten recently? Is that it? The Lycan virus hasn't had time to assimilate completely?"

Andre shook his head. "She bears the mark."

The mark.

Damn it all to hell and back, how could he have missed that?

Mason went down the pathway of his memory, and narrowed his vision on the woman caught in the trap. He observed the bare skin of her tanned torso spattered with blood and followed the shape of her throat to her shoulders and down her arms. There, he found what he was looking for, saw in his mind's eye what hadn't registered at the time.

Small punctures of whitened scar tissue marred the suntanned skin, looking like indentations made by the bite of a large dog, in the circular shape of a full moon. On her right upper arm.

It was the sign of a genetic Lycanthrope, and called a Moon Mark. Only Weres from old families whose blood dated back to the beginning of time carried the inherited scar, just as immortals as old as himself carried their own special detail.

Nevertheless, genetic Weres were not the norm. Most werewolves were Weres because they'd been bitten by other Weres. A good percentage of werewolves in the current century carried diluted blood in their veins. Like vampires did. Cut from the same cloth because some genetic Were, way back, had to have bitten a human to have started the whole mutant ball rolling.

Which of my brethren has done the same thing?

Which one of the sacred Seven immortals had sunk his teeth into human flesh, against the vow he had taken, exchanging blood, reducing the purity of its concentration?

Maybe this had been done out of loneliness, with companionship in mind and a longing for intimacy that hadn't worked out. Maybe whoever had taken that bite then tried to create another companion, and those females did the same, outside of the inner circle. Whatever the reason for that first broken vow, the indiscretion had initiated the creation of a population of bloodsucking fiends.

As Mason eyed Andre now, he wondered if genetic Lycans cared about which of their kin had dished out that very first nip, in the way he cared about the first puncture of a human's neck by an immortal's fangs, and which one of the Seven had done it. He wondered if any of the old Were families hunted for the spin-off from their own ground zero.

"This one is special," Andre said with a revered emphasis only one genetic Were would use for another.

Andre's frown was contagious. Mason felt a similar crease line his own brow.

"Yes," he agreed. "She is."

He had always known of Andre's strength and prowess, and was willing to bet that Andre carried the mark of the moon somewhere on his body. He was also quite certain that mark would be what helped to place Andre in the position of alpha in this pack.

But was Andre attracted to the wolf in his guest, and trying to eliminate potential competition by telling him these things about the female in his shack?

"My question stands in regard to your intentions about this woman," Andre said.

Mason could not answer. He found that he wasn't sure what his intentions were, or why he also felt protective of a wayward female trespassing in his territory. It was blasphemous for an immortal to long for a member of another species' clan, even though the blood wars between wolves and vampires had been a relatively recent development in history's long march, and caused entirely by the mutants on both sides.

His own maker hadn't created another female immortal. The Seven were men. There was no one of his own kind to dull the sharp edges of his longevity, no companion of the opposite sex. It seems that his maker had eliminated that final temptation.

Temptation? Hell, now that he had met a female Andre suggested was a blue-blooded she-wolf bearing the potential for power, was it possible that all her contained, untried power was the source of her sweetness? That she wasn't actually as fragile as she seemed at the moment, and would soon grow into her birthright?

As he stood there, Mason found himself developing a new affinity for Andre, a sympathetic bond that circumvented the concept of a truce. Andre was genetic royalty of sorts, a true Lycanthrope, unlike many of his werewolf cousins. As such, Andre was a born leader. This marked female inside the shelter would be a good match for an alpha of Andre's caliber.

Mason's fangs snapped tight with the thought. He clenched and unclenched his hands, feeling the thrill of danger within his reach, and fending off a budding rise of apprehension.

He wasn't sure he wanted Andre to have the female in there, no matter how alike she and Andre were, though he couldn't define why he didn't want her paired with the silver wolf. The only thing he knew for certain was that if this woman was allowed to pursue her sister, and find out what she had become, the action could very possibly set them all back to the Dark Ages.

As could his own interest in her.

He looked at the cottage, contemplating that.

Refusing her plea for help had been difficult. Those large, pain-filled eyes of hers had provoked cravings he had assumed were long gone, lost in the annals of time. Seeing the fear in her eyes, as well as the anguish, had made him realize that he harbored empathy for her plight, alongside every one of his physical yearnings for her that appeared to intensify with each passing minute.

Christ, he remembered the sweetness of her breath. He was covered in her blood, still damp against his skin. He could hear her jumbled thoughts, when such communication should not have been possible.

Whether or not she was a wolf, he and that female shared some kind of bond that placed their future on the head of a pin. He had put the fluid of the immortals inside her, and it was doing its work too well.

Indeed, his thought now was to brush Andre out of the way and charge back inside. Who knew what would happen if he acted on that urge, or how what came after would go down?

"You must keep her from me," he said to Andre.

The Were nodded, his eyes as dark as the night. "How far will I have to go to do that?"

"As far as it takes."

Mason ran his tongue slowly over his teeth, lengthened with his thoughts of her, sharp for want of her. He ignored the thunder inside his chest.

"You've had years to perfect your control," Andre suggested soberly.

"Far too many years, perhaps," Mason restlessly agreed, trying to ignore that warm, sultry wetness on his thighs.

"So be it, then," the Were concluded. He added, with a glance to the house, "How long will she be in danger?"

Over the pulsating, rapidly increasing need to possess the female inside Andre's house, Mason said earnestly, in a voice like steel, "Every damned minute she stays."

Chapter 5

Faith felt as if she were moving.

She felt the familiar smoothness of a taut, bare chest, cool against her cheek. An impression came of being carried in two strong arms. And of wind on her face.

A raging heat coursed through her, intense, fluid and disturbing. The thoughts so recently creating havoc in her mind had gone silent, leaving her adrift in a dark, unfamiliar place where tall strangers rescued trespassers and breathed life back into them.

Just such a breath coursed through her now, and a phantom pressure of the lips through which that burst of life had flowed. Certain she would find this strong stranger if she looked, Faith was afraid to open her eyes. On some primitive level, she wanted more from him than merely her life back. Deep down, she harbored a strange connection to him.

Was this a dream or déjà-vu?

Her stranger's voice swam inside her mind, sharing the space. "Keep me from her," she heard him say in a strangled tone, and she wanted to argue, because his vehemence lacked the ring of truth. Her rescuer was thinking about her. A desire for further closeness sat in the forefront of his mind, recognizable because a hint of the same desire flowing through her.

If he wasn't there now, Faith was sure he had touched something close to her, and that he was nearby. Her awareness of his presence brought with it the echo of a fading command. "Rest." And also a name. *LanVal.*

Grasping that name as if it were a magical talisman that would free her from her burdens, Faith fought against the bonds holding her and let her eyes flutter open.

Unable to immediately recognize her surroundings, it took her a moment to figure out where she was. She wasn't in any stranger's arms, but lying on her back, with her head on a pillow, in a cottage in the French woods.

Reality rushed back with surprising swiftness. Faith pushed herself up, panting with the effort, hoping she had merely blacked out, and that Mason LanVal would still be here. He'd told her that other business called, but damn if she didn't still feel him, as if he had just touched her. As if an imprint of that touch lingered.

To her dismay, no one stood beside her. There was, in fact, no one else in the room.

A dream, then.

Wanting to stand up and get to the door, Faith realized that she couldn't manage either and that it was absurd to think she could. Even with the seemingly miraculous relief from the worst of the pain, she remained weak. Her muscles were quivering.

The room's curtains were closed. Candle flames fluttered on the tables. She felt the night outside as clearly as if she had swallowed some of it. If she couldn't get outside and get some air, the next best thing would have been to throw open the windows and let it in.

Let *him* back in.

Mason LanVal had to be out there, somehow a part of that same darkness she wanted to feel on her skin. The strength of his presence remained. She felt choked by the warm fuzziness of the small room she'd found herself in, added to whatever Andre had given her to curb the pain that should have been overwhelming.

She craved the night suddenly, now more than ever. Her spirits had always risen when the sun went down. In Miami, relief from the glaring heat and humidity of the day had been a universal acknowledgment celebrated by most of her family, who had laughingly labeled themselves Night Creatures.

Except for Hope, Faith recalled with sadness. Her younger sister had hated the hours after sundown, and partied hard wherever lights glittered the brightest, trying to ignore the dark. Maybe the concept of fear was what separated her from her sister the most profoundly. Hope had preferred to hang out with people she considered to be stronger than herself, and Hope's definition of stronger differed from her sister's. In Faith's mind, Hope's habit of riding motorcycles at breakneck speed was tantamount to numbing fear, rather than Faith's own practice of firmly raising a middle finger to it.

The desire to be part of a group, instead of seeking alone time, had been another of Hope's habits in the past few years. With Faith in medical school, and then on rotation as an intern, spending long hours and nights away from home had exacerbated Hope's rebellious steak.

Faith blamed herself for Hope slinking away from any kind of viable relationship. Although she had barely turned twenty when she'd been given custody of her sister after their parents had died, Hope had only been an impressionable teenager. She'd needed more guidance than Faith had been able to provide.

Blame, however, only took her so far toward explaining away Hope's exceedingly rash behavior. She wasn't Hope's mother, after all, and hadn't known how to fill those shoes. She might have done a poor job of supervising, but in any case her influence would have been proved limited. She had done the best she could to try to make up for Hope's suffering, and for not being there with Hope when their parents had died.

She'd been sure a trip to Europe would enliven her sister, and separate Hope from the rough crowd. The expense of the trip had been paid from her first real paycheck as an M.D. She'd put Hope on the plane with an organized group of like-aged young women and waved goodbye. Hope hadn't acted stranger than usual. Nor had she balked at the gift. What Hope had done was jump ship. Three days into the trip, just across the French border, Hope had left the tour without a word to anyone and disappeared without a trace.

Faith couldn't stop thinking about this because here, tonight, Hope had been running through a forest, in that same darkness the girl had always despised.

The possibility seemed ridiculous. How this had happened was the question, ultimately pointing in the direction of Hope either having been abducted, or else she had taken leave of her senses.

Both of those options were as terrible as the realization that Faith hadn't caught up with Hope out there. She'd bungled the whole thing by getting hurt—another damned delay in the quest to find her sister, when she'd been so close.

Whose house was she in? Who was this other man? She hadn't even known the identity of the provocative stranger with the unsettling aura until she'd heard his name. But she had at least found Mason LanVal, a man who, after entrusting her to this place and toying with her senses, had turned down her plea for further assistance. It had seemed as though he couldn't get away from her fast enough. Could she damn him for his refusal, though, when he was the sole reason she was alive?

Still, after refusing her, LanVal remained close by. She knew he was there, just outside this house. His closeness continued to harangue in subtle ways: the remembered words of assurance, his gentle touch on her fading life force.

Slumping forward with her head in her hands, Faith whispered, "Now what?"

"Now," her gray-haired host said, entering the room looking more serious than before, "you get better."

This was not the man she wanted to see. Faith worked to hide her disappointment.

"Thank you for what you've done to help me," she said, hoping she'd be able to get answers from this man, if not the other one.

He nodded graciously.

"Please tell me where I am, exactly," Faith said.

"You're in my home, about a mile from where you left your car."

LanVal had carried her a mile, in the night. An impossible feat, in spite of his solid wall of muscle. And although she was small, a limp, lifeless body weighed a ton.

"How can I be sitting up, talking to you?" she asked, her nervousness escalating when she remembered how LanVal's wide, bare chest hadn't registered exertion.

"Perhaps you weren't injured as badly as you thought, and were merely terribly frightened by what happened, as anyone would be," her host suggested.

"A logical idea, I suppose, except that I'm a surgeon and know better. I know what that trap did to me."

"Ah. Yes." After looking her over carefully, he changed the subject. "Are you in pain?"

"Plenty. Dulled to a manageable level. I know that's not usual, either. I did crack a bone, right?"

She watched her host cross the room to the table. Though his hair was the color of a silver nickel, he moved as agilely as a young man as he reached to pick up a bottle of white liquid, then crossed back to hand the bottle to her.

"Used this," he said. "Made you swallow half a glass, then rubbed it into your wound before setting your bone. It's partially to blame for soaking up the symptoms of your pain."

Faith peered at the bottle, which had no label and emitted a disgusting smell she couldn't identify. "What is it?"

"Old family recipe that doesn't work on everybody."

"How did you know it would work on me?"

"I took a chance."

Faith rubbed her forehead to ease the ache between her eyes. Thinking had become so damn difficult. None of this made sense.

"I'm sorry. I don't mean to sound rude, but an old

family recipe, no matter how much you believe in it, couldn't have replaced the blood loss."

"No, not by itself," he admitted with a shake of his head. "Other things helped."

As Faith awaited further explanation, thinking he'd surely give her one, she took the time to really look at the man. He was tall and broad, with noticeable lengths of hardened muscle beneath faded jeans and a worn plaid shirt. His shirtsleeves were rolled up to his elbows, showing off forearms punctuated by several raised veins. Bodybuilders, when pumped up, showed off veins like that.

"Who are you?" she asked.

"Name's Andre."

"Are you a doctor?"

"A healer of sorts. No real training, as you'd know it, but good enough for the locals."

"Why did Mason LanVal bring me here instead of to a doctor?"

"It's a long way to the nearest clinic, and few folks out here drive."

"That's unique, isn't it, in this day and age?" Faith said, thinking how Andre's excuse corroborated LanVal's.

"I believe it's more a case of choosing to remain reclusive. No automobile means no temptation," he said.

"Are you going to answer my question about the blood loss?"

"Not yet, I think. Why don't you first tell me who you are."

Faith couldn't reach the persistent ache inside her skull with her fingers, and wished she could. She had to take her time and answer this man's questions. Of course he'd want to know who he was treating and housing.

"Faith James," she said.

"An American surgeon?"

"From Miami."

"You're a long way from home."

"I came here to find Mason LanVal," she said. "I needed his help, but the request didn't go so well. He's supposed to be good at finding missing people."

"LanVal is indeed good at that, but he's also a man of few words, and more reclusive than I am."

"Why won't he help me?"

"LanVal is his own man. He doesn't seem to excel at the finer points of inquisitiveness about the people he stumbles across, like I do."

Blinking brought on a bonus streak of pain behind Faith's eyes. The meager light in the room suddenly seemed way too bright. She couldn't bear to look at the candles, and felt confined in the small space. Her hands continued to shake.

"What else do you want to know?" she asked.

A short span of time passed before Andre said, "First and foremost, I'd like to know why a genetic Lycanthrope doesn't know she is one."

Silence seemed to swell in the room after that grouping of nonsensical words, as if the question had the ability to awaken something inside her that she hadn't been aware of her entire life. The sensation of finding a secret was like the unfurling of an idea she couldn't get at, or a problem she couldn't grab on to.

She knew her color drained further… She was aware of every inch of its downward rush.

What had he just asked her?

She couldn't focus properly. Maybe it was that ger-

minating ghost of an idea she couldn't reach that was
adding to her confusion. Something was trying to get
out of her, trying to make itself known. Faith revisited
the idea of whether the man beside her might indeed
have slipped her a hallucinogen and then had taken
one himself.

None of this was normal. She had no idea what he
was talking about. Nothing short of a transfusion could
have compensated for the blood loss she'd suffered. No
medicine in a bottle could help with that.

She again looked around, searching for hospital
equipment, finding none. She was holed up in a small
living room, its walls hewn from logs. There were a
couple of chairs nearby, the table with the candles on
it, a stone fireplace and the carved wooden cot she
was using as a bed. She was shirtless, her arms and
chest bare, with a blanket tucked protectively around
her. Her skin had been cleaned of the blood she'd shed
in the woods.

Had Andre done all of this?

Where the hell had LanVal left her?

The room seemed to spin with unanswered questions, accompanied by a faint ringing sound in her ears.
Concentration had been shattered, sidestepping her
finely tuned process for understanding things others
couldn't. Yet smack-dab in the center of everything,
Mason LanVal's elusive presence filled her mind, larger
than life, minus several details. She didn't know what
he looked like, having never seen him in the light, so
how did she know he was tall, dark, unearthly handsome and not at all what she had expected from a name
scrawled on a piece of paper?

Andre cleared his throat. The gray-haired healer had
repeated his question and was awaiting an answer. But

the question she heard made about as much sense now as it had the first time he'd voiced it, and only added to her discomfort about being left in a stranger's care.

She looked to Andre again, grasping at his question.

Why didn't she know she was a...*genetic Lycanthrope?*

Had everyone in France gone stark-raving mad?

Mason anxiously tossed the hair out of his face and stared at the exterior wall of the house. Inside, Andre was circling his prey, entering dangerous territory by stirring things up if his patient was, in fact, ignorant of her ancestry.

Wolf? He felt her heat signature through stone walls at least four feet thick. A swirl of heat, as misty as a mirage, caressed his partial nakedness, bringing with it more reminders of things best left forgotten. Silken pageants. Crowds of cheering people. Summer sunsets stretching across a distant horizon.

Although he hadn't hidden from the sun for over a hundred years, and never had to sleep in the earth or a tight, dark space, like vampires did, he preferred the night. He revered the quiet, the breezes, the brilliance of stars overhead and the freedom to move about more or less undetected. In the dark, he somehow felt less alone. Fewer humans moved about. After all these years, his existence was easier if he didn't have to see many people.

Being near to the female inside Andre's house brought back more of the things he had missed from his days as a mortal. This female was blood-lure and missed heartbeats. She was the tickle on the base of his neck that foretold an oncoming storm. He wanted an explanation for these things. He wanted to go in there and take her back, rub his face in her hair, rake his fangs across her moist, full mouth. The urge to do those things was incredibly intense. He actually took a step toward the door.

No barrier could keep him from her if he willed it. No pack of werewolves was powerful enough or stupid enough to try to hold him back from something he desired. He had been one of the strongest humans in his time, before his resurrection as an immortal, and had had centuries to perfect his skills since then. Strong, pure, undefeated…that's how he had once been described.

What about lonely? Where does that fit in?

There had been a time long past when women had offered themselves to him in payment for his services, and as a reward for his prowess in tournaments and other courtly deeds that made him seem a shining example of knighthood. Many an evening, women had crept into his room, their white skin drenched in luxurious oils. They had lain beside him with their bare legs spread wide. Their hushed voices had coaxed him to mount their waiting bodies, all of them wanting to experience whatever his magic was.

Sometimes they came to plead for his protection. At other times they begged for grisly deeds to be performed on their behalf. It was usual for two or three women to arrive at once and parlay for the best position on his sheets. Curving white rumps. Ripe, pink-tipped breasts positioned near his mouth.

But it was because he had shunned these temptations that the call of a higher power had come. And after he had accepted his fate, court life became an inconsequential thing of the past. A barely memorable faded dream.

He and his brethren had fought for more serious stakes after taking the vow in life-altering battles. Knights, mercenaries, the Seven creatures of the night became an infallible army. But the awareness of what they had become and the constancy of their unrequited thirst beat at them.

The brilliant glow of the thought of immortality eventually faded. Years later, the Blood Knights dispersed. For the protection of the blood in their veins, and because they'd grown weary of the reminder of the things they had done, the Seven had scattered themselves to the four winds.

Where at least one of them had become a traitor.

Now, centuries later, this female in Andre's cottage single-handedly threatened to tempt him from the path he had been treading upon for far too long in a fight that went on forever.

Why now?

Why her?

As the questions piled up, Mason swung his head into the breeze, listening farther off, hearing a disturbance. The distant stealth of false shadows, corroded with a malicious stink, became an unmistakable calling card.

"Vampires."

Monsters were roaming the woods in search of dinner, and were currently too close to Andre's house not to be considered a nuisance. Yet the time wasn't right to teach them a lesson. If he removed a hundred vampires without taking down the creature who had made them, more vampires would follow.

He had waited a long time to find that one source.

All this time...

Mason gazed at the house with regret. Although he'd

tried to wash his hands of the woman inside, and in spite of what he'd told her, both his vow and his quest, prior to and after becoming an immortal, made it impossible for him to refuse her plea for aid. The banner he'd once fought beneath had carried the legend *Might for right.*

If she'd asked for anything else, he might actually have excused himself. But she wanted to find her sister, not knowing that sister had gone to the monsters. This made her request a plea for help against the same creatures he had sworn to protect the population from. How could he make her an exception?

Andre's patient was ill. The big wolf would have to tug the wolf out of her in order to further speed her regeneration. When his own blood gift to her wore off, awakening her bloodline might be the only way she'd save her leg. Fully healed, she would be off-limits to anyone outside her clan. She'd be a wild thing until she got her beast under control.

Until that time however, and holding to those same truths he had given up his life for, Mason could not actually back away. He had to help her. God help him, he wanted to help her.

He had to start now.

So rich...her scent...

Mason looked down at himself, at the blood saturating his jeans. Breathing in its unique fragrance, feeling its effect all the way to his ongoing erection, he kept his gaze locked to the curtained windows of Andre's house.

He knew how to begin. In wearing the blood she had lost before he'd introduced a drop of himself into her system, he would act as a decoy. The vampires would follow her scent on him, and he would lead them away from Andre and the...

The what? Object of his desire?

Wincing over the sentimentality of the thought, Mason turned away from the glow of lights. Whatever *she* really was, her heat had found him as easily as if the drop of blood he'd put inside her reached for him, instead of the moonlight she should have preferred.

Her heat coursed through his veins like an influx of exotic liquid. His body constricted with need as the silent rustle of the monsters in the distance crept closer.

The female was stable enough for him to leave. He knew this. His blood had helped her more than he'd anticipated, and quickly. He could give her more of his blood to ensure her full recovery and to see to it she circumvented the wolves, but if he did there was that chance he might be the one to bring into existence something else altogether, something even the vamps next door couldn't reproduce by biting her sister.

His immortal blood, in quantity, if given to a potentially potent she-wolf, would create not just an abomination but an unstoppable one. Truly, a big, bad wolf.

Then again, maybe Andre was wrong about her. The Were had been wrong once before, and it had nearly cost him his arm.

Feeling a scratch of shadows in his mind, Mason snapped to. It was time to take care of business.

"Come and get it!" he whispered to the vampires, wheeling gracefully on his long legs.

Before hearing the soft echo of his own taunt, he was off and running—for the time being, leaving the seraphic taste of femininity and his lust for a delicate, beautiful, blonde behind.

Chapter 6

A harsh cry went up behind Mason as he moved, the whoop of a frenzied male vampire who had caught the scent.

Mason ran quietly between the trees with a slow, steady pace. Though he possessed the greater speed, he didn't want to outdistance the monsters. He had to stay just far enough ahead to keep them coming, and keep them distracted.

He heard them. These typically silent creatures were forgetting themselves. Half-crazed with craving, they sent up foul cries as they searched for tracks in the wind and sniffed up blood particles like a drug. Other forest-dwelling animals instinctively ran for cover. Nothing was safe with ravenous vampires on the loose.

The night rushed past as he skimmed the border between the forest and the distant town, leading a merry, deadly chase. He was circling them in a wide arc back toward the estate where the nest had taken up residence, hoping these beings, human once, and now consumed with inhuman appetites, would be confused enough to force their master into the open. This had been Mason's goal all along—to find the intelligence behind the creation of this nest. To meet the maker of these local monsters.

Maybe, he thought now, fate had played him a timely hand after all by bringing him the female. The uniqueness of her blood was a certain aphrodisiac. A heady draw.

As he ran, Mason sensed something else in the dark coming in rapidly from behind to form a rustle of movement running parallel to his path. With this notice came the scent of damp fur, and a glimpse of black, brown and gray movement sliding in and out of the diffused beams of light from the moon in the branches.

Wolves.

On all fours.

Not just any wolves, either.

With no full moon overhead, the only beasts able to change at will, and into the four-legged shape of their early ancestors instead of furry man-beasts, were the most powerful of the genetic recipients—the strongest Weres who had morphed so many times they could do so whenever they chose, into the shape of choice.

These had to be some of Andre's pack, here to make sure he wouldn't return to the cottage, to the woman Andre shielded there. He, himself, had given Andre the order to keep him away.

Indeed, Mason reasoned, inhaling Were scent, the female had to be special if she needed this much protection. But then, he'd already guessed as much.

He laughed out loud at his own rebellious thoughts,

a sound that brought a corresponding growl from the throat of a large, black-furred predator with incandescent eyes.

Andre knew who he was dealing with, after all, to send the best.

Surrounded by the wildness of the wolves and the thickness of the night, Mason felt the slow rise of his own beast, that part of himself kept safely sealed away at the center of his being, only bits of which had ever seen the light. The harsher parts of what he was were beginning to simmer, stirred up by the unmistakable odor of vampire.

He felt a tangible sense of impending significance, as if the air around him sang a vitally important song he was just beginning to hear. That song had evil woven into its melody, as well as a kind of a call to arms that spoke of carnage and sacrifice.

Who was this call meant for? The vampires? The wolves? Himself? He slowed to a jog, realizing that the voice in his head was driving the action behind him and dictating the path the vampires were to take.

The adrenaline rush of enlightenment brought him up short. Suddenly, Mason knew what this singsong voice was, and what sort of creature wielded the power behind it. He recognized the intelligence of its design, as well as the length of its reach.

In front of God and everything he held sacred, had he found the vampire maker he'd sought? If not one of his brethren, this had to be a creature fairly close to the original source of Mason's own blood lineage.

His patience had been warranted.

The wolf companions had stopped beside him, no more than ten feet away, and were milling about, growling low in their throats. When their huge, primal eyes looked beyond him, Mason instinctively knew they hadn't been sent to drive him off, as he'd first surmised. Neither was their wolfish presence a warning meant to keep him from Andre's cottage. These wolves had been sent as backup.

Why? Because Weres despised vampires as much as he did and would patrol the woods? Because they knew about his agenda and approved? Because Andre, sensing something in the wind, had sent them as a pledge? A pack, as needed, in exchange for a female?

These wolves were offering up their support, sensing trouble in that foul, tainted wind. They were offering their assistance, if not their complete trust, to an immortal, against whatever tide was approaching.

This was often the way in battle. Enemies united, in spite of their differences, against a greater cause. But in that moment, Mason felt in himself the spark of a new type of hunger. Not a gnawing thirst, but a need equally profound. He hungered for the friendship he'd never had, and for a continued bond with others, however tenuous. He hungered for the female he had placed in Andre's care—a hunger that if acted upon, would lose him those other things and perhaps even his standing as one of the Seven.

Most of all, he hungered for the blood of a villain. The bane of his kind. The creator of chaos. His mind raced, as it often did these days, with old, unanswered questions.

Did anyone care about the purity of the blood anymore?

Was he the only one of his kind left? He couldn't feel his brothers out there.

What good was protecting for centuries the very thing that had kept him apart from the world, and living on that world's fringes?

How would *she* react when she found out what he was? If she knew her sister had willingly adopted fangs, would she recoil from his own pale flesh?

That last thought birthed an image of honey-colored skin pressed tightly to his own white flesh, on a bed of scarlet silk. A female's body heat able to warm his soul's constant chill. Warm fingers on his face. Slender hips beneath his. Long legs opening…

Trouble and distraction. This female was all that. She was temptation, just as he'd feared, and here to test his willpower against the plans he had set in motion to catch the immortal that had forsaken his vow. He had to forget this female and set other, far more serious grievances to rights. What were his own needs, when measured against the world's?

He stood with his finger in a dyke. If he removed that finger and vampires continued to breed unhindered, a blood tide would be unleashed. Without checks and balances, a world in peril would have no hope left.

As Mason stood among the wolves, listening to a voice in his head that wasn't his own voice and was likely a harbinger of doom, he shunned the mesmerizing heat of the thought of the woman he had rescued, as it continually reached out, in spite of the distance separating them, to touch the empty spot in his soul. The spot where he had once upon a time considered love to be a goal in itself.

"Well, then, shall we face the monsters?" he said to the anxious wolf pack in a gritty voice, needing the widening scope of a new distraction.

* * *

Mason LanVal had gone. Faith wanted to cry out for an absence that created a hole in her safety net, stripping away some of her confidence, bringing fear back as she lay stranded in a strange place.

She would have stopped LanVal if she could, though he'd already done plenty by saving her life. She had no right to expect anything further.

But there was something else. In thinking about him, and in reaching out to him with her mind, she felt him out there in the distance, just as she'd felt him in the room. She was aware of the swell of his anger and the rawness of his need. What was he doing so far away?

Her pulse quickened in response to her own needs. Her hands tugged at the blanket. Biting back a shout of pain that her conscience warned was too outrageous, Faith looked up to meet the open curiosity of the man beside her. Andre. She'd nearly forgotten about him. At that particular moment, his observation was an unwanted intrusion that kept her from thinking about LanVal, out there somewhere in the dark.

Yet Andre's eyes drew her, because she hadn't faced the madness of his last question.

"He's gone," she said.

"But not forgotten, it seems."

Faith looked to the door, hoping to be proved wrong about LanVal's disappearance, expecting him to change his mind because she wanted it so badly.

"I can't feel my leg," she said. "I can't feel much of anything. But I can feel him."

She didn't expect her host to respond to that, and he didn't try. She was the surgeon here, and knew better than to expect another miracle. She knew better than to believe in miracles at all. At the same time, she seemed to have been the recipient of one. She was alive.

"Am I going to a hospital eventually, Andre?"

"I'm not sure they'd know what to do with you at the moment," he replied, perched on the edge of the bed, his body eerily motionless.

"What does that mean?" Faith pressed, wondering if there was time to ponder the idiosyncrasies of backwoods people.

"Can you tell me, Faith, was there anything unusual in your upbringing? Anything unusual about your family?"

"Are you asking for a medical history?"

"A history of sorts, yes. Answers to be found in the details of your family tree."

"Would it change your treatment in any way, or get me out of here any quicker?"

"No."

"Am I a prisoner?"

"Of course not. You're too ill to be moved any farther by hand and foot. You know that."

Yes. She knew, and remembered that no one here had cars or phones.

"My parents were healthy," she said. How many times had she fed these same questions to her patients at the clinic and hospital? "They were never ill. Not one day. No heart problems, no inherited diseases."

"You speak of them in the past tense."

"They're dead."

"I'm sorry. May I ask how long ago they passed?"

"Six years ago, this month."

"What happened to them?"

"A hunting accident happened. A tragedy."

Andre's face showed concern. "Please tell me about it, if you can."

"What has this to do with anything?"

"Please," Andre said gently.

She could speak of it, Faith told herself. This far away, and with Hope missing, she could say the words that had brought her and Hope to this moment in time.

"They were camping in the mountains. Hunters, illegally carrying guns, shot wild, thinking to bag deer. My mother and father were in the line of fire."

"Hunters," Andre said at length, as if finding hidden meaning in what she'd said.

Faith was urged on by the sympathy in his eyes. "I've never spoken about my parents or the accident to anyone. I got my sister into counseling, but she kept her pain tucked away. My sister was there, you see. Hope survived by hiding from the gunfire, then she ran to get help."

"That's the sister you're searching for here?"

Finding empathy in Andre's eyes, Faith nodded. "Yes. She hasn't been the same since that accident. I've tried to watch out for her, and it hasn't gone according to plan. It seems that some things never do."

"So, after coming here, your sister ran again from something unpleasant. And you've come here to find her."

The truth of that statement was a terrible sting, because she had considered this, of course. She had wondered if Hope had run away for good this time, attempting to outdistance the demons that had plagued her since the incident in the woods. The idea had merit, but was in the end partially nullified by the fact that she'd seen Hope here, in the kind of place her sister had always feared. Hope had been there, in the trees, in the dark, alone. She had dived headfirst into her nightmares.

"She's all I have left," Faith said wearily. "The last of my family."

Pointing to her arm, exposed above the edge of the wool blanket, Andre said, "Do you know what that is, Faith?"

"A birthmark."

"Does your sister have one like it? If so, it might help us to identify her."

Identify her. Did Andre mean when they found Hope's body? God, what a tragic, unthinkable, unacceptable outcome.

"No. She doesn't. Not really. She had a similar mark tattooed on, in order to be like us."

"Us? Your parents also had similar marks?"

"My mother had one."

The birthmarks had been a personal link between her mother and herself. A private bond. Hope had been jealous about this when she was younger, so her mother had drawn a mark on Hope's little arm with henna and a pen.

Andre began to roll up one of his shirtsleeves, taking it all the way to his shoulder, exposing a stretch of smooth tanned upper arm skin.

Faith sucked in a sharp breath. "What is that, Andre?"

"Birthmark."

"It's the same as mine. In the same place."

"Yes. So you see, Faith, you're not alone, after all. We're family, of sorts. Maybe even very distant relatives. This mark proves it."

Really! This was nuts! Faith tried to throw her legs over the side of the bed. Too weak to support herself, and with the broken bone, she ended up hanging over the edge of the cot, on her stomach. Pain rushed back with a force that left her nauseous and shaken.

Andre had a birthmark like hers.

As he lifted her up and settled her in place, Faith's mind continued to whirl. After checking her splint, Andre covered her up again before he sat back down. He continued to watch her, as if waiting for something. Another major freak-out, maybe?

"I don't know what you're talking about," she said, needing to break the awkward silence. "Family?"

"Why doesn't your sister have the mark, Faith, if most of your line bear it?"

"What line would that be? Are you saying you have the mark because you're a James, too?"

"No. Not a James. I'm from another branch of the tree. A male-dominant line of the clan. There has to be two lines in order for Lycans to match up."

That answer sent Faith back into memory to warm nights and beach days, where she found a remembered sliver of an image.

Her father had a mark on his body, too. Early on, he'd teased about having had it installed to match her mother's "beauty mark," so that her mother wouldn't think of the whitened ring on her skin as a flaw. The joke was an ode to family intimacy. Her father had gotten a tattoo, he'd said, which he kept covered up so that no one else could see it.

But it hadn't been a tattoo. Faith had known this all along. It also had been a mark similar to her own. All three of them had this birthmark. Her father, her mother, herself. Only Hope was missing it. Eventually, Hope had gotten a more permanent copy of the earlier henna artwork by having the mark tattooed on.

And now it seemed that this man beside her, in France, so far from home, had one, too. Not just any mark, either. The same one. Exactly the same.

"What do you mean? Two lines matching up?" she demanded, sure she would have to revisit the concept of full consciousness, because this was downright insane.

"A male Lycan line and a female Lycan line are necessary in order for us to procreate," Andre said.

This sounded like gibberish to Faith. Was he talking about sex? Her nerves hummed like plucked strings, another special confirmation of truth. Whatever this man was trying to tell her in his cryptic manner, he was steering her toward a truthful, if whacked, enlightenment.

What was so special about males and females of certain families mating? Was he talking about royal families?

"What does *Lycan* mean?" Her voice sounded nothing like hers, and rang with the tinniness of panic. Explanations were to come, she supposed, explanations that might hurt terribly. Already, she wanted to hide.

"It's the name of a certain kind of being, Faith. One who carries the genetic code of a wolf inside them."

Faith leaned back into the cushions in an attempt to distance herself from the ongoing madness. Unable to avoid Andre's scrutiny, and hogtied to a splint that kept her from charging out the door, she felt her anger rise. Anger beat the fear back. Always had.

"Maybe you live out here in the middle of nowhere without a phone or a car because you're a lunatic," she said defensively. But Andre wasn't completely nuts, her instincts told her. He was attempting to lead her slowly toward whatever point he would eventually make. He was being kind and thoughtful while making shocking allegations, then carefully monitoring her response. He was feeding her information piece by piece, so that she'd have an easier time digesting it.

Perhaps sensing her distress, he held up both of his hands in a gesture of placation and lowered his voice. "I'm supposing your parents liked the nighttime hours, and that when you were younger, they often took you out at night to feel the wind and view the moon."

Her parents had done all of those things, instilling in her their love of the nighttime that Hope never shared. But how would this man know it?

She stared back at Andre, who sighed and picked up the bottle of white fluid. Pouring a measure of it into a glass, he handed that glass to her, along with a gesture for her to drink.

"Well," he said. "LanVal brought you here so I could set your leg. I have done so, and I'll watch over you until you're better. As for the rest, we can talk later, when you're feeling up to it."

Faith looked at the glass. "I won't die if I drink this?"

"Not tonight," he replied with a grim smile.

And Faith believed him. Through the strange, disturbing thoughts that were attempting to line up in some sort of reasonable order, she thought—

Birthmark. Lycan. Wolf in the blood.

She definitely wasn't sure about the current state of her special gifts. The injury had to have messed up those perceptions, because it seemed to her that Andre, for all this kindness, was insinuating that he was a werewolf.

Lycan.

Wolf in the blood...

And that what he was trying to tell her was that she was one, too.

Chapter 7

The wolves, each one of them weighing over a couple hundred pounds, set themselves in a wide circle around Mason, giving him plenty of room. The rippling of their fur in the breeze echoed like layers of darkness folding in on itself. The gnashing of their teeth sounded like small bones snapping in half.

Mason stood poised beneath the trees. The oncoming vampires were an assault on his senses. They were evil things, incomprehensible creatures. Ancient instincts from his days as a knight left him feeling colder and far more separated from the rest of the world than his warm-blooded wolf companions. In his past, he'd been a hunter, a predator deadlier than all the rest. With his blood running cold in his veins, he very much felt the part of the predator now.

He willed himself into a static stance and leveled

his gaze on the path, predicting how this first meeting with the neighboring bloodsuckers might go.

When the unsuspecting vampires arrived, they flowed to a stop. Seeing him, their voices trailed off with surprise and startled displeasure.

Mason counted five gaunt, corpse-pale faces attached to skeletal bodies. All five were younger than thirty in human years, and none of them radiated power. These were new vampires, probably not hungry really since they prowled the woods nightly, but ruled by the need for hunger all the same, and driven mad by the dichotomy. All of them were males. Faith's sister wasn't among them.

"What do you want here?" Mason asked in a voice carrying the chill of iced marble.

Dark, lifeless eyes searched his body for the blood they'd scented, confused that the smell didn't match with what stood in their path. They had counted on finding this blood. The youngest of them whined his displeasure.

"Not for you," Mason said. "Go home."

None of these monsters should have dared to outright defy this suggestion, able to sense the power behind the venom in his tone. Yet as the centuries went by, Mason had found that attitudes, along with a freakish acceptance of disobedient behavior from the world's youth, had translated into nearly degrading rudeness. Everything was for the self and the selfish. Turn that sort of careless youth into a vampire, and you got these five, one of whom stepped forward with its tongue out, hoping for a lick of Mason's arm, where the blood had caked to a dull maroon.

With a speed faster than even their eyes could see,

Mason had the young sucker by the throat before its stringy hair had settled against its brittle shoulders. A lesson was overdue, it seemed. These new vampires had to be taught to respect whoever was in charge.

The vampire flailed its arms and hissed through its short white fangs. Chuckling sardonically at this pathetic show of courage, Mason tossed him back to the others as easily as if he were a discarded jacket.

He wanted to do so much more to the creature. It wasn't personal, and just the way things had turned out. These five were mindless and no longer able to think past the thirst driving them.

Intelligent vampires had a choice to shun this sort of cult behavior, and a few special ones did. The decision on attitude had to be made in that first minute, when their eyes reopened to a new life and their bodies reanimated.

Over time, he had come across several special vampires living more or less peacefully in their surroundings, moving through time with their own kind of grace. This fledgling he'd just tossed to the ground hadn't made the choice to behave, a decision that seemed to have been shared by the rest of the nest Mason had been watching. Maybe it was a purposeful recruitment on the part of their master to snare the least intelligent youths.

Mason considered it astounding that these five had made it this far, and hadn't killed themselves by walking into their first sunrise. Mindless, unthinking, uncaring *and* deadly was a recipe for disaster.

"I don't believe you heard me," he chastised. This time, his message got through.

The other four vampires snapped their fangs in distress as they backed away without helping the downed vampire to his feet. From the shadows, the wolves advanced menacingly, their bodies hunched low to the ground.

The five fledglings, high with bloodlust and the wet dreams of a chase, now realized they were bested, and by an entity far beyond their reach. They disappeared silently in a back draft of angry, fetid air.

The five of them would carry the message of Mason's presence to their master, of course, which meant that the next step in his plan had been prematurely set into motion. He would have to pay a visit to the chateau sooner than expected.

"We should make sure they get home safely," he said to the wolves. "Wouldn't want them sniffing up the wrong path."

He was sure the big black-furred beast with a hide like a bear's nodded. Then Mason found himself again alone with his disconcerting thoughts.

There were five new vamps in the nest. Added to the others he'd seen recently, their number had risen in this one month alone to twelve; a dozen hungry vampires in a region that couldn't support the presence of even one of them, and shouldn't have to. Plus, somewhere in that nest was a new female unfortunate enough to have been named Hope.

Angered by the encounter, the hairs on the back of Mason's neck rose. As he stared into the distance in the direction of Andre's abode, his thoughts turned to the female in the Were's care. If she invited her wolf in, and healed as swiftly as other Lycans did, she might be up in another day or two. When the moon approached its full phase, her Lycan blood would boot her energy into high gear. She'd be stronger, dangerous in her own right and possibly a hindrance to his cause. If she tried to take matters into her own hands in regard to her sister's retrieval, she'd also be a thorn in his side.

A beautiful thorn.

He shook his head to dismiss the thought and lifted his chin to accept a new stream of insight. It wasn't only anger over the vampires causing his skin to twitch, it was the realization of the beautiful thorn having already sunk her claws into him. The tingle he felt racing up and down his spine was her, dragging her nails across the plane of his back in order to capture his full attention. She was calling to him, mind to mind, body to body, in a whisper that had already replaced the mysterious voice driving the monsters.

He could not listen to her. If he heeded her call, accepting that the drop of blood shared between them had somehow created an unexpected, ongoing bond, then she would be far more dangerous to him, to his vow and to his plans, than anything he could recall in his long lifetime. She would be *with* him, connected to him, part of him. She would know his whereabouts, and possibly what he was thinking. Her presence, however ephemeral, would raise his thirst and keep him hungry.

Mason turned from the thought. He had to get her blood off his body, get rid of her touch. Having a she-wolf threaten the goal of a Guardian was absurd.

Nevertheless, he turned back before taking a step, puzzled, searching the dark and wondering why he had almost headed the wrong way. Back to her.

It didn't take Mason long to reach his sanctuary. His house was nestled deep in the woods, and as dark as he'd left it. Remnants of an earlier fire issued filmy, ribbonlike wisps of smoke through the chimney that easily dispersed in the air.

He found the odor of wood smoke comforting. He had never allowed himself the luxury of a permanent home. A funny thing, Mason thought now, since he'd had so much time to wade through.

His travels had taken him through several countries, and spanned many years. If there had been a favorite country, city or town, he couldn't afford to think about it with a job that kept him constantly on the move.

However, this diminutive chateau on French ground, with its stone facade and cheerful mullioned windows, came as close to the concept of home as any place in recall. The woods were fragrant and secluded. He wasn't often bothered by outsiders. He could be, he had recently decided, if not actually happy, then at least less restless here. That was something.

Or maybe he had come to the same conclusion about all of the places he'd stayed, in order to survive time's passage.

The great room welcomed him with an enveloping darkness, lit only by a faint glow in the hearth. Though it was late summer, Mason stood in the center of the scantily furnished room, longing for warmth. Actual comfort was a distant memory.

The surprise was how *her* scent filled the room here, too, in a space that should have been private. He was drenched in the very essence of her, which made it impossible to forget the surprising thrill of their closeness in the woods, when he had pressed his lips to hers. For the hundredth time, he recalled how her sleek body had felt, when nestled in his arms. It was hard not to concentrate on the rightness of those things. Distance remained his only option for self-preservation.

He kicked off his boots, unzipped his jeans and pressed the bloody pants to the floor, thinking it would have been better to have shed the clothes outside, rather than bring *her* in.

Now that he had brought her into his home, he was certain she would haunt him in his one remaining place of solace. Hell, she was haunting him already. She was making him want her, when an injured she-wolf shouldn't have been considered succulent or sensual by anyone other than her own kind.

He waved off where that thought was headed with a slice of his hand through the air. "Enough!" The declaration echoed faintly in the room, as if unsure of itself.

"It's about your sister, and why she would want this," he remarked, trying to make himself believe that, when he knew better. Nothing of what he was feeling was about the lost sister who had run off with vampires. It was about the unwieldy laws of attraction between a male and a female, an attraction he likely had tweaked without meaning to, and for which he was now paying the price.

What would she think of him in that moment if she saw him standing here above the pile of clothing he'd carried her in? "Standing here, amid all these bloody rags."

Blood remained both a link to her, and a barrier. The sight and scent of it was a turnoff to humans. He'd seen them gag and faint with the merest glimpse. Tenured cops and gendarmes were often affected the same way. So were medics, doctors and surgeons, until they'd been around the fluid long enough to build up a wall of immunity.

"Blood." He said the word again and slipped his thoughts to the sister. Given nearly everyone's fear of blood, why would a young female turn herself over to bloodsuckers? What would cause anyone in their right mind to purposefully cross that line without full knowledge of the outcome? Emotion? Anger? Loss? An intrinsic fear of death? The assumption that any degree of life was better than the unknown alternative?

Maybe the key phrase in need of attention here was *in their right mind*. He knew nothing about Faith's sister, other than that Hope was a young American with at least one family member caring enough about her to place her own life in jeopardy in order to find her rebellious sibling.

Oh, yes. Faith had done that, tonight. She had placed her own life in jeopardy. These were dangerous times. Roaming these particular woods had become a suicidal act.

Mason hesitated. Then he said "Faith" aloud again, as though he were trying the name on for size.

This was the first time he had permitted himself to say her name, and the resulting disturbance in his chest was noteworthy. His beautiful thorn had been named after a concept he was all too familiar with. He had relied on his faith all this time to keep him moving forward. He had clung to his faith for most of his lifetime, anyway. Perhaps her name was an omen.

If Faith hadn't possessed the medical training to tie off her injury before he found her, she might be gone now. He might not be staring at her blood, on his clothes, on his floor, and wondering what had gotten into him to make him so distracted. So obsessed.

"Only one thing to do about it."

Mason picked up the blood-soaked jeans. He carried them to what was left of the fire in the hearth, knelt down and tossed them in. Then he used the sheer strength of his will and the remembered words of his vow to stop himself from retrieving them.

Maintaining the purity of his immortal blood was paramount. He couldn't afford to be further distracted. Look what happened when the blood of the undead was spread around like a common virus. "You get too many fangs."

It took a while and much stoking for the worn denim to catch fire. Once it did, Mason got to his feet, only partially satisfied. He wasn't free of her yet. His legs were tinted with the blood that had seeped through the jeans. That blood was now tacky in texture, and no less erotic than when he had first scented it. It was her blood. One small bit of Faith. The part through which her life flowed was treacherously branding his pale flesh.

What he needed was a hot shower, something electricity was needed for, and yet another missing luxury. Dreams of scalding water, along with a perpetual fire in the hearth, were necessary parts of his life in all seasons. Ways to experience heat, even temporarily, were meager comforts in a world that had grown cold and distant. Fire and water and heat…his only weaknesses.

Until now.

Until a small, beguiling female with an unusual scent had stumbled into these woods.

Mason glanced down at himself, at his throbbing erection. The wetness and the color of the blood striping his skin had to have been what made him so thoughtful, and any blood would have done the same.

"It doesn't have to be hers," he said, to solidify this.

But his body was telling him a different tale. His body knew the truth. It was indeed Faith's blood that set him on edge, as it was her presence in the night, in the woods, that had triggered the first of his unwieldy physical responses. The touch of her skin to his, and the smallest blood transfer, merely a drop, had sealed the deal just as surely as if he had been inside of that drop.

He was, in essence, already inside her.

"No," he added to the growing list of protests. He would not give in to the compulsion to possess her. He was so much stronger than this. He had ignored more powerful women in his lifetime, and had unwaveringly adhered to his path. He had been chosen for his strength of body and mind, and could manage this.

The question, though, was whether he wanted to manage.

"Treacherous fiend!" he said with a glance to the shuttered window. "Let her go."

Then he turned from the comforting snap of the flames, heading for a rinse of cold water he would use to christen himself back to being the kind of immortal he had been for a very long time.

Werewolf.

The idea set off an alarm that reverberated throughout Faith's body.

She ran her hands down her thighs beneath the blanket, not daring to touch the very private place where the warning ended up. She didn't know why the word affected her like this. She had never been able to see inside herself. The gift of filtering extraperceptions didn't work that way.

Werewolf?

Andre hinted of nonsensical things in elusive syllables to which she couldn't tune in because she was sensing the mental touch of someone else, coming to her from a distance. And she was reacting physically to the arrival of a silky, magnetic, if completely theoreti-

cal, breath of coolness on her skin that was less than
reality and so much more than a wish.

Mason LanVal was thinking about her, and his
thoughts were intimate.

Her body responded with a sexual quake. Moisture
gathered between her breasts, unrelated to her fever.
And though the room had grown cold with the suggestion of unfathomable mystery, Mason LanVal's attention burned through it all as slickly as if her dark
stranger had actually penetrated her body.

"No!" She heard his vehement protest. It plunged
into her vulnerable mental softness with a thrust that
left her breathless.

"Let her go!" She heard him say that, too, as if he
had to convince himself.

LanVal was talking to himself, and the intimacy of
his remarks were affecting her personally, in private
places relegated to a lover's touch. In lieu of a hand between her legs, his whisper brushed her there. Instead
of his lips sliding across hers, she felt them move from
a damnable distance.

He was urging himself to leave her alone, while
fighting that directive, and somehow, she was hearing
his thoughts, sharing his turbulent emotions. Either she
had tuned in to him for some reason, or her imagina-
tion truly had been as irreparably damaged as her leg.

Her attention veered to the doorway. His voice might
have come from there. But it hadn't. A bond had been
established when he had rescued her, and something
between them had been left unfinished. The unifying
spark tying them together still burned. Although Mason
LanVal left her here, he hadn't let go of her completely,
no matter how much he wanted to.

Was he like her, then? Possessed of extra senses that

were bringing them together? That seemed the only explanation for the tumultuous, deep-seated thrill she was experiencing.

And if she was hearing him, he might also hear her. If she called him back, surely he would come.

LanVal, she sent to him, concentrating hard, testing her theory.

Anxious, she awaited his reply with her eyes closed and her thighs pressed together.

Noting a tug on the blanket, she opened her eyes to find not Mason LanVal, but a lined face beneath a shock of gray hair, and a pair of green eyes peering into hers. Andre. The madman.

"I don't want any more." Faith held up the glass he had handed her. "My head needs to be clear. If that means accepting the pain I'm supposed to be experiencing, so be it."

Andre didn't argue, though his forehead creased. He wasn't going away. He had promised to stay and watch over her, as she would have done if the tables had been reversed.

"Tell me more about the birthmark," she said to temporarily take her mind off the man who may or may not have heard her silent call.

"There will be time for explanations," Andre said. "You're looking wan, and rightly so. What you need right now is more medication, and rest." He alluded to the glass in her hand.

Faith shook her head. "You can't leave something lingering like that, and then refuse to explain. Please tell me more about what you think you are."

As Andre appraised her with heavy-lidded eyes, Faith could have sworn she saw the hint of a grin lift his lips.

"My concern is why you don't already know what the mark on your arm means. I have to wonder why your parents didn't tell you, and prepare you for what lies ahead."

Andre's concern was palpable, and maybe his half-assed stab at answering her question by asking another question made sense in some alternate universe, but not in this one. She was ill, not stupid. She was frustrated, and very close to shouting.

"I suppose," Andre slowly continued, "that voicing my concern is hypothetical, even useless at this point. I'm just sorry I have to be the one to tell you about yourself."

About herself? She was well acquainted with that subject. For instance, she had always been a fighter, and more or less a loner. Being born with the ability she had for opening herself up to faculties above and beyond the norm had made those other traits requirements. She had always been different.

How neat was it to know what friends really thought, or what scandals a date really had in mind? That someone came to your tenth birthday party only because they were told they had to, in order to keep up appearances in the neighborhood? What did anyone know about what it was like to sense so many dark emotions in others and in the world around her, to an almost heartrending degree? How about rampant emotions like hate and jealousy?

Andre had no idea how diligently her mother had worked to prepare her for the life ahead. Danika James had spent years soothing, cajoling, and at the same time coaxing this gift out of her daughter. Fine-tuning it. And when Faith had matured, and become aware of how this gift could be nurtured and used for her benefit, then she had lost her mother.

She'd found a modicum of peace, and what had seemed almost like happiness, in medical school, and then as a doctor. In a practice that was inherently competitive by nature, she was able to work on her own, and was free to utilize her special talents. In diagnosing and treating others, she had found a useful place, and a reason for believing in her gift.

Now, here, and a long way from home, she had virtually stumbled upon a person displaying a similar trait in Mason LanVal. The prospect of this kind of shared experience was a thrill, and left her feeling less alone.

She wanted LanVal to return and tell her about himself. She damned herself for getting caught in the filthy trap that had robbed her of her mobility, and was sure the white stuff in Andre's bottle was leaving her with a false sense of well-being.

And though Andre waited for her to say something, LanVal had withdrawn, like a lover who had promised, teased, laid his skin against hers and then pulled out suddenly, leaving her panting and unsure.

Who are you? What are you like, really?

She was sure Mason LanVal was tall and broad shouldered, with stern, chiseled, aristocratic features surrounded by masses of midnight-black hair. His arms were uncommonly strong, and had carried her more than a mile to Andre's house. Were these accurate descriptions, or simply wishful thinking?

Was it crazy to imagine she had merged with Mason LanVal's thoughts?

Maybe she was the mad one here.

He had given her his shirt. Remembering that, Faith searched the cot and didn't find it. Looking to Andre for the explanation, she found him waiting patiently for her wits to make a comeback.

"He won't return," Andre said, as though everyone in the vicinity could read minds. "He doesn't belong here. He isn't like us."

"Does he know what you think you are?"

If her question sounded rude, she wasn't going to take the time to try to soften it.

"More to the point," Andre said, "he knows about you."

"Knows what about me?"

"That you're a Lyncanthrope. A werewolf. Only genetic Lycans bear the Moon Mark, which is what that birthmark on your arm is. Only genetic Lycans can pass that mark down through a family tie."

It was, Faith thought, useless to respond, since what Andre had proposed was so appallingly absurd.

Still, she again felt the annoying flicker of heat that came with having heard the truth.

"And what is he, if not like us?" she asked, challenging how far Andre would go with whatever this game was.

"We simply call him the Guardian."

"That's not half as bad as what you're saying we are."

Andre nodded, his eyes bright with what Faith took to be secrets. "Drink up, and rest. What's in that glass won't harm you. I won't harm you. I can't say the same for LanVal, but you're safe here, while his attention is elsewhere."

"You're insinuating that he is a danger to me, after helping me get this far?" she asked.

Andre said nothing more.

Faith turned her attention to the milky liquid in the

glass, trying to decipher its chemistry. The fluid had a slight shimmery cast to it, reminiscent of the silver metals once used in medications in the older days.

Unlike some other metals, silver couldn't really hurt her in moderation, and might only show up as shiny silver patches in the dermis of her skin. If taken in quantity, however, it could lead to a condition called argyria; to seizures, ulcers and even death.

Andre had said he'd also rubbed this liquid into her wounds. Wound dressings with slow-release silver compounds in them were still used in some clinical settings, though the FDA had banned usage in over-the-counter medicines. If it was the silver in this liquid that was helping her, had the medical community lost touch with a valuable, semi-miraculous healing aid?

"Why do you call him a guardian?" she asked.

"Because that's what he calls himself. And that's what he is."

She thought of LanVal walking the woods in search of people to help. She thought of his strong hands pulling animals from the traps, and either helping them to safety or setting them free. The images were disturbing, as was the final one that arrived in Technicolor.

Hope. Out there in the night. Caught in a trap. Bloody and hurting and scared.

She could hardly bear that image, but what could she do? She wasn't any good to anybody like this. She was now trapped here in blankets, instead of that damn bear trap.

Lifting the glass to her mouth with shaky hands, she asked over the rim, "What does LanVal guard?"

"I suppose you might say he guards the world. As much of it as he can, anyway."

Andre was serious, Faith saw.

She took a sip of the bitter liquid and made a face. The stuff tasted of burned bark and tree roots. A faint after-burn of alcohol, similar to taking a gulp of a really bad martini, left her throat feeling raw and abused. But she drank again, downing the remaining portion, figuring it would be better to get the gag reflex over with all at once, and that it would be far better to pass out than to be plagued by guilt and nightmares.

Strangely enough, the choking reflex never came. Instead, and immediately after swallowing the last drop of Andre's filmy potion, a growing lightness took over her limbs, matched by a similar airiness in her head. The ache behind her eyes winked out. Her stomach calmed. The room stopped revolving.

As Andre took the glass from her, Faith said through numb lips, "What does the world need protection from?"

LanVal was there again, in the question, in the woods, tearing off his shirt for her to bite on, opening the weighty, bloody trap, lifting her into his arms.

Although she wasn't completely certain, and was starting down the rapid descent into a medicated sleep, Faith thought she heard Andre answer her question about what the world needed protection from. But this, too, had to be the workings of his milky concoction. Because what she thought she heard him say was:

"Vampires."

Chapter 8

He was looking for a brutal-minded killer, not a lover.

Chanting that mantra to himself, Mason wound his way through the trees and brush, careful to check for traps, obliterating those he found in the best way he could. He would return later to remove them. Just then, he was driven toward another task where caution and timing were crucial.

There was a monster on the loose. A prime vampire with delusions of grandeur. Getting closer to the nest might enable him to find out more about this creature, and required caution.

As objectionable as it was, there were reasons a strong vampire might set himself up as king. Surrounded by other blood drinkers, a master with more than a few brains and a head for leadership could gather minions at a dime a dozen. He might gather them even faster if he created them himself. If he didn't want to get his fangs dirty, he could instruct his fledglings to bring him his meals. And if he wasn't hungry, he'd have his servants create more of themselves, enabling that master vampire to skip the recruitment part altogether.

Only a bloody beast would think in this way, and this master was more than a mere beast, Mason knew. He'd felt the monster's reach, had heard the voice driving frenzy into the young bloodsuckers. This master was intelligent, vicious and on a roll.

Dappled moonlight struck Mason's skin as he walked beneath the tree canopy in silence. These same circles of light were like lunar kisses to the wolves, kisses that could alternately mesmerize or torture them, depending on the strengths of their own genetic makeup.

He'd seen werewolves tear their own morphing flesh apart trying to stop a painful transformation. He'd also witnessed alphas of Andre's status blend seamlessly from one shape to another, as if they only had to choose one. But Andre's kind of strength was rare. And werewolves weren't really wolves, only an interesting crossbreed.

On the other hand, vampires maintained a portion of the appearance of the humans they once were, which made them able to walk among mankind if they chose, and if they kept to the darker spaces. The problem being, there were plenty of those darker spaces.

Most werewolves were able to live within society, hold down jobs and have houses in neat neighborhoods, except for the two or three nights per month when the wildness, dictated by a full moon, came upon them. There were, of course, bad wolves among the lot. But the Were clans had ways of dealing with miscreants.

Most vampires seemed to have ditched all connection to civilized behavior over time, and were reduced to stalking the nighttime hours. But then vampires were walking undead. That made a huge difference.

Undead. The thought produced a rerun of a disturbing idea. If Faith's sister had Were blood in her, and the master vampire in this nest was as powerful as Mason assumed he might be, the combination would be worse than he had feared. If vampires bit Faith's sister during a full moon phase, she would be a beast, frozen in that beast's shape, with fangs and an insatiable thirst for blood.

Hell, what would such a thing look like?

His attention stirred, Mason brought his head up to sniff the air. "Andre," he said, sensing the distant approach of the Were. He repeated the greeting once Andre had arrived, adding, "How did you find me?"

Andre tapped his nose with a finger.

"Who is watching over her while she sleeps, Andre?"

Fresh from his run, Andre seemed a brooding, watchful presence. Mixed into the Were's own special scent was the odor of his recent meeting with others of his pack.

"Gregoire is there," Andre said. "One of the strongest of my kind, he is backed by another."

"Good."

Andre cocked his head. "How do you know she sleeps?"

"The voice in my mind is silent."

"Her voice?"

Since Andre's tone held a hint of surprise, Mason knew better than to say anything further on the subject of his unusual connection with Faith.

"Why have you come?" Mason asked.

"To tell you that her sister doesn't bear the mark."

Mason studied the Were. "It helps lessen the stakes

somewhat," he said, turning over this news. "Are you sure?"

"Faith confirmed it, but I had figured this already," Andre confessed.

"Yes. I thought you might have. Otherwise, you wouldn't have let the other girl go."

"I'm not sure about lessening the stakes, LanVal," Andre continued. "The sister isn't completely human, either. Not Were, nor human."

Mason recalled the white-faced young woman in the woods who had run by him.

"Does Faith know you saw her sister?"

"I failed to mention it, as a matter of fact," Andre replied, "figuring there would be a better time for her to possess that information."

Mason found himself liking Andre more all the time.

"Does Faith know that her sister isn't like her?" he asked the Were.

Andre shook his head. "Family faux pas, on a grand scale, I'm thinking. Could be her sister was adopted. Also could have been the result of something that happened when she was young."

"Could Other blood have overridden a Moon Mark?"

"Nothing can remove the mark itself, but as you well know, LanVal, blood issues can be tricky, complicated things. A scratch, a bite, a brush with something else…"

They weren't off the hook. But if Faith's sister wasn't a genetic werewolf, and wasn't fully human, what was she?

"Why are you telling me this, Andre?"

"In case you skipped a step on the ladder of your own agenda because of the need to catch an abomination."

"And if this sister is one, still?"

"We don't know what she'll be when the bloodsuckers get through with her."

"We let her go," Mason said.

"Yes, we did. Or at least, I did. As soon as our backs were turned, she must have gone to them, as if she had come here for that very reason. As if she knew they were here."

Mason felt a tingle of apprehension return, this one located between his shoulder blades, at the site of his blooded tattoo. The discomfort telegraphed to him that Andre was hiding something.

"What is Faith's sister?" he asked the Were.

"I'm not sure," Andre replied.

"A tastier meal than a human, nonetheless?" Mason suggested.

"Catching anything in these traps other than animal, human or Were is fairly rare. Haven't you known this to be so?" Andre replied.

"In all my time on earth, which is considerable, I have never run across a species unknown to me. But my mind has been focused in one direction for a very long time."

Andre grinned. "I assumed you might be long in the tooth, LanVal."

Mason got the joke that fit on so many levels, and almost smiled back—which caused him to wonder if he remembered how to smile. Long ago, he had smiled often, finding mirth in all sorts of things. Maybe he was, he concluded now, as rusty as the traps in these woods. It had been necessary for him to kiss social skills goodbye once he'd left his former life behind, and his new existence had to be kept secret.

"Do you know what I am, Andre?" he asked.

"I have a fair idea."

"Do you want to know if you're right?"

"Not necessarily, as long as we're on the same side."

Mason accepted that with a nod. "Are you willing to help the sister if she isn't Were?"

"Doing so would be helping my own clan in the long run."

Again, Mason caught a hint of secrets on the wind, though none of them showed plainly on Andre's features.

"How far are you willing to go?" he asked the Were.

"As far as the chateau's bloody hallways if that's where this current path leads," Andre said.

"Even if there's a big surprise waiting there?"

Andre grinned again. "I don't take kindly to pots of wolf stew on their gilded plates, or traps that cause the bloody, broken limbs of any beast. So I'll be waiting for word."

"And when it's full?" Mason waved at the moon.

"Even better," Andre concluded. With a smile and the flick of his hand, he sprinted off, leaving Mason alone with his centuries of haunted memories in a shallow puddle of silvery light.

"Where are you? Please come back." Faith's plea arrived as a whisper, ruffling through the hair at Mason's temples before drifting through the chambers of his heart.

He stood beneath the trees like a carved stone sentinel, watching for movement, sorting through the threads of his past; the parts of it that would keep him from a woman whose voice conjured up a new restlessness.

Haunting memories...

The dancing beams of moonlight through the

branches, so reminiscent of a room full of candles, sent Mason backward to a time he didn't often revisit.

His death and rebirth. The things that kept him removed from the rest of the world.

The pictures in his mind were vivid enough to touch and, as always, possessed their own pungent smells.

He had accepted the invitation to the Castle Broceliande on the assurances of his friends of its reputation for bestowing favor upon knights in service to the crown. Would he attend them, the invitation inquired, written in red script and accompanied by a handsome young squire of regal bearing. And would he be pleased to attend them right away.

He had been intrigued.

He'd found the castle secluded deep in the forest of the Bras-De-Fer, on French shores. The beautiful stone edifice was surrounded by perfumed gardens that sent lush fragrances through the cool autumn air. Tiered fountains sang to welcome him.

He'd thought it strange that no people were milling about, enjoying the rare beauty of the place, and odder yet that no one waited in the great hall to greet him, though the squire in attendance to him on this journey didn't register concern.

Broceliande was a small castle fortress, he'd found, fortified inside with intricate buttresses and two sculpted towers. The walls, both inside and out, were composed of irregular cut and quarried French limestone, creamy in color and pleasing to the eye. But the castle's interior reflected none of that lightness. There were few slit windows spaces.

The chamber given to him was high up in the beams, a resplendent, lavishly decorated room with ornate furniture and exotic fabrics in palettes of gray and blue.

Candles, carefully doled out in all residences, including the royal courts, due to the scarcity of tallow, were in shocking abundance here, awaiting nightfall, ready to chase away the most persistent shadows.

Shadows.

Mason winced at the memory of his own naiveté and raked his hair back from his face. He wasn't sure why the memory was so painful. After all, he had agreed to the pact that had been offered to him, if not completely willingly, at first. He had, in truth, believed the offer and the strange countenance of Broceliande's occupants to be some sort of charade. All courts loved games.

They had come for him at dusk. Three beautiful people, comely to the last detail. Their throats, fingers and wrists glittered with jewels that served to highlight pale, perfect flesh that hadn't been privy to the gardens of delight created for them outside. These were people, it seemed, who slept away the day and rose when the sun went down to indulge their every whim.

On the surface, in physical matters, he had fit right in—with his tall, sinewy physique, sculpted to hard muscle on the fighting fields, and the black hair that reached to his shoulders. But his own questioning intelligence had soon seen through their disguises. Castle Broceliande's occupants may indeed have been royal by birth, and as handsome as fallen stars, but they were no longer human.

And it was no game they played.

Mason ran his fingers over the chilled skin of his face, and again tilted his head to look up at the moon. So far from that distant place, and that time, the chill persisted each time the image of the castle's inhabitants came to him. The incredibly white faces of the woman and her two male companions. The scarlet lips covering gleaming teeth. The thick, deep red liquid swirling in their golden goblets.

Broceliande's occupants had been a surprise. A revelation. And his visit there had turned out to be so much more than he could ever have imagined.

In that windowless castle, he had been handed a challenge, a quest, and he had paid for its acceptance with his life. In return for this favor, he'd been given an opportunity relegated to the very few who had only hoped for such an event in their dreams. He had beheld the Grail, the holiest of all relics, its elusive presence among humans rumored to have the power to heal a land in turmoil. Whoever viewed this relic, legend foretold, would be blessed. It was said that whoever drank from the chalice would be resurrected, as was the Grail's original bearer. Born again.

Castle Broceliande's inhabitants had been afraid to sip from that cup. Their lives had already been extended by other means, and not in the way they had foreseen. Where they once had desired peace and life everlasting, after their own resurrection, they also began to crave the taste of blood.

They became what would soon be known as vampires, but with parts of their transcendent souls intact. They would live this new kind of life forever, without aging and with their physical beauty in place, but could no longer walk in the daylight or feel the sun's warmth. Nor did they dare to mix with others, fearing the intensity of their strange hunger. Lacking the need for food, yet ravaged by a new and relentless thirst, Castle Broceliande's three occupants began to feed from each other.

Their blessing, their self-imposed quarantine and their unusual cravings eventually became a tiresome horror to them. By the time Mason had arrived, they had secluded themselves from society for fifty years, and had been drinking each other's blood for more than a hundred. They had grown weary of their ghoulish existence.

But the ancient blood that had permanently stained the chalice brought a new kind of life force altogether, they promised.

Their objective had been to pass this gift of immortality on to seven fresh, stronger souls, already proved in worth elsewhere. They would pass their gift to men, and the men they chose were knights who would, by necessity, become celibate monks, reclusive bearers of the holy magic of the sacred chalice.

Afterward, only one of the seven Blood Knights would know the whereabouts of the Grail, and that one was to be charged with the task of keeping the artifact safely out of the hands of others. This task was multidimensional, and a parable in itself. Was it the Grail that needed protecting from the mortals in search of it, or did the mortals themselves need protection from the magic of the Grail?

The quest seemed both beautiful and terrible. Mason had understood this, as had the other six knights. And he, Mason LanVal, had been charged with the ultimate task. An unbearable quest. Immortal life, while carrying on the principles of Good, in whatever form that took, while acting as Guardian of the secret transgressions of the holy Grail. Forever.

If not a religious calling, it was something freakishly similar. So many people during that time and after had spent their own lifetimes searching for what he had once held in his hands. What had touched his lips.

But the castle's blood-drinking occupants hadn't known for sure how the knights' resurrections would work. When the Seven drank from the cup, they had indeed become something bigger and better, and also strikingly similar to the Three.

Deed accomplished, the lives of LanVal and the other six Blood Knights continued on. And would do so until such a time as they decided, as had Castle Broceliande's occupants, to either end their own lives or pass this dark, perhaps even treacherous, magic on. Doing either of those things would necessitate that the Seven come together, face-to-face, to break the bond.

Yet one of the Seven had tried, unsuccessfully, to stretch that bond out of recognition, on his own. As a result, parts of the world were in peril.

"Help me!"

Faith's new call shook him up, causing the memories to dissipate. The timbre of her voice haunted him more than all those other memories, telling him to pay attention to what this meant. She may have been the sole reason he'd gone back to take a second look at himself and his decisions. Some part of him desperately wished he could again be just a man, a mortal, and able to be with her for one single lifetime.

Yet if Faith wasn't human, where would be the sense in that wish?

He found it impossible to ignore her. She was connecting to him via their mystifying union, and asking him to go to her, with Andre and his wolves standing guard. He had issued the order for the Weres to keep him away. He'd given them permission to use whatever force was necessary to accomplish that.

But he was pulled by her call, and wary of the barriers separating them. A leopard could not change its spots. He could not go back in time to make different choices. He was what he was.

Lifting his chin to listen, Mason heard nothing further, felt nothing further, and didn't like it. He was alone again in his own skin, with a silence too final. He'd been left with a craving for Faith that rivaled every hunger he had ever known.

He knew what she wanted. He would find her sister, do this for her, not just for justice's sake, but so that he could see Faith again.

"Little wolf," he whispered, pacing in a small circle. "Are you there?

Although no answer came, not even the mistiest touch, his heart continued to pound. Both of his shoulders twitched.

He couldn't wait to see her again.

Had to see her again.

"Just this once."

Chapter 9

Faith had fitful dreams bordering on the edge of nightmare.

Both in and out of consciousness, she saw Hope's face flash by in fleeting streams of light. She heard her own voice calling out over and over in a panicky chant for her sister to stop running. She again saw the whiteness of Hope's face and the twisted expression on it. The fear on it.

She opened her eyes with a start.

"You're going to be all right," Andre said, though it took a minute for her to process who had spoken. "Bad dreams tend to hover over illness."

Andre stood by the fireplace. The candles had burned out. The room was now lit by the soft glow of a fire Andre had likely kept stoked for her with another show of kindness.

"Have you found her?" Faith asked. "Hope?"

"We're looking," Andre said.

They were working on finding her sister, and Andre had said "we." Had Mason LanVal changed his mind?

Her heart rate spiked with the thought of LanVal's capable arms reaching out for Hope and bringing her back.

"You'll need to drink more of this." Andre set a glass beside her. "It's time. The body mends faster at rest."

Faith had no intention of drinking more of his concoction. She needed to think, to make sense of what she'd seen on Hope's face. If Hope had been afraid, why hadn't she stopped?

Damn it, why didn't you stop?

"I'll be outside this door," Andre said. "I'll hear if you call."

When he had gone, Faith gathered up the blanket, needing to see the true extent of the damage she'd taken to her leg, and whether there was any way—any way at all—she could move, at least as far as a neighboring phone.

Her hands stopped pulling. She looked up, pulse starting to race, knowing without a doubt that Mason LanVal had heard her call and was coming for her.

The scent of wolves spiced up the forest. They had marked their territory afresh after their run-in with the vampires.

Vampire scent underscored the other smells with a virulent punch of metallic agitation. They'd gone back to their nest, but some of them, or their brothers, had returned to the night not long afterward. Would a young female be among the scavengers looking for prey? Mason wondered. If so, he'd eventually find her.

First, he had to take care of something. He had to

pull a tenacious thorn from his side, and nderstand how that thorn had worked its way in. In order to do that, he had to tiptoe around Andre's pack.

He slowed when the overlaying wolf scent became stronger, and paused to take stock. It wasn't easy to pull one over on a werewolf. Almost impossible, really, unless you had a couple hundred years head start on stealth, plus the blood of immortality in your veins.

Willing himself into stillness, Mason concentrated on Andre's house, just over the rise. Faith was there, her presence like a glimmer of light in the dark landscape.

Andre and the others had gathered outside where they would feel freer. The wolves he'd met earlier were no longer on all fours. In all, three big werewolves in man form guarded the door as Faith's capable bodyguards. Not exactly a cakewalk, and risky for a small party of young vampires…but doable odds for a Blood Knight.

Mason grinned, but not out of self-satisfaction. He and these fearsome Weres were on the same side, save for one little thing—a female named Faith, and his access to her.

For the sake of this small corner of France and the people in the towns populating it, he couldn't push the wolves too far off their agenda. Nor could he lay claim to one of their own, though Faith's hidden identity was open to interpretation, he supposed, if she didn't know about herself and had never changed her shape.

He strode on, jaw set, hands fisted. If Faith was Lycan, he wanted to see evidence of it. Sometimes, seeing was absolutely necessary for believing.

He paused to eye the structure of Andre's cottage from the path beyond it and inhaled a whiff of air to get his bearings. Then he frowned. The darkness here had a foulness to it that hadn't been present earlier. That foulness battled for his attention, because it was the sudden, none-too-subtle poison of vamp pheromones not too far away that clogged up the freshness of the breeze. The Weres had noticed it, too. Their heads were up. They looked like statues in their motionless state of hyperawareness.

"Call the pack." He heard Andre's directive.

A howl went up from the throat of a black-haired man of middle age and towering height, whose body was far more powerfully built than the rest of those present, and twice as formidable. All three Weres were as large in their man shapes as they had been as wolves. When they'd meet somewhere in the middle as were-wolves—neither fully wolf nor man—they'd be the stuff of nightmares to anyone stumbling by.

However, having them in readiness for a second vampire intrusion into their territory hampered Mason's objective of seeing Faith. Also problematic was the persistence of an ungainly troupe of teething vampires who didn't know their place. The Weres could handle the fledglings, of course, with their hands tied behind their backs. And soon, as an ode to the forthcoming Blood Moon, there would be more Weres on the way.

Taking advantage of the few rare seconds of opportunity, Mason approached the cottage from the back and scaled a wall to the roof. From there, he swung himself down to a window, opened it quietly and slipped inside.

The room was in near total darkness, its meager illumination coming from a fire in the hearth. For that bit of luck, Mason was thankful. Faith wouldn't be able to see evidence of the interest he could barely hide.

He was virtually pulsing, trepidation and secret longings mixing to warp the surrounding air. His fangs were extended.

Faith was sitting up on the cot in the corner. Her anxiety made her glow like she'd swallowed a light beam, and that light seeped out of her pores. She was wide-awake, her huge eyes open. Her breathing was shallow.

She had been waiting for him, sure he would come, using that uncanny sixth sense she possessed that had allowed her to locate him earlier that night. She was aware of his closeness now. He had helped to fine-tune these extraordinary senses by providing an infusion of some of his own.

"LanVal."

Her voice was equally vibrant and defenseless, husky and smooth. Hearing it stopped his thoughts momentarily.

"You called," he said, like a servant might, without moving toward her. But every cell in his body demanded he touch her, taste her, find the reason for this inexplicable bond.

"You heard me?" Her tone suggested she couldn't believe it and that she feared she might be dreaming this encounter, just as she might have dreamed the last. Her next question was whispered. "How?"

He had no answer for her that she would understand. Beyond that, he didn't know why the link had lasted so long. One drop of his blood surely couldn't have fused them together for so long. Yet he sensed his blood still there inside her, moving through her system, influencing her in ways new to them both.

Was it possible that his feelings for her were born

of a more simple explanation, such as his body merely recognizing the missing drop of his blood and wanting it back?

"Will they hear us?" She glanced to the door.

"Yes. Their hearing is extraordinary."

"Because they are werewolves?"

She'd spoken the last word with the audible dread of an outrageous belief. "Yes. Because of that," he replied, watching her, thinking her truly exquisite, even with her silky hair in a damp, tangled disarray and her oval face taken over by her wide, luminous eyes.

"You can't sleep?" he asked. "It's late in the night."

"Are you all mad?" she tossed back. "I asked Andre that same question."

"What did he say?"

She brushed the question away with her hand. At the moment, to her, the answer was of no consequence. But she didn't realize that madness was an integral part of the heart of the matter. Things, entities, she might consider nightmares did live and take part in her world—a world that was, for her, about to unravel at the seams.

Because she was one of them.

"Well, I suppose everything is open to debate," Mason said. "You must know, however, that everyone here has your best interests at heart."

"Not my sister's?"

The swiftness of her comeback surprised him. She wasn't half as sluggish as she should have been, given what had happened to her. Her mind buzzed with perceivable activity. Like him, she had swallowed a storm system that was electrifying. There was a chance much of this was the direct result of his chancy blood donation. Some of it, though, could just as easily be the wolf in her beginning to blossom.

Had he awakened her long-hidden beast by blood or touch? All that confusion tumbling inside of her could be evidence of the escalation of the activity of her own internal chaos. It also could be, he again reasoned, that the single drop of immortal blood added to hers had been the key to opening what lay dormant at Faith James's core.

Whatever had happened between them, it was too late now to regret or analyze it. Nothing was to be gained by going back.

"Then it's true," she said. "You don't deny there are such creatures as werewolves."

"Those, and more," he replied. Short of breath and nearly powerless in his resolution to keep himself from her, Mason remained wary of the brightness and intensity of an attraction that refused to dim.

"Andre said you're not like them," she said.

Mason heard what she didn't add. *And not like what Andre thinks he and I are.*

Did she want him to declare himself sane, and free of Andre's delusions? If so, she was awaiting explanations she'd never get. Now that the Were had taken the first step by telling her what she was, things had been set in motion. He felt the wheels turning.

But it was obvious to him that Faith didn't believe Andre. Her confusion reached Mason like an open extended hand he wanted to grasp. If he took that hand, though, they might both go down, their objectives obliterated by the intensity of the physical needs raging within them.

"I'm not quite like them, that's true," he said.

Her relief was instantaneous and visible. She blinked slowly, then closed her eyes, waiting for the passage of several erratic heartbeats. Closing her eyes was an action of trust, Mason realized, and that trust beat at him fiercely. She didn't know who he was or what he was. She had no knowledge of the extent of his cravings, his longings or the ravenous hunger. She knew nothing of the insatiable thirst he had always denied.

"Andre isn't telling me something important." Her voice was again like the caress of a wayward breeze, arriving to stroke his lips. Mason leaned toward her, straining to keep back, wanting to respond to her remark. But their time together was too short for explanations that would cover centuries. Andre was outside, and Weres could discern a whisper from great distances. A werewolf's hearing was its strongest trait. The only reason Andre hadn't already barged in was probably due to the blasphemous odor of vampires in the wind.

Mason knew all this, and yet Faith was waiting for him to fill her in. Any answer might serve to ease her frantic mind.

"Andre withholds information for your own good," he said.

"You know what that information is?"

"In part," he admitted, taking the step forward he had willed himself from, drawn by her expression and her heat.

"Take me to her, LanVal."

With that same uncanny insight, Faith had guessed at what news they were withholding from her, and that it had to do with her sister's whereabouts.

"It's far too dangerous," he said, his fingers beginning to twitch with the anticipation of reaching her side.

"Is Hope dead?"

It might be so, and not in any way you might envision. So, how can I answer your question?

He did not speak the thought, afraid it might shatter the fragility of the moment.

"Do Lyncanthropes have her, too?" she asked.

Lycanthrope. Another word she hardly got out as she groped for answers no one was providing.

"No," he said. "As strange as it sounds, if she were with Lycans, she'd likely be as safe as you are."

"Am I safe?"

"Yes." *From others, at least. Not necessarily from me. But then, you know this, as well, don't you?*

He could see her thinking. Her forehead creased slightly. Her eyes narrowed.

"You know where my sister is," she said, desperation returning to darken her tone.

Mason felt the rapid rise and fall of each stroke of her heart. He watched those pulses visibly lift the skin just below her left ear as if they were signals from a homing beacon put there to tempt him that way. He heard the thump in her chest, loud in the small room, and felt his own heart speed up to match her rhythm, molding to hers, thrumming in sync with hers—a phenomenon usually reserved for chasing prey in the woods.

But Faith James wasn't prey. She was a female who had somehow imprinted herself on him, for good or ill. He could not lie with her. Nor could he lie to her. Although he wasn't able to tell her everything, he couldn't be untruthful while harboring the beat of her life force inside his own chest. The rhythm of their frantic duet made him feel stronger, more alive, more like the man he had once been in another lifetime. Her nearness brought back those useless, forgotten moments of regret over what he had become.

"I believe I know where your sister has gone," he

conceded, and was rewarded—or was he damned?—
by her gasp of breath that lifted the blanket tucked
around her.

One bare shoulder emerged, crossed by the thinnest
slip of a lace strap. There was no marring of its satiny
smoothness by a Lycan mark on the exposed portion
of this arm.

His gaze traveled to the deep, lush V of space between her collarbones, and to the stretch of tanned
flawless skin beneath that may have been further evidence of her latent Lycan blood. The moon liked her
children to be perfect, and ensured this was so by eras-
ing external flaws touched by her light. From what he
could see, Faith James was already a physical manifestation of perfection.

His fangs ached damnably. His entire body ached,
though he had never known illness. It was obvious
she was strong, ripe, maybe even willing to accept his
closeness. Her extra senses were failing her now.

Soon, when her bone and tissue had regenerated,
she would run, naked, with the Weres in the moonlight.
Her golden skin would shine.

Mason willed his boots to remain nailed to the floor,
tossing off the enticement of that thought, and of catching up to her out there. His body shuddered against the
tightness of his hold. Faith had no idea how vulnerable
and sensuous she looked, and how very hungry he was
for those things.

"Have you seen her? Tell me the truth," she whispered uncertainly, perhaps sensing the riot beneath his
stillness.

"I have seen her," he said.

Her features loosened slightly, some of pain's trac-
ings eased away by this revelation. In spite of every-

Paranormal Reading...

TWO BOOKS FREE!

Each of your FREE books will thrill you with dramatic, sensual tales featuring dark, sexy and powerful characters.

We'd like to send you **two free books** to introduce you to the Reader Service. Your two books are worth over $10, but they are yours free! We'll even send you **two exciting surprise gifts**. There's no catch. You're under no obligation to buy anything. We charge nothing – **ZERO** – for your first shipment. *You can't lose!*

Visit us at
www.ReaderService.com

YOURS FREE!
We'll send you 2 fabulous surprise gifts (worth about $10) just for trying "Paranormal"!

The Reader Service — Here's How it Works:

Accepting your 2 free books and 2 free gifts (gifts valued at approximately $10.00) places you under no obligation to buy anything. You may keep the books and gifts and return the shipping statement marked "cancel". If you do not cancel, about a month later we'll send you 4 additional books and bill you just $21.42 in the U.S. or $23.46 in Canada. That's a savings of at least 21% off the cover price of all 4 books! It's quite a bargain! Shipping and handling is just 50¢ per book in the U.S. and 75¢ per book in Canada.* You may cancel at any time, but if you choose to continue, every month we'll send you 4 more books, which you may either purchase at the discount price or return to us and cancel your subscription.

*Terms and prices subject to change without notice. Prices do not include applicable taxes. Sales tax applicable in N.Y. Canadian residents will be charged applicable taxes. Offer not valid in Quebec. All orders subject to credit approval. Credit or debit balances in a customer's account(s) may be offset by any other outstanding balance owed by or to the customer. Please allow 4 to 6 weeks for delivery. Offer available while quantities last.

thing that had happened to her, and what she'd been told by Andre, Faith believed him. The fact that he had rescued her was foremost in her mind. That they had met, flesh to flesh, also had meaning for her, as if she knew instinctively that he would continue to help her.

Still, she had not discerned nearly enough of his nature. She didn't know that she had been kissed by immortality, teased with a lethal fang into surviving. She failed to see that his blood maintained the bond that had sprung into existence between them.

Faith wasn't ready to hear and accept what such a bond meant, or see what he saw in it—the euphoric highs, crushing lows and the undeniable flaws. She couldn't possibly predict what might happen when that bond dissolved—knowledge both he and Andre possessed, at least in part.

And at the moment, with his heart beating fast and his fangs dropped, his desire was to go to her anyway, and to quiet her agitation in any way he could. He ached to bury his fingers in her hair, nestle his face against her neck, right above that pounding pulse—and then allow himself to gingerly explore her other intimate places. He wanted to console her, whisper calming things to her that wouldn't necessarily turn out to be true and recite phrases about happy endings.

All that, and he didn't dare move, out of the fear of hurting her further. Though this female named Faith might have placed her faith in him, he no longer completely trusted himself. There was one more thing he wanted from her. An awful thing. A damned, unconscionable, forbidden thing.

Just one taste of your blood, in return for mine.

Sweet Jesus! He wanted to feel her blood winding through his veins. Feel her inside of him. He craved the sensation of her essences mingling with his own in a new and profoundly powerful way—an action substantially more intimate than taking her to bed would be, although that came close.

Oh, yes. He wanted her in bed, too, so badly that his fingers continued to curl against his palm, and his body continued to throb. He was sure that time had done this to him, by catching up with him at last. In his mind's eye, he saw daylight streaming through a vow that had become noticeably transparent.

"What can I do to make you help me?" she asked, her lovely eyes averted. "To get you to help my sister?"

"Nothing," he answered. "There is nothing you can do that will see me any more committed to the task at hand than I already am."

Tearing his gaze from her, he looked quickly to the door, then silently cursed the sudden distraction dividing his attention.

Andre was outside that door, and about to enter.

Bloody bad timing!

He had only moments more with Faith. Precious few seconds, after so many lifetimes spent waiting for the mother of all distractions that could very well prove to be *her*.

The idea shocked him, and he wasn't sure why. Eventually, even his maker and her friends had given up on life, worn down by time's unkind passage.

Instead of backing to the window, Mason found himself beside Faith's cot. Before she had drawn a startled breath, his cheek was against hers. He had touched her before knowing he'd done so.

Her skin was as smooth as velvet, and somewhat cooler now, on the downside of fever. Her sultry dampness was inviting. For a brief span of time, he was at a loss as to what mattered most. Hold her, help her, bite her, leave her. Kiss her.

If he hurried, concentrating hard enough to avoid the other monstrous cravings, he could probe her mind, feel in her body what he needed to know about her. Were? Human? Lost? Hurt?

Why do you mean so much to me?

He feathered his fingertips first along the line of her jaw, then over her trembling chin. Her mouth was open, maybe in an unspoken protest. On her pale lips sat a metallic residue, beaded like silvery stars, created from the medicine Andre had fed her. Silver…an old foe.

Her exhaled breath was soft and warm. Her body was tense. He badly wanted all of this, and all of her. His need for the information he lacked fled as his lips found hers. If God or the devil wasn't causing the lightning strike that ran through him, melding their mouths together, then why couldn't he tear himself away?

Her lips were like nothing he had ever experienced—hot, full, resilient and as wet as her blood on his thighs had been. Yet he had already known how unique she was, as well as the degree of temptation she presented.

She relaxed beneath him, sighing, accepting and then finally opening herself up to his rash behavior as if she had no plans whatsoever to oppose him. The quick rise of her excitement left Mason with the overwhelming need to push for more.

He had to kiss her. His desire was for a real kiss, long and savage. With his lips pressed to hers and his mind open, he'd be able to either comprehend the mysterious allure that had taken hold of him or end it here. No lies could be hidden inside a kiss. It was rumored that eyes were the mirrors of the soul, but that was not the only way to that elusive spot. Lips pressed to lips, and a few precious seconds of shared breath, could also lead him to truth.

Merely an experiment, Mason told himself. *Necessary.*

He increased the pressure of his mouth on hers, absorbing strike after strike of electrical charges that jolted his insides. Their tongues met. She held her own. But the kiss wasn't nearly enough to ease the rise of his passion. The kiss had upped the stakes tremendously and was, he supposed, an answer in itself, an end in itself, if only temporarily. They both wanted this.

Faith tasted not of full moons and wolfish lunacy, but more like untried passion tethered to a short leash that was beginning to fray. The female beneath him was strong and outgoing on the outside, and curiously fragile beneath. She had a fighter's temperament, evidenced in her refusal to give in to pain, and yet he had a fierce desire to protect her from the outside forces she would soon have to face.

She wasn't used to asking anyone for help. She wasn't used to trusting others. And bloody hell if he hadn't become part of those outside forces she needed protection from.

Mason saw all of this so easily. It didn't matter to him what she was, or what she would soon be. He desperately wanted what he had never had. Closeness. True companionship. Love.

Such things weren't reachable in five seconds, or twenty. Maybe not even in terms of years. He couldn't allow himself to think too long or hard on what had been so easily disguised as hunger. Longing for what you couldn't have tended to drive people insane.

In retaliation of these findings, he nearly took Faith

James there, in body and soul, on the cot in Andre's house. He had been fighting himself for too long, and it had come to this.

God help me. I have strayed in all but what matters most.

And Faith trusted him. She was telling him so in the only way she knew how—by responding to his ill-timed ardor.

Trust.

Maybe Faith also wanted to gauge him, judge him, comprehend what this sudden attraction meant. Maybe she'd agreed to this small slice of personal intimacy for the same reasons he had. For information. In the name of knowledge.

Is that it, Faith?

What will you make of this?

He crushed her mouth brutally with his own, unfurling the raging needs held in check for so long, recapturing the excitement and anticipation caused by the acuteness of their attraction. His tongue danced with hers, teased hers, and neither of them tried to pull back.

Where will this kiss lead?

He was determined to go to wherever it took him. And when confronted with the full brunt of his desire, Faith accepted him, reacting in kind with a force of her own as if she hadn't been sick or injured or created from an alternate cell sequence.

Her warm lips clung to his. Her tiny teeth nipped at his mouth, as though her tether to sanity had been further stretched and was in need of an outlet for her anger.

All the while, her bare arms wound around his neck like clinging forest vines, pulling him closer, inviting him in with the erotic friction of the meeting of their bodies.

The kiss was everything all rolled into one—life and death, sacrifice and bliss. Mason couldn't drag himself from her. For the first time since his rebirth as an immortal, he was experiencing real warmth, freely given. He had not made her do this, had been no puppet master here, and no fire in the world had the power to match the moment.

He became stuck in time, as if the woman he was with had slowed it. He felt that he belonged here, in this blissful pause, after having straddled centuries. It was as if this one action, this one ongoing kiss, had caused the birthing of some completely new thing, and was therefore incredibly important.

Greedily, he went after it all.

But just barely enough of his defenses were left intact to hear the click of the door latch behind them. Metal on metal.

Andre was there, and about to come in. Even slowed time wouldn't give Faith and him more of it.

Arguments would ensue when Andre saw them. Details would emerge that would be damaging to them all. Damaging to this.

Mason slid his arms beneath Faith's body, ready to scoop her up and take her from this place. What mattered to him was holding her and exploring what had sprung into existence with the blistering heat of this embrace. He had indeed discovered the ultimate temptation at last and in the least likely of places. He was sure of it. He felt changed, somehow different.

With his mouth ravaging hers and his tongue running over the points of his fangs, careful to keep them from her, he heard Andre bark orders to someone.

It was a wake-up call to a lapsed reality, a warning

that Mason had taken things too far, too fast, in an unstable situation.

Faith was injured and shouldn't be moved. Her life might depend on her recovery. Besides, where would he take her? If he took her home, there would be no one to protect her if vampires came calling while he was away.

Faith was Lycan, with a special full moon on the way. He didn't know how to help her with that.

Bloody hell! He couldn't take her with him. He had to leave her here for a while longer, in Andre's care.

He had to leave her.

But I will, he silently swore to her and to himself, *return to claim you.*

Oh, yes. He would do that.

His wounded lover, perhaps sensing his withdrawal, made a sound deep in her throat that further stirred the prickling sensation at the base of his spine.

That sound was a low, guttural growl.

Christ, she was one of Andre's brood!

Yes. There. He saw it now, in her taste, her heat, her willingness to fight the world and in the speed of her recovery so far.

Damn it to hell and back, she was a werewolf.

And, more insane than the acknowledgment of her secret, was the recurring acceptance of the fact that he may have wanted her all the more because of it.

What sort of protector did this make him? What sort of ally—when werewolves, unlike humans, were fair game in love and in war?

No time to deal with these issues. Faith.

Not your fault, mine.

He could not have her. His rational mind told him so. Did he have to listen, when there were so many things he wanted to do for her, with her, *to* her?

Now is not the time. A postponement, only. Then we'll get to the bottom of this.

"Heal, little wolf," he whispered. Loving the silky feel of her hair against his face and the quiver of her mouth as he left it, he backed away, his body painfully erect, hurting and hungry.

From the open window, he repeated, "Little wolf," willing her to look at him, needing one last meeting of their eyes.

"I know nothing of that. Nothing," she said.

Holding her gaze as her throaty voice faded off, Mason watched her waning energy fail her at last.

Chapter 10

The growl came from behind him as he hit the ground. Mason spun around to see the black wolf, in wolf form, facing him from the copse of trees. Beside that big animal was a silver-pelted wolf, similar in size, whose coat reflected the shine of the moon over their heads. Both were blocking Mason's path.

"Andre," Mason said, acknowledging the Were.

The silver wolf snapped his teeth fiercely with a force that would have torn cleanly through a human, had there been a human present. The black wolf mirrored the sentiment with a grisly rendering of his own ability and willingness to bite.

"You'll have to speak in English or French in order for me to translate that," Mason said.

The silver wolf turned, took a few steps, then looked back. Its black counterpart growled again, deeper in its chest this time, as it circled Mason in the same way

Mason had seen him circle the vampires earlier that night.

Was this an attempt to herd him toward the trees? It seemed to Mason the wolves were waiting for him to follow them, clearly not calling him out for his most recent indiscretion.

The hairs on his arms bristled, this close to the wolves' rush of adrenaline. He set his features to a neutral expression, a difficult feat after having minutes before encountered so many tantalizing, long-abandoned feelings with Faith.

"You know what the vampires are up to?" he said to Andre.

Anxiousness continued to roll off the silver wolf's body in discernible waves, oscillating the fur on his wide back.

"Faith will be protected if we go," Mason said. *Not a question.*

The wolf's luminous eyes gleamed as he tossed his head.

"Carry on, then," Mason directed.

Dread, excitement and an image of Hope, whatever Faith's sister might have become, fostered his necessity to follow the wolves, when part of him longed to be back at Andre's house. But the Were had found something important. That much was clear.

Had Andre found Faith's sister?

The idea brought discomfort, and he wasn't ignorant of the reasons why. He hadn't promised Faith he would find her sister, though this had been her request. And he had never brought up what would happen when he did find her.

Faith's trust was unwarranted. Their kiss had proved nothing. The answers lay in the unspoken details they had not gotten to, sidelined by the meeting of their mouths and the insufficient amount of time they'd spent together.

She had asked if he was like her. The question haunted him. He wasn't anything like her. He could count centuries on his fingers, but didn't have enough fingers or toes to tick off the scores of vampires he had taken down in this one century alone. Faith was a physician whose own credo, an oath she also would have sworn to, was to save lives at all cost.

He had lived for hundreds of years, while Faith was young, and therefore relatively new at life. Where he considered himself world-weary, she was so very much alive. And though he was alive in most respects, with a beating heart and lungs that required oxygen in order to pump his blood, he wasn't truly alive in other ways. He didn't age. He couldn't be hurt in the same ways that mortals could.

He, too, could slide through the gray zone between worlds, if he chose. A beating heart wasn't required for his existence. But to drop into that beatless, silent state, like the heathens at the neighboring chateau, he'd have to survive on the blood of others.

Heartbeat or bloodfest. That was the choice. And once a blood-drinker, always a blood-drinker.

To his credit, he was innately faster and stronger than most beings walking the earth of whatever species. Perhaps the purity of his purpose was what kept up his strength, on what he had always assumed was the correct path toward his destiny.

A being apart. Like no one else here.

And Faith was a werewolf.

Iron couldn't sideline him, while it had injured Faith so brutally and easily.

Still, saving as many human lives as possible had become his objective, once he'd seen the problem with the original wording of his vow and as time changed the world's needs. He and Faith shared similar goals of trying to keep as many mortals alive as possible. That was something.

His thoughts took another turn.

Faith desperately loved her sister, who might already be gone. Even so, Faith now would have family of sorts when Andre finalized his story and the full moon worked its magic.

He was alone, as he should be. A monklike existence was necessary in order for him to move about and carry out his tasks. Adherence to that plan had lasted all these years—though he was still a vibrant enough man when faced with the possibility of finding *the one*.

Lifting a hand to his head to stop the thoughts, Mason hoped to God that the drop of blood he'd given to Faith would be gone soon. Because if it wasn't, and he upheld his promise to come back and get her, with Andre and his wolves on the prowl, who could predict what might happen?

"Not like them, and not like you," he whispered, shaking his head to rid himself of the remnants of the fragrance clinging to him as tenaciously as Faith's arms and lips had mere moments before.

"We are so very far apart on nature's scale," he whispered to her. "Yet we are, I believe, two lost souls in need."

And souls, unlike anything else, are incapable of being fooled.

Mason pressed his hair back from his face with a renewed resignation. Now was not the time for reworking his own foundations. Giving Faith blood, and the aftereffects of that decision, were chances he had been willing to take.

Andre barked his anxiousness.

Mason nodded to the wolf.

The smell of dead flesh singed the night air, and Mason knew what to do about that.

With a gasp of smoky air forced into her lungs, Faith pushed herself off the edge of the cot. From there, she made it to the chair beside her by hopping on one foot, but no farther. Her uninjured leg shook so hard it threatened to cave.

Mason LanVal's image wavered before her eyes. His presence remained all around her as if his virile masculinity had left an imprint on the air, reinforcing Faith's waking dream theory. He had been way too handsome. Unearthly gorgeous. Not in the least a crusty recluse.

Black hair, long, straight and shiny as volcanic glass, hung past his ears, curtaining pale skin perfectly molded over sharp aristocratic features. Large eyes, dark in color, intense, had searched her own as if trying to see past skin and bone.

She reached up to finger her mouth and found it swollen. She winced, but wanted more of the same.

LanVal had been fully clothed this time. His broad chest and shoulders strained at the fabric of his shirt— like his wiry energy, not so easily contained. He had the leanness of an athlete, an unmistakable overlay of hard muscle and the ability to capture her with just one kiss.

Mason LanVal had slipped in and away again, engaging her in a moment of moral weakness. She had allowed him to see just how vulnerable she could be. She hadn't fought off this sensual invasion of her body. She hadn't even protested. On the contrary, she was thinking of nothing else, and the scope of those thoughts needled her as much as her injured leg did.

Who the hell was he, and what did he want?

When will you return?

The realization of how badly she wanted him to come back overlapped the rest of the mysteries. She knew she was in trouble here, beyond her injury and Hope's strange disappearance. The world had been turned upside down, with talk of werewolves and vampires and guardians tossed in for good measure. Mason LanVal was a part of that mystery. The man Andre had said was the guardian of the world.

LanVal was gone, and luckily, Andre had not returned to check on her. She was sure Andre would have read the dread her face had to be showing in reaction to this whole ordeal. A flash of white in the night, a trap, a rescue by a gorgeous stranger and a gray-haired healer werewolf in possession of a probable cure for half the world's ills, who believed her to be just like him.

Every damn bit of this was a nightmare. Even the kiss. *His* kiss.

Impossible things were going on here, and she was stuck in place. She might be vulnerable in her current state, Faith wanted to shout, but she wasn't beaten. At the hospital, she held human organs in her hands on a regular basis and reconnected delicate blood vessels finer than thread. Did LanVal think she couldn't handle a kiss?

Again, she fingered her lips, able to smell LanVal on hands that had clung shamelessly to him, seemingly independently of her will. But her will had been present and in working condition, in spite of the necessary haste of finding her sister. She had just taken a detour, that's all. Incurring massive wounds and finding out you're a werewolf could have sidetracked anyone.

She felt stronger now, and suddenly, as if by putting things in order, she'd been hit by a wayward stream of accessible strength. Her body continued to shake, at times with the intensity of seismic tremors, but her pain had ebbed, withdrawing along her neural pathways in some kind of fantastic early retreat. Another mystery based on a complete impossibility…as was lusting after a man who had just dishonored her status as a patient in this house.

His aura was wrapped around her. The excitement of having had his body close to hers and his breath in her lungs had not dimmed. In the midst of all this unbelievable chaos swirling around her, Faith felt the kindling of a raw new hope.

Whether dream, coma, or medically induced phenomenon, she'd been caressed by luck. She had seen Hope near here. She had survived being caught in a lethal trap. All good signs. Omens, pointing out that she was on the right track. And then there was LanVal. Was he a dream or a promise?

She glanced down at herself, able to see enough by the light of the fire to notice the professionalism of the job Andre had done in splinting. LanVal had brought her here for this, but maybe there had also been another motive.

If this was indeed reality she had opened her eyes to, Andre had been right about one thing. She hadn't needed a blood transfusion. Although she had heard the crack of her bone and seen the pooling blood on the ground, there was a chance Andre had been right about something else, too—that she hadn't been injured as badly as she had supposed.

"I know better, but what if I'm wrong? If I'm wrong, I can move. At least, I can try."

There was nothing in the room that could be used as a crutch. She'd have to manage somehow to get to her feet and stay there. She would be on her feet when LanVal came to her again, and look him in the eyes. He would come. Every one of her bones, broken and whole, told her so.

She straightened up slowly, holding on to the back of the chair. It might have been premature to assume she could get to the door without knowing what she would do when she reached it, Faith quickly realized. Just standing up carried the promise of ending up face-first on the floor. That, and she was nearly naked, wearing only her underwear and blood-spattered bra. How far could she go like this? Where would she go, in any case?

Impatience had always been a weakness, her greatest flaw, and another inherited James family trait. Her parents had taught her nothing, though, if not that she had to take her life and future into her own hands, flaws and all, and deal. Given that advice, was she supposed to allow a broken bone to stop her from doing just that?

Other than short bouts of dizziness and a general wariness of what actually made up the liquid in Andre's precious bottle, she felt levelheaded enough, now that LanVal had disappeared. She felt ready for action, ready for something to happen. "Anything."

She made a correction. "Certainly not a race through a patch of foreign woods in the dark, though."

She could no longer sit still. The room reeked of wood smoke, snuffed-out candles and illness. It smelled of wool blankets and wood carvings and whatever that antiseptic was that Andre had washed her down with.

The room also carried the musky scent of masterful, mysterious men, like Mason LanVal.

"No explanations for any of this?" she said aloud to him. "What do you want from me, if you aren't going to help me find my sister? A sexual encounter, in exchange for saving my life? Well, dream on!"

As LanVal's face faded, her sister's face replaced it.

"Were you running away from home, Hope? From me? What have I done?"

She hunkered down on those thoughts, as if they were images passing before her eyes.

Hope had been present when their parents had been killed. She hadn't. Hope had witnessed the horror of their bloody demise—an event that might very well continue to unbalance the girl, even after a couple years of therapy.

"Merely a mind coming unhinged, then?"

Faith snapped her head toward the door, hearing a scrabbling noise. Andre? Andre's pet?

Willing her good leg to hold her upright, wrapping the blanket around her body and checking her balance one more time before lifting her hand from the chair, Faith hopped toward the sound.

"But then," she muttered cynically with the exertion, "why would someone with wolf blood in their veins need a pet?"

Chapter 11

The night carried an eerie atmosphere of disturbance. In honor of this, Mason's fangs hadn't retracted. Anger and anticipation kept them ready. Andre wanted to show him something, and Mason supposed it wasn't going to be good.

He had a disgusting image of pale vampire tongues lapping at the dried blood of the rusted trap, and of slim ghostly figures, like the fledglings he'd encountered earlier, fighting each other for leftovers. Those actions were the epitome of what he hated most about his job.

Wondering if Andre had the same image in mind, Mason kept the silver wolf in his sight lines as they hurried through the trees. Although the night was clear, it felt like a storm might be brewing. The air was thick with the smell of ozone.

Andre's pack moved quickly, efficiently, and again with the intimidating appearance of low-slung shadows.

Their supple bodies were created for this sort of chase. In the dark, Andre's fur glowed slightly, as if it had soaked up celestial light.

Mason wondered what a she-wolf would look like. Faith couldn't be a wolf on all fours, like the creatures beside him. Nevertheless, she would be a strong were-wolf if the mark on her arm meant what it was supposed to mean. And she would hate him if he harmed her sister, with a werewolf's long memory. Perhaps even more so for what had just transpired between them.

Stepping over a fallen sapling, his attention snapped up. Andre issued a bark. Andre had seen the speck of white in the distance that Mason had been aware of for some time. The speck, resembling a floating bit of ambient light, was, in fact, their prey.

"Way too easy," he muttered, picking up his pace, noticing how the woods around him seemed to be holding their breath, as he was. In the silence, he heard the wolves' padding strides and his own unsettling thoughts.

Why would Faith's sister be out here? He was certain it was Hope up ahead. Familiar with every path and tree in these woods, Mason saw where she was heading: back to the scene of the crime.

He could stop her now. Put her out of her misery. Get it over with, and scratch one of them off the list.

And lose Faith forever.

He tuned in to this female's vibration, heard the pounding of her blood in her veins and the small sounds she made. She was running fast, but not fast enough to outdistance anyone in shape, on two legs or four.

The area reeked of vampire. The scent on the wind was sour, like old clotting blood, interspersed with a perfume he recognized. On the surface, at least, the female up ahead smelled like her sister. Surprisingly, no stink of death clung to her, but no one survived a week in close proximity to vampires without becoming one of them. Especially a female.

She slowed.

Mason caught up and eased to a halt in a thicket of trees several feet from this apparition. They were at the trap that had snapped Faith's bone. A bloated moon, high above the treetops, cast filmy shadows across the small circular clearing in the brush. A hint of the former saturation of Faith's blood trailed to him along the ground like a creeping mist and wound around Faith's sister's ankles.

Standing among the wolves as he scanned the area, Mason again confirmed to himself that vampire presence was what kept his flesh tingling. Several vamps had been here recently, only minutes before, and were gone now. The nest hadn't been here in full force, as he might have expected if the fledglings had tattled. There was only one figure out here, alone.

Hope James was a startling picture. Impossibly thin, she was composed of angles and sharp planes, in a silhouette overwhelmed by a waist-length tangle of jet-black hair. She was clothed in jeans and a white shirt ruined by a vertical striping of blood.

Smelling the blood, Mason fisted his hands.

Hope's face was as gaunt as her body, and pale to the point of transparency. Her sunken eyes were surrounded by bruised circles of dark skin, similar in color to the tresses curling near them. She looked sick, starved and ghostly.

"Hope," he said.

The wolves growled menacingly beside him, obviously not recognizing Hope as one of their own. But they waited with him for what would happen next, sensing his hesitation.

This wraithlike female stared at the trap as if unable to comprehend what it and the dark pools on the ground beside it meant. When she finally met his gaze, she offered no greeting. Her expression remained blank. She didn't try to run away.

The same skeletal hunger worn by the rest of her new companions hung about her, with slight, noticeable differences. Her eyes were not glazed over with the madness of having died and then woken to another kind of life. She did not hiss or cower when confronted with his presence and that of the wolves she should instinctively have feared. Hope James, with her big tormented eyes, defiantly met the directness of his appraisal.

Curiously, in spite of the blood soaking her clothes, and against all odds that should have pointed to the contrary, Faith's sister wasn't a bloodsucker. Not yet.

"Hope," he repeated.

The female, who didn't look anything like her sister or radiate the same kind of scrambled energy, pointed to the trap with a questioning expression etched on her delicate, bloodless features.

"Faith will be all right," he said, and thought he saw relief cross her face—an emotion that would have been highly usual in a vampire.

He had, in his travels, come across vampires who blended in well enough with humans, and only took from human society what was necessary for their survival. Intelligent, elegant creatures, closer in line to the source of pure blood, who took precautions against creating more of their kind and smelled almost human themselves. He had no qualms about those creatures, and felt more than a little sympathy for the kind of existence they led. But the farther away a vampire was from the original bite of the pure-blooded immortal, the fewer human qualities they possessed.

Faith's sister smelled *off,* even without the familiar stink of death. More bloodsucker trickery? Had her chemistry been altered in some appalling new way? What sort of master vampire would have the talent to do such a thing, if it were possible? Was the vampire who had set himself up as king of this nest up to it?

Mason avoided looking to Andre, who had been right. Faith's sister was exhibiting strange traits. She wasn't a vampire. There was no aura of wolf around her, either. So, what did that leave?

The metallic tang of the blood soaking her shirt dispersed particles of that blood in the air. The wiry, staid energy in Hope's stance suggested she either might be stronger than she looked, or running on reserves, despite her emaciated appearance. She seemed sad, wounded, possibly hurt beyond his ability to comprehend whatever ordeal she had suffered. She looked haunted. It occurred to Mason that she might not be able to speak, even if she wanted to.

From the sound of the silver wolf's continuous growls, Andre had to be thinking along those same lines. *Unknown. Different.* The Were was telegraphing his wariness through his throat.

"I can't tell you where Faith is," Mason said to Hope. "You can't go to her. You know this."

She understood. When she nodded, her hair fell across her face in a dark tangle of black strands studded with bits of leaf and plant, lending her the outward aspect of a wild, untamable thing. Her face seemed paler, almost frozen by fear.

He tasted that fear.

Tearing his gaze away, Mason again looked to the silver wolf. Andre had known Faith's sister wasn't human when he set her free. It was possible the Were had an idea about her origins that he didn't care to share.

It was damned inconvenient for Andre to be unable to speak. It was just as inconvenient that he didn't choose to capture Faith's sister now, on the spot, or do anything to her at all. She really didn't stand a chance out here. She hadn't been turned, but the odds were lined up against her.

His hesitation in dealing with anything from that nest was uncharacteristic. If he let Faith's sister go, as he had done with the earlier fledglings, his presence was no longer hidden, and immediately suspect. It was likely he'd have to face Hope at another time, after she had gained more strength.

He didn't want to see Faith's reaction when she found out what had happened to her sister. He couldn't shake the sensation of Faith's mouth against his, and her arms wrapped tightly around him, as if she clung, not only to his strength, but to her expectations of his reputation.

You don't know me...

Neither, it suddenly seemed, did he know himself.

He wanted to be back there with Faith. He wanted to save her from further heartbreak. He wanted to live up to her innocent expectations, and the acknowledgment of that came as a complete surprise.

Mason turned his head. In a blur of speed reminiscent of the advantages supernatural creatures possessed, Hope James was suddenly gone. There one second, and not the next.

Instincts automatically kicking in, Mason went after her with the wolves at his heels.

* * *

Robbed of necessary breath by the effort it took her to get to the door, Faith leaned heavily against the timber frame. If she truly was lucky, she'd make it back to the bed. If not, she'd have to hit the ground and wait for Andre to find her there.

"For the record," she muttered, "sprawling on the floor is not an option."

She reached out a hand, then drew it back to stare at its treacherous, ongoing, shaking routine. After wiping it against her thigh, as if the shakes could be eliminated with a good rub, she reached out again. Closing her fingers over the old-fashioned door latch, she yanked hard.

The door opened a crack. Wedging her shoulder into the open space, Faith sucked in the fragrant night air and gasped when a beam of light hit her in the face.

Icy-cold at first, then turning hot, the light dripped downward to reach her bare neck and a small patch of skin not covered by the blanket. Despite the woolen cocoon, her shaking advanced to a whole new level. Her heart began to pound with a steady drumming that gradually got stronger.

This had to be a reaction to Andre's milky medication, she reasoned. The energy she'd needed to get to the door was fighting against the sedative. Either that, or she was having some kind of allergic reaction.

Processing the symptoms, Faith glanced up, shielding her eyes, and saw silvery beams of moonlight slipping through the treetops. She was surrounded by forest like the one where her parents had been killed.

The light slipping through the branches carried a sound, a faint buzzing noise that seemed to hover inches from her skin. This, she thought, seemed illogically magical, in a medicinally instigated kind of way.

Another sound accompanied the fainter one. The kind of sound a watchdog made when warning strangers to back off its territory.

As Faith looked beyond the doorway, the animal growled again, closer this time and twice as menacing. Something brushed against her legs, causing her to panic.

The largest animal she had ever seen was mulling around Andre's front door, way too close for comfort. Watching it closely, afraid to breathe until it moved off, Faith gasped when moonlight lit the animal. Larger than a coyote, more the size of a lion, its brown furry body rippled with muscular tension. Its bright eyes were trained on her with a predatory keenness.

Wolf.

God. What had Andre said? Lycanthrope. Lycan.

She didn't have the energy to go back through the doorway, and nothing handy to use to scare this thing off. When the beast growled again, the sound was echoed by another one, lower in tone and not too far distant.

These animals might have smelled the blood from her injury and come calling. One bite from something this big, and she was history.

Another thought came. A strange one.

Wolf in my blood.

Pulling apart her clenched teeth, Faith faced the closest animal directly. "Relax," she said. "Andre says I'm one of you."

After that totally ludicrous remark, she waited for whatever might happen next.

The figure in Mason's sight lines knew where she was going. He refrained from shouting for her to stop.

He'd seen the fear in Hope's eyes and didn't want to imagine what would cause her to go back to the vampires who hadn't accompanied her to the woods. She could have run in any direction, or asked for his protection. Did Hope know the bloodsuckers could easily catch up with her if they wanted? Was she tethered to them by the extremes of her fear?

Because she hadn't asked for his help, and because she was now headed for the chateau, on her own, it was entirely reasonable to conclude she couldn't be trusted. It was plausible the vampires were using Hope James for some nefarious purpose of their own. If he was to help anyone here, he had to figure out what that purpose was.

He kept his eyes on the white form, maintaining a slight distance while his mind scrambled for a hold on the problem.

He recalled wondering, when he'd first laid eyes on Faith, if she'd been herded toward that trap for his benefit. He'd considered whether Faith might have been bait, either for the Weres or for himself, with the elimination of all of them in mind.

Since baiting him hadn't worked, and he was here now, it also could be that Faith's sister had inherited the roll of wounded female enticement, sent to lure the unsuspecting males of whatever species.

There were so many ways this could go. He backtracked, thinking further on the possibility of lures and baits, deciding that this nest's plan might have worked, after all, in a way he hadn't realized. Faith had been rescued and taken to Andre's house, which could very well have been part of a demented master plan to find where the werewolves gathered. If hunting old enemies proved the direction of the plan, he had sealed that deal.

Which was it, then? Injured females as a trap for immortals, or werewolves? What did these blood-drinkers have in mind?

There also remained the possibility of vampires expecting Hope to lure her sister here for the sake of having more females in their nest.

All these scenarios were nasty and despicable, especially if Hope James had been a willing participant in any of them. Luring Faith here would mean that Hope had to hate her sister deeply.

It was possible, he supposed, for there to be enough dysfunction in a family to pit sister against sister in such a way, and for that dysfunction to have taken the James sisters to the point of no return. But he had perhaps gummed things up with his little blood donation that indeed must have confused them.

And now, they had sent Hope out here to pick up the trail?

He thought about Hope's haunted eyes, and couldn't quite believe that scenario.

So, if Hope wasn't willingly taking part in this deadly recruitment, why hadn't she run away from her grim fate? Why hadn't she asked him for help when she had the chance? One word would have done it, or one meaningful move in his direction. She hadn't even tried to save herself.

He was inundated with thoughts and possibilities, with no clear path to the right one. Whichever way it went down, the goal of that nest was getting murkier by the minute.

Mason stopped walking. The wolves passed him by, circled and returned with their fur raised and their ears pinned back. They looked to him with almost human expressions of frustration on their faces.

Wolves, he thought. Hope James hadn't been bitten, when the odds were against this. And she might have been sent here after the wolves.

"LanVal, you ignorant bastard," Mason whispered as he followed Faith's sister and became engulfed by darkness.

Chapter 12

The wolf Faith had just spoken to as if it had the capability to understand her asinine introduction backed away from her. Tossing its big head, it looked up past its long muzzle…and began to change shape.

"No, wait!" Faith shouted in alarm, unable to stop the progress of what was happening however hard she wished she'd wake up.

The sound of cracking bones split the quiet as the wolf heaved itself onto its powerful hind legs. Seconds later it was standing up. The fur covering its body disappeared, leaving in its place a man's glistening flesh, slick with sweat.

Faith watched in disbelief as the muzzle reformed into a prominent-jawed, wide-browed face. The big bad wolf no longer faced her. A naked man did.

"I'm Lucas," he said unselfconsciously, as if shifting from one shape to another was of no consequence. "That's Gregoire by the trees."

Rigid in the doorway, with her attention fastened to the man who was also a wolf, Faith cried out in confusion. What she had just witnessed could not have been real. There was no way a wolf could become a man. No rational mind could seriously believe it. This had to be the result of the drugs Andre had given her, or her injury causing havoc in her system in a way she hadn't fathomed.

More time was melting away while she wrestled with these nightmares, time she needed for finding her sister. Hope was out there in the dark. In the trees. She sensed this. Andre might have gone to search for Hope, but would the naked man beside her know anything about that?

"You should go back inside," Lucas said, his voice surprisingly gentle, calm and assuring, for all his great size. He made no attempt to cover himself.

Faith tried not to stare. "Andre?"

"Not here at present. Do you need something?"

Yes, she needed something, Faith wanted to shout. A psychiatrist. A time machine. A wheelchair. A phone, car or helicopter. A sister whose actions made sense. And then there was Mason LanVal, with his thoughts stirring her insides, no actual presence necessary. Which of the things on the list she needed most at the moment was the question currently stumping her.

"Do you know LanVal?" She was actually afraid to look too closely at the man who had introduced himself as Lucas, for fear he might unexpectedly change back. If she looked closer, would she find leftover fur on his neck, or a human mouth full of a wolf's teeth?

If this man had wolf in his blood, and she did too,

was this kind of transformation what she had to look forward to?

Not possible. Has to be a mistake.

"LanVal. Yes," Lucas replied. "We know him."

"Can you get him to come?" she asked. Then what? What would she do? What excuse could she invent for wanting to be near him when Hope hadn't been found?

"LanVal is with Andre and the others," Lucas said. "There was a disturbance. They went to check the traps."

Traps. Plural. Faith's heart jumped. If there were more of those devices, Hope might have been subject to the same fate. If so, and Andre and LanVal were out there checking the contraptions, surely they would find her sister.

Andre had told her Mason LanVal guarded the world. Maybe Andre had meant he guarded the woods. It was possible that LanVal saved people and animals on a regular basis from these traps.

"We're gearing up for the full moon," Lucas said. "The rest of the pack will arrive soon."

He'd said pack, as in a wolf pack. Traps and packs— all part of the same madness. Faith spoke just to say something, to keep from shouting. "Full moon?"

"A special one," Lucas replied.

"What's special about it?"

The moon was a ball of light that regularly orbited the earth, and that most people took for granted. Except for surgeons, of course. Surgeons knew better than to operate during a full moon phase, aware of the effects such a moon had on the human body. A full moon's pull on human blood was similar to its effect on ocean tides. In medicine now, as in the olden days, a full moon had to be respected.

It was entirely possible, however, that French woodsmen who shunned technology revered the old ways. Ancient ways predating science and astronomy.

"A Blood Moon comes," Lucas said.

Faith shivered, not liking the sound of that.

"This type of moon rarely occurs," he explained in his heavy accent.

"Why?"

"One transition per month for most Weres is difficult enough. Two fulls, one right after the other, is a deviation from our normal routine. For Weres unused to shifting, this tends to double the emotion. You will find that the mind can easily be overruled by the cravings of the body."

Faith for sure did not want to know what a werewolf might crave. Nonetheless, she said, "And the *blood* part?"

"It's what is sometimes shed with the arrival of that second moon."

Blood Moons! She and a naked man were having what amounted to a casual conversation about werewolves morphing and the possibility of more of them soon running rampant, as if those things were real and not merely supernatural fantasies. Lucas had spoken matter-of-factly and as though he knew about the lunacy of a Blood Moon firsthand. And Lucas had said, *"You will find,"* as if she really was one of them.

Lucas. Another nutcase in a *pack* of nutcases?

Faith couldn't help taking another glance at the sky as she steadied herself in the doorway. "What about vampires? Would a moon like that affect them, too?"

"I'd assume it might be a bad time for bloodsuckers, as well," Lucas said. "More so if there are Weres nearby."

Again, an image of LanVal, handsome, black-haired and strapping, crossed her mind. *Not a wolf. Something else.*

Something worse?

This time, when Lucas grinned, there was a fierceness to his expression that made Faith shrink back into the doorway. Werewolves and vampires were enemies, then, and it made her wonder where regular old humans fit in, and what would turn up next. Winged fairies? Fire-breathing dragons? She doubted if a wolf trap, with its big jaws, could catch and hold something as ethereal as a fairy.

She glanced up at the sky, as if sudden illumination had come from there. The words *wolf trap* resonated with a particular sting. Had someone out here set those traps, hoping to catch wolves? Real wolves? Maybe, along more sinister lines, somebody in the area hoped to catch any and all trespassers, even Andre and his friends.

Faith's heart skipped again, missing a groove, leaving her breathless. Her mind was flying, searching for a place to land. Questions came, one after the other, too rapid-fire to consider any one of them for long.

Were the traps a sadistic twist on the word *sport?*

She sensed a startling spark of rightness in the idea, and felt more color drain from her face.

"Do you need help?" Lucas asked.

"No. I'm okay," Faith assured him, afraid to let him get close, fearing that whatever condition he had that made him a wolf might be contagious.

Mustering the energy necessary to get back through the doorway, taking a shuffled hop on her good leg, she decided this little sojourn hadn't helped at all. For all the effort it had required to reach fresh air and take a look around, she felt worse and much more confused.

Andre's house was guarded by a pair of were-wolves—at least one honest-to-God shape-shifter. It seemed to her that Mason LanVal must have known about this, and that he might have brought her here for this very reason. He'd called her his *little wolf.*

He thought she belonged here.

"Madness!" she whispered, straining to breathe, once again not getting far on her one good leg.

She was out of commission and, for all intents and purposes, locked in. It looked like Hope's immediate future lay in somebody else's hands. Since she couldn't make it to the cot, she prayed it was in Mason LanVal's hands Hope might land, and that his reputation with the police was warranted. She hoped her own belief in him was warranted.

Her good leg finally gave out as she turned. She barely noticed when a rolling growl of displeasure rumbled up through her diaphragm.

Andre snapped his sharp teeth precariously close to Mason's right leg, missing by a centimeter. The silver wolf wanted to chase Faith's sister, and was looking for whatever potentially pertinent detail kept Mason in place at the moment.

"Conversation time," Mason said to the wolf, the fine hairs at the nape of his neck still bristling from the strange encounter with Hope James.

Andre growled his reply.

"In the flesh, Andre," Mason said. "There's something we need to work out."

The silver alpha tossed his head, barked once, then flowed fluidly into his human shape with a series of crunching sounds that made Mason flinch. After stretching his broad shoulders as if they were only a stiff nuisance, Andre returned Mason's attention.

"I'm going to pose a question," Mason said.

"Which I can see you might have already answered for yourself." Andre's voice hadn't caught up with his human shape, coming across half bark, half gravel.

Mason shrugged off the comment and said contemplatively, "What would keep vampires from turning a young female in their midst?"

"Shouldn't you know that?" Andre returned.

"One would think so. However, since the question also potentially involves *your* kind, Andre, the answer eludes me."

"She's not a wolf," Andre reiterated.

"Nor is she a vampire. I find that extremely odd. Don't you?"

Appearing to consider the remark, Andre stepped closer. "You don't think they've tried to turn her?"

"The blood on her shirt wasn't hers."

"No," Andre agreed. "So whose was it?"

"I don't know."

"Puncture marks?"

"None that I could see, but there wouldn't be any by now, in any case, if she had been turned. Wounded vampires heal faster than Weres do. Which brings us back to the same question of why Hope isn't a vampire, and why she's allowed out here, alone."

Andre's brow furrowed in thought. "Two options immediately come to mind. She either tastes bad, or she's some kind of creature we don't know about that is immune to the damage a pair of fangs can do."

Andre's option had been one Mason had considered

early on. But he saw that the Were wanted to add something else that had occurred to him in afterthought.

"You have another idea?" Mason asked.

Andre shrugged his bare shoulders as if already negating what he was about to suggest, and then spit it out.

"There's a possibility she's a Hunter."

Hunter. Capital H. Yes, that was the third option Mason had landed upon just minutes before.

"Not just any Hunter," he proposed.

Andre looked to the other Weres, all of them fully furred-up and listening none too patiently.

"Faith is Lycan," Mason went on. "Her sister is not. If Hope isn't something out of ancient lore that we know nothing about, and the vampires haven't made her one of their own, then we must explore the prospect of Hope having been bred to become something the vampires might temporarily find useful."

Andre held up a hand to stop the irrational reasoning, but Mason was aware that Andre had been following closely, and that the Were had not missed this latest insinuation.

"How could a family of Lycans raise as one of their own a creature designed to kill their own kind? The idea is preposterous," Andre said.

"Nevertheless, it remains on the table as a viable reason for Faith's sister being alive and showing herself to us."

Andre snapped his teeth in distaste. "We feared an abomination. If the bloodsuckers chewed on her a while, she'd be just that, no matter what else she is or isn't."

"Yes," Mason agreed. "So, maybe they've postponed their ritual for purposes of their own."

"Such as?"

"I was hoping you'd be able to tell me that," Mason said.

"You believe that nest is after werewolves?"

"I don't believe this nest would send a Werewolf Hunter after me," Mason said. "Do you?"

"A Werewolf Hunter isn't stronger than a vampire, LanVal. She couldn't have fought all of them off in order to stay alive."

"Precisely. So why isn't she a vampire, and why is she running around out here?"

Andre took a second glance at his companions.

"If she is a Hunter, she would possess certain intrinsic building blocks that would make it easy for her to find you and your pack," Mason said. "Isn't that true? Maybe even lure you into the open like she did tonight."

"Speculation," Andre said, though Mason could see the Were was considering his words. The wolves had indeed been lured out. Twice.

"Do you have a better explanation, Andre?"

"We've done more than our share of damage to that nest."

"Yes. In that case, could they be seeking revenge?"

"If they were, and Faith's sister is a Hunter whose job is to pry us out of our den, why didn't the vampires attack now, tonight? Their stink is everywhere."

Mason waved up at a sky mostly hidden by the trees. "Hardly more than a week until the moon is full again. This one is special, isn't it? They could be waiting for all the members of your pack to gather in one place, and in the meantime, be looking for that place."

"Then they'd either be fools, or idiots or both," Andre said. " It would take an army of them to take us on, full moon or none. Even then, they wouldn't stand a chance. Beneath a Blood Moon, when we're at our strongest, the fight would take minutes."

"What if there are more than twelve vampires in the nest, some of them hidden, and it's to be an all-out war with the Weres they're planning over territorial rights?"

Mason looked toward the chateau. "I could be wrong, of course, but there isn't much time to figure this out. We need Faith to shed some light on the options."

His focus shifted past the wolves to the direction of Andre's cottage. In that moment, with the tiniest action of looking her way, Mason felt the thunder in his chest return. He felt a sudden spike in his heart rate and an unusual tightening in his throat.

Faith was calling to him, waiting for him, counting on him.

He tried to shut her out so that he could think.

"I'll speak to her," Andre said, and it was obvious to Mason that the Were, so practiced in the art of shifting, had picked up on Mason's sudden change of attention.

"Yes," Mason muttered, with another reminder to himself that an immortal had no right to interfere in Were business, even though Were business had become entangled with his own agenda.

He'd actually been relieved to discover that Hope wasn't a vampire, whatever else she might be. He was glad his hand had been stayed. He had never taken the act of killing for granted. He didn't terminate the undead for exercise, but for the objectives set by his vow. In spite of the fact that the task set to him and his brothers had long ago become daunting, he had held to that vow as much as possible, for as long as he could. The same thing couldn't be said of one of the others.

Same old question of fading loyalty resurfacing.

Why? Because this nest shouldn't have been a problem. If there was any kind of plan to draw the Weres out, with thoughts of annihilating them in one fell swoop and then afterward moving their deadly aggression to the surrounding towns, it was a sure bet the prime vampire in control here was more intelligent than any prime ought to be. Plans weren't the usual province for bloodsuckers.

The whole thing didn't feel or smell right, and wasn't moving in the right direction.

"A Blood Moon approaches. That's always notable," Andre said.

Mason nodded. They both felt a change in the wind. More layers of strangeness were piling up instead of being peeled back. A routine nest-flushing had quickly taken on more ominous connotations.

Luring a Hunter to their chateau—if that theory panned out—had taken intelligent design, as well as the skill to pull it off. Werewolf Hunters weren't a dime a dozen. Like Vampire Slayers, Hunters were rare. One in a thousand? One in a million? To have found one as far away as the States and then gotten her here was too intricate a plan for the average undead brain to have conceived.

If Hope had been a Slayer, the nest would not have survived. Because of the telltale hint of their odor in these surroundings, that wasn't the case. He had not sensed that instinct in Hope James. Nor had she looked at him with a Slayer's lust for the kill in her eyes.

Even if she were to be proved a Hunter, there were more important things to worry about. Who the master vampire in that chateau might be was the top concern. Second to that, and almost an inconsequential part in comparison, was the fact that if Hope wasn't a Werewolf Hunter, her identity remained up for grabs.

In either case, there wasn't time for dallying or room for mistakes. Andre and his pack were the good guys in this case. One dead werewolf by a vampire's hand would be one too many.

Distracted again by the sultry voice in his mind calling to him, and the physical reactions twisting him with the need to comply, Mason turned his head. Faith's voice rang in his mind and burrowed deep under his skin.

He shut his eyes as her voice washed over him and heard, beyond her husky, familiar tone, Andre's flow back into an alternate shape. As the wolves raced off to confront Faith about her sister, Mason spun toward the chateau.

Closing his mind to the unforgiving heat of temptation, balling his fists against an urge to go to Faith that was so strong within him, it was uncomfortable…

Wanting to take Faith away from all this, and to hell with the rest of the world and its problems…

He let the wolves run. And after making sure they were gone, he strode silently down the path Faith's sister had taken.

Chapter 13

Faith felt Mason LanVal close himself off from her. The unexpected loss of connection was like the slamming of an iron door. Cold rushed in.

She had dragged herself on her backside to the fireplace and sat panting with the achievement. Fatigue had leeched what was left of her energy. Images of wolves gnawed at her mind. She didn't probe beneath the blanket to find out what further damage she might have done to her leg. LanVal's sudden disconnect had shot down thoughts of her own safety.

He seemed utterly gone. Sealed off from her and beyond reach. The sudden sense of aloneness was a shock. She hadn't realized the extent of the bond between them until she felt that door close.

In this new silence, she heard the rasp of her own breathing and the crack of the fire. She heard wind in the trees outside, and the distant bark of an animal—

those things quickly pushed aside by an insistent stab of pain originating below her knee.

Her recent efforts to move were catching up. She was far from home and among strangers, with no way of getting help other than what had been offered here. She had left her purse in the car, with her phone inside. There was no access to transportation. She was, therefore, forced to remain stationary. No matter how many times she had been on the other end of an injury like hers in the hospital, assessing and taking charge of things, she now had been rendered helpless.

How many hours had gone by since she'd turned onto that hellish gravel road? Seemed like hundreds. Losing track of time was never a good sign in any kind of recovery process.

"Faith?"

Andre's voice. He was here, opening the door. She wanted to cheer. She also wanted to throw something at him for being an eccentric recluse, and for being a werewolf.

She wanted to have a tantrum and get to her feet. She wanted to cry. Not so much because she was hurting, but because with her own eyes, she had seen a wolf change into a man.

Tugging the blanket closer to her, Faith held tightly to its ragged edge, knowing she couldn't afford to fall to pieces. The only protection she had in all of this was her sense of self and a werewolf's worn wool bedding. Somehow, she'd have to make do with just those two things. She was responsible for her sister, and had to pull through. At the very least, she owed allegiance to her parents for their unwavering faith in her.

"I'm here, Andre," she said.

Listening to the muted sound of his footsteps on the floorboards, she said warily, "You didn't find her."

"I'm afraid we did."

Andre's reply was a further torture. Something in his tone.

"Is she all right?"

No hint of the calm acceptance she'd tried for registered in her voice. By the light of fading fire, Faith clearly saw the grim arrangement of Andre's features. His weariness pressed against her as if they had actually touched.

"She was searching for you," he said. "At the trap where you had your accident."

"At the trap? Searching?" The idea caused a rush of anguish, but her prayers had been answered. Hope was alive. She could let go now, or stop holding back the things LanVal had directed her to tamp down.

"Where is she, Andre? Here? Outside?" For all the good news, she was still so very cold.

"She's nearby. Not here," Andre said.

"Why didn't you bring her to me?"

Andre sat down on the chair beside her, his expression far too solemn for good news.

"We couldn't bring her here, Faith."

We. She latched on to that because Lucas had told her LanVal was with Andre. He hadn't let her down.

Tears gathered in the corner of her eyes that she refused to shed. Another surprise. The last time she'd cried was at her parents' funeral. So many tears of sadness and loss back then. And now tears of joy, of relief, born out of frustration and fear.

Hope was nearby. Andre would tell her all about it. The back of her neck chilled up with nervous anticipation.

"Has she been hurt, Andre?"

"Yes. She has been hurt."

He was avoiding her eyes.

"What happened? How badly is she injured?" Her voice had risen in pitch. The ache in her leg worsened with every shouted syllable.

"She's not like you," Andre said. "We need to better understand what she is in order to confront her."

"Confront her? I came here to find her and to take her home. That's all that matters."

Andre nodded soberly. "I'm afraid that isn't all that matters at the moment, and those circumstances prevented us from bringing her here."

"Can you take me to her?"

"I cannot," Andre answered reluctantly, Faith thought, and at the same time firmly. "Can you tell me more about her, and what might have brought her here, to this area in particular?"

"I did! I put her on the tour! I agreed to the itinerary!"

Hearing the emotion that cracked her voice, Faith shut up and let several beats of silence go by before starting again.

"What do you mean by *she isn't like me?*" Her hand came up abruptly, as if to stop him from answering that question before she could get a grip on what she knew he was going to say. "Are you implying that you didn't bring Hope here because she isn't Lycan?"

It was easy to see she'd hit the mark. She read in his features what she needed to know.

"You're not serious," she whispered. "Tell me you're not serious. This has gone far enough."

But it hadn't gone far enough, Faith knew. The mystery was, in fact, just beginning. As much as she wanted to delete it from her mind, she'd seen evidence of the things Andre was suggesting. A wolf really had changed into a man, outside this house. Not a dream. No hallucination. She had witnessed this unbelievable transformation. And if that was possible, nothing else—hell, the whole world—might not be as it seemed.

"Andre?" she said, when he didn't immediately reply.

He had told her she had Lycan blood in her family tree. If that were true, would she eventually become like that beast guarding the door?

If she was anything like the creature outside, like Lucas, surely she'd know it. Something like that couldn't stay hidden all these years. And now, Andre was telling her that Hope was different?

Well, this wasn't news. She already knew how dissimilar her sister was. She had always known it. They had been Night and Day from the beginning, remember? Through the years that gap had widened considerably.

So what?

So what if Hope wasn't a stargazer, and had never been strong, at least on the outside? Or that Hope hadn't been born with a circular scar on her arm. Why did it matter that Hope preferred urban surroundings to nature, and preferred to keep to herself?

Did it matter if her sister was taller than most of their family, and smaller boned, with black hair in a house full of blondes? Siblings were often miles apart in appearance, personality and temperament. Weren't they?

Okay. She slowed her speeding thoughts and brought them to a standstill to take stock. She wasn't an idiot, and she'd been trained to sift through details until specific clues stood out. Andre, her senses told her, wasn't talking about any of those trivial differences that had come to mind—like personality clashes or hair color. He had told her that she was a Lycanthrope, and was pretty much adamant about that...so "different" in this circumstance meant he was telling her Hope wasn't.

"Not like you." Andre was suggesting that Hope had missed the odd curse both of the people in this room had supposedly not avoided. Which should have been a good thing. Hope wasn't a damn werewolf. Not even remotely bad news enough to warrant the expression on Andre's face. Yet Andre wasn't happy.

Another fleeting thought arrived, maybe out of self-defense. If anyone in the James family actually looked the part of a supernatural creature, Faith thought, she would have placed bets on her sister. She, herself, might be the daughter who inherited the James family's access to an extra set of senses, but Hope had her own secrets. She knew this for fact.

And a lot of good those extra senses had done *her* in avoiding that trap in the first place!

Hope, bereft of those honed James perceptions, hadn't stumbled into its iron jaws. *She* had. In spite of the fact that Hope had gone missing, Faith was the one sitting here, facing a self-professed werewolf with a mark on his arm that matched her own. She was the one Andre said had wolf blood in her veins.

All of these points needed to be faced, argued, proved, because none of what had gone on here made the slightest bit of sense, and sure as hell didn't make a difference in the long run. Andre knew where her sister had gone. She would get Hope and go home. Leave all this stuff about werewolves behind.

But I have seen it.

God, help me. I've seen a man change shape.

"You do see there's a problem," he finally said, his voice and the concern in it the perfect hook to bring her back to that lingering feeling of dread. Yes, Hope had always been a problem. Always the moody, wild child. But never Lycan.

When she shook her head, not wanting to hear any more or think on this further, the room began to spin. Around and around things went, a whirlwind of colors, sights, ideas, sounds, sensations, protestations.

Mason LanVal.

Wolf.

Hope.

Andre, across from her, seemed to await the return of her wits.

The madness had to stop. She had to get her sister and get out of here before she really started to believe this was her life.

But something else nagged at her already over-whelmed mind. Was it important? Did it make any more sense than anything else? It had to do with her sister, and with Andre's wary expression.

When she spoke, it was to ask the question thrusting up from the core of the whirling cyclone, in a tone hollowed by doubt.

"What is she, then, if not like us?"

Night filled in around Mason as he tracked Faith's sister. Beneath the heavy overhead branches of the older part of the woods, the darkness took on the density of a bottomless pit, sprinkled only here and there with tiny sparks of light.

A savage foulness tempered the air, but he was used to this and moved with an agile, practiced determina-tion. Chasing enemies was what he had trained himself to do. The role of protector was the mold he had fitted himself to throughout endless centuries, an ideal that kept him going forward. Besides, hadn't it repeatedly been noted by worldly philosophers that it was never wise to glance behind at the past, since there was nothing to be done about it?

An immortal with an endless life span had to heed that notion or go mad. Castle Broceliande, and what had gone on there, had to remain buried. He couldn't regret his decision to take on this new life. Those regrets had only surfaced because of *her*.

His jaw tensed over that. His muscles twitched with a sudden desire to be near to Faith that was so overwhelming, he nearly turned back. Particles of her sultry heat spanned the distance separating them, tying them together, leaving him wanting. The ache he felt for the curve of her mouth, the softness of her skin and the brilliant gleam of her gaze was like an irreparable wound to both his heart and the constancy of his vow. Although the wolves would protect her with their lives, he wanted to be the one to elevate Faith above all this. He'd have given anything at that moment for calmer times, with Faith in his arms.

He was jolted from the severity of those longings by a new flash of white that returned him to the chase.

He saw Hope's running figure as he rounded a bend—the same ghostly flash Faith must have seen through her windshield.

This time, as he thought Faith's name, he dismissed his thudding heart. The chateau, with its bottom-feeding residents, had to be the goal in the forefront of his mind. No one in the area would be safe with this nest in action, including Faith and the Weres. He had to find out what was going on. The responsibility was his. He had been born for this. There was no other reason for being what he was.

Mason easily closed the distance between himself and Hope James. She wasn't so very fast or fleet, after all. Maybe she was reluctant to return to the nest she didn't really belong to. Maybe she thought she had no other choice.

It was clear she didn't sense him coming. When she was near enough to touch, Mason reached out a hand.

Chapter 14

"Are you familiar with the term *Hunter?*" Andre asked.

Having expected an awkward reply to her question about her sister, Faith almost laughed at the consistency of the mysteries continuing to pile up. The word Andre had emphasized had no immediate meaning.

"Hunter?" Her patience worn thin, and with anger beginning to fill the void that patience had left, Faith shook her head.

"There are people who carry the Lycan gene in them, and others who carry certain variations," Andre said.

"Go on," she urged. "If she isn't a werewolf, and you haven't mentioned the word *vampire* in the last hour, why are you waiting while I struggle to grasp the meaning of what a Hunter might be?"

"Because Hunters killed your parents," he said.

A slow beat of time passed, then another, without any hint of where this was going.

"What kind of variation are you talking about?" Faith finally asked.

"A species always has its opposite. The idea of an opposite, in this case, is the plan nature has set in motion to keep the numbers of any particular species under control. For every type of being, there's another type equipped to ensure that balance is kept."

Faith waited impatiently as Andre paused for a breath.

"Vampires have Vampire Slayers as their opposite, and Weres have Werewolf Hunters," he said.

Hunter. Suddenly, the term made Faith uneasy.

"Hunters and Slayers are genetically altered humans," Andre went on. "Enhanced beings whose genetic codes specifically allow them to sense and identify the species they're connected to."

"Good. Keeping populations of Others down has to be a good thing, right?" Faith interrupted. Then she wondered how keeping the balance came about. The opposite of life was death. Was the answer of how to keep a species under control to be found in the word *Slayer?*

At least they weren't talking about vampires here.

"You think my sister is a Werewolf Hunter?" she asked, not liking the way that idea sat so heavily on her mind, and wondering why she hadn't laughed at any of this.

"It is possible she is," Andre replied.

"Aren't you sure? If Hunters can identify and pick out those they hunt, as you said, don't the hunted get a chance to see them coming?"

"Rarely. Only in the oldest, strongest lines is there any kind of built-in recognition."

"There seem to be a lot of discrepancies in your world. If I'm Lycan, as you say, wouldn't Hope be Lycan, as well, if she's my sister?"

"That's where things get tricky," Andre said.

"Are you kidding? Only there?" Cynicism again, in the name of frustration and all that was holy. But the urge to laugh had fled. Andre didn't comment on her outburst. His features merely projected sadness, a seemingly earnest emotion.

Surprised to hear herself ask, "Why tricky?" she blanched.

If Andre had noticed her change in pallor, he gave no indication as he got up, walked to a dresser and pulled out some clothes.

"Mother to daughter is how Hunters and Slayers get their strength," he said, setting a folded shirt and a pair of pants beside her.

"Can Lycan mothers produce Hunters?"

Faith needed to see Andre trip over the inconsistencies. At the same time, she was curious about how intricate this story line was, and how long it could go on.

But she was thankful for the clothes. Carefully, she wrapped the shirt around her shoulders and stuck her arms through the holes. When she'd accomplished that, Andre helped her pull the pants over her splint.

"No," he said. "Lycans cannot produce Hunters. That's why your sister must have been adopted."

"You mean *if* Hope is what you say she is."

"Hunters have Lycan blood in them, Faith, in infinitesimal amounts. This infusion ties them to us. The story goes that every hundred years new wolf blood is necessary to reinvigorate a Hunter's own. Since pure wolf DNA isn't really compatible with humans, getting blood from a Lycan is the only way Hunters can get the strength they need to continue the hunt.

"There are few Hunters because most human systems, even the special cases destined to be Hunters, often fail to assimilate and acknowledge what's inside them. Only a very special few adapt to the invading blood cocktail and develop the desire to do something with it."

"Their mission is, what, to destroy each werewolf they come across?" Faith asked. "Go out of their way to do so? That doesn't sound like nature's path toward evolution to me. Infused, you said. How does that happen?"

"Blood has to be taken from a genetic Lycan, chemically cleaned, then separated into the tiniest portion, which is then injected into their veins. This infusion seems enough to carry on through several generations of family members. When its strength dilutes, the process has to be repeated."

"Surely Lycans don't provide that deadly cocktail willingly."

"They do not. But even those of us from the oldest families recognize the need for checks and balances as the populations of rogue werewolves continues to explode."

"What makes a rogue?"

"A bite to a human by a werewolf."

Faith thought about that. "Have you ever met a Hunter, Andre?"

"Not personally. No one has been bitten here, and my pack prefers to keep ourselves tucked away from the outside world, as did our parents."

"Until I sent a Hunter to France. To your doorstep."

Andre's features fell. The ensuing silence seemed poignant. Faith needed to fill it.

"Even if Hope was adopted, she never exhibited aggressive tendencies," she argued stubbornly. "To my knowledge, she's never seen a gun up close, or been in a fight."

"If untrained, she wouldn't have to hold a weapon. All she'd have to do is find us and point the way for someone who can."

Faith shook her head. "If you think my sister is one of those special beings, and she jumped a tour bus to come to these woods, you'd have to believe she had found out about you and your friends and that you're not fully human."

Though the idea sounded absurd, Andre remained silent, as if considering it.

"How could she know that? She had never been to France," Faith continued. "She was on a tour she had no knowledge of until I told her about it. Who could have relayed your secret? In any case, how could she possibly have ended up here, in this remote spot? We're from Miami, and have never been out of our state. My parents were kind souls who taught us values. I make my living by helping others. The sister I know couldn't hurt anyone."

"You might be right," Andre said. "For your sake, I hope so."

She wasn't about to let that comment go unprotested.

"Hope was with our parents when they died. She's seen the carnage and has spent time trying to deal with what she witnessed. After what happened out there, no one in their right mind would wish the same result on anyone else."

"I wouldn't think so," Andre agreed.

But? She waited for what he didn't immediately add, knowing there was something. Whatever it was that Andre kept to himself sat like a stone between them.

And then she got it. Knew what he hadn't said, and why.

With trepidation and complete disbelief, Faith said, "As a Hunter, bred to go after her opposite, you're surmising, or at least addressing the possibility that my sister may have had a hand in my parents' deaths."

Sorry she'd attached wings to such an unconscionable notion, she hastily added in a tone of self-defense, "The deer hunters who killed my parents were after meat. The police told us so."

Hell, she thought, Andre was trying to goad her into believing her sister was a homicidal maniac when there was no reason to believe it. Hope's participation in that horrible event wasn't possible. Hope had been a teen. Adopted or not, those parents had been Hope's parents, too.

The gaze Andre turned on her was disconcertingly appraising. The sadness he'd worn since entering the room down-turned his features, and was thick enough now to be disconcerting.

Faith touched her lips to keep from speaking, shaken by the fact that she had argued over ideas so bizarre. She didn't believe anything that had been said, and wasn't about to take any of this further.

She was afraid to believe, because…

Her leg had healed considerably in a few hours' time.

She had seen a wolf change into a man.

And she was all too aware of the moon, hovering outside as if waiting for her to acknowledge its presence in some special way.

Closing her eyes and squeezing them tight, she said, "You think my parents were werewolves, that I inherited a gene from them that makes me one. You think that my sister is a being who has been created to kill us, so that the world isn't overrun by Lycans."

She took a deep, calming breath. "Taking that to its illogical conclusion, if Hope were to be proved a Werewolf Hunter, she may have been compelled to harm her own parents, adopted or not. Is that right, Andre? Have I left anything out?"

"Yes," he said. Just that. A universe of meaning in that infuriating one-word reply.

Faith wished to God she had the strength to get to her feet. She wished she had the nerve to shout "Bloody murder!" But she was dazed, stuck in a never-ending loop of nonsensical facts that, despite their bitter taste, had a certain sorry rightness to them.

"No one ever mentioned the possibility of Hope being adopted," she said weakly.

"And you never checked?"

"Why should I? I didn't care. She's my sister."

"In hindsight, perhaps not the perfect relationship," Andre proposed. "Hunting would be in her blood, and unavoidable. The way wolf is in ours."

"How would that even be possible? Besides, you're admitting that nothing is certain, and that it's all guesswork. None of this might be real."

Andre kept his gaze level with hers. "What did you think of Lucas? He said you met."

The question drove her back against the wall. Groaning from the strain, Faith groped for the edge of the blanket, now on the floor beside her. It seemed imperative, suddenly, that she find warmth.

"Do you want to know why I've kept you here, Faith? Other than helping with your leg?" Andre said.

If she could have opened her mouth, Faith thought, she'd be screaming.

"I gave you silver," Andre said. "In small amounts, before we've changed shape for the first time, the restorative powers of silver are nothing short of miraculous. You've noted that yourself. No doubt you've also come across references to the use of metals in your studies. Am I right in assuming so?"

Faith didn't move, couldn't even nod.

"Silver has a dual purpose for Lycans. It can at first aid in healing, but its main effect is to bring out what's hidden inside us that makes healing possible," Andre explained. "Silver acts as a catalyst for young Lycans, kicking metabolism into high gear and enhancing our ability to mend. It can only be used on those of us who have never transitioned, never changed shape. Once we have shifted, silver has a reverse effect. An adverse one. It becomes deadly for those of us who come into contact with it in any way."

"Like the silver bullet legend in the movies?" Faith remarked, looking to the curtained window, listening for Mason LanVal's missing voice. "You're going to tell me that's true?"

"Indeed, it is. A silver bullet can kill us. A silver chain can sap our strength, or burn us to the bone."

"The moon is silver."

"The moon..." Andre exhaled a slow breath. "The moon rules all of this. No one knows why. Perhaps she tugs loose from us what we wear on the inside, like the silver in the medicine does, only on a grander scale. Setting our inner beasts free."

The physician in her made her respond to that. "How

does a beast take over a person's body, Andre? If it's not a separate entity, buried inside, what is it?"

"We believe it's an emotion so vivid, so intensely rich, that it temporarily takes us over, unlocked, freed, if you will, by the pull of the moon."

"That man outside was no metaphor for harking back to our animal beginnings. He had fur. And the moon isn't full tonight."

"Variances," he said, "come with experience."

"Not all of you can change shape without celestial influence?"

"Very few can."

"So, what you gave me in that bottle is fueling the fire of my own immune system in a new way?"

"Yes. Starting it working overtime."

"You said you took a chance that your medication would work for me."

"If you weren't what I thought you were, the medication would have had little or no result, and your leg would have had to be amputated."

Another truth, and it left Faith feeling sicker. This was what she had feared all along—an answer as to why she hadn't died in this forest.

"So, I'm healing because I'm not really human. I'm a supernatural creature who doesn't know it."

She was going to offer up a further argument, and opened her mouth to do so, but stopped herself because she couldn't come up with any other viable explanation for her speedy recovery. She wasn't able to think of a reason for Hope to be running around in a forest at night, when they had both shunned wooded places after their parents' death. There certainly was no explanation as to why her sister hadn't stopped when called, or for the look of fear she'd seen on Hope's pale face.

God. Did Hope know she was a Hunter, or whatever the hell else she might be that didn't involve the term *Homo sapiens* in the strictest sense?

Did Hope know about *her*? That her sister was part wolf?

Goose bumps formed on her arms. Faith swiped at them with her hand, then let the hand fall. There was no way Hope could have harmed their parents, just as it was an impossibility that Hope could have known about the existence of werewolves in this remote corner of France.

Prove it, her analytical mind demanded.

Show Andre he's not right about this.

Call his bluff.

Thinking that, Faith held up the wrist of one shivering arm. After looking it over, she ran a fingernail across it hard enough to draw a faint line of blood.

See? I bleed like anyone else!

Her relief was cut short. The gibe she'd been about to make fizzled as she watched, fascinated, the wound first begin to tingle at its edges, then close as if it had been zipped shut.

Holding her breath, not sure she'd ever be able to breathe normally again, Faith saw the wound disappear. Gone. Erased. Leaving no trace.

With trembling hands, she yanked up the bottom of Andre's loaned pants.

The damage to her leg had seemed irreparable when she'd first glanced at it. Already black and blue by the time she'd awakened here, in this house, large slices of muscle and skin had been missing from her shin. There had been stitches where she supposed the bone had broken through the skin. The seriousness of the injury had been all too evident.

She felt her way down the splint now, a device molded from a piece of wood as smooth as glass. Pressed against her calf muscle and stretching from her knee to her ankle, the splint was tied with strips of white linen, which were in turn held in place with lengths of surgical tape, slightly damp with an ingredient she placed by its smell.

The silver medication.

Her gaze followed her fingers. She was shocked at what she saw. The soft pink of healthy skin showed through the gaps in the tape. Some bruising remained, but not enough to mask the fact that the wound had sealed shut, the disarming rupture barely visible.

She wiggled her toes and saw them move. Not the typical aftermath of major trauma to a leg bone. Nowhere close. Her leg was nearly healed, its damage inexplicably repaired.

No human being could recover this fast. It wasn't possible. Breathless, and with her heart racing, Faith realized that unless she'd been here weeks or months, instead of hours, Andre had to be telling the truth.

She was a goddamn werewolf.

What came to mind in that instant wasn't anything about Hope, or about the mystical properties of a werewolf's healing powers. Her first thought hadn't been about any of that.

She wanted to know about the man at the core of everything that had happened so far. Mason LanVal.

If these woods were filled with supernatural creatures out of myth and legend, and folks around here knew about them, even accepted them to some degree…then what kind of creature would LanVal turn out to be?

He had unbelievable strength, enough to carry an

unconscious woman a mile through the dark without even breathing hard. He had a direct channel to her thoughts and the ability to speak directly to her mind if he chose. He was possessed of an uncanny ability to make her bypass current problems in favor of wanting the touch of his mouth to hers.

But what sort of being hid himself away from the world and called himself Guardian? Communed with police and werewolves?

And why did she want him, and all he might be, so badly?

With what little strength she had left, she slammed into LanVal's closed mental door, shoving it open, fighting her way through the darkness separating her from him.

She found him in the dark. Felt him. And through him, something else. Something tall, pale and surrounded by a red-tinted aura of Otherness. Something familiar, yet not quite right.

Hope.

LanVal! she silently cried to the man through whose eyes she looked out at the world with horror and recognition.

It was Hope. He'd found her.

But…

The feeling of Otherness wasn't only tied to the being he held tightly to. She saw this, as well. Tasted it. Tasted *him.* The man she hungered for, the man with the ability to make her disconnect from everything important to her wasn't human, either. Not a man. *Damn it, not a man.*

She hadn't only been deceived, she'd been foolish, rash, stupid. She had walked out of the known world and into a new one, and was stuck in purgatory for allowing this to go so far.

If she wasn't fully human, and neither was anyone around her, the rules most humans adhered to no longer applied.

Who are you? she called balefully.

And what are you going to do with my sister?

Chapter 15

Hope James was as cold and brittle as her posture suggested. Touching her was like latching on to bone and sinew, rather than the flesh and blood of what had to have recently been a relatively normal young woman, at least outwardly.

No one, Mason thought, especially a physician, could have allowed a sibling to drift this far from the norm without seeking substantial help from others in the medical community. Therefore, Hope's rapid physical and mental downturn must have been recent enough that Faith missed the signs. As a Hunter with latent blood, it was possible Hope had just become acquainted with what that title meant, either by force or necessity.

Mason felt a frigid coldness rise from deep within his body as his fingers closed firmly around Hope's arm. A chilled arm, the circumference of a child's. In what felt to him like slowed motion, Hope whirled to-

ward him with her hands raised. She began to pound at
him with her fists, making no sound, not even a startled grunt of anger.

She was unnaturally strong, given her gaunt appearance, but not strong enough to physically harm
him with her attack. Although her limbs arced with
an agitated speed that picked up in pace as she dug in,
it seemed to Mason that her heart wasn't in this protest and that she might merely be reacting defensively
to being tracked.

"Easy," Mason cajoled, wary of giving her the shake
that may or may not have knocked some sense into
her. Whatever her purpose for being out here, she had
clearly been mistreated.

"I want to talk to you. I won't hurt you," he said.
Not now. Not yet. Not until I know what you are. "Do
you need help? Can I help you, Hope? You see, I know
who you are."

Her struggles ceased as abruptly as if someone
had pulled the plug. Her hands fell to her sides. Her
thin shoulders slumped. In her dark eyes Mason saw
a gleam of tears. And yet she didn't reply to any of his
questions.

He pressed on. "Are they waiting for you? Do you
know what they are? Have they hurt you?"

Dull, lifeless eyes stared up at him. Around those
eyes, her skin molded tightly over prominent cheekbones in an expression suggesting his presence and his
questions were painful to her. But beneath the obvious
hurt and the haunted cast to her eyes, Mason perceived
an awareness that caused his own skin to chill further.

She was indeed subtly something other than one
hundred percent human. It took him seconds to find

what he sought while surveying her damaged exterior. At first, he didn't dare believe what his senses told him.

He turned her body toward his so that she faced him fully. And there he sighted the evidence of the horrors she had been through, as well as the reason she hadn't spoken. Hope's lips had been sewn together. Small white stitches—two in each corner, and two in the center—sealed the swollen flesh of her mouth together.

The needles required for this act of atrocity had been small, the result no less ungodly painful. Several pin-size holes were caked with dried blood. The uneven stitches that remained had been tied off with tight, tiny knots of silver thread.

Mason dropped his hold on her. He hadn't seen anything like this since the Inquisition, and the reminder of that appalling time made him shudder all over again.

Not wanting to lose her, he grabbed Hope by the waist and got another surprise. Coiled around that waist, beneath her shirt, close to her skin, was a length of slender chain. He didn't have to guess what its links were made of.

The discovery made him recoil.

Silver could no longer harm him enough to cause real damage. Very few things could. But with wolf in Hope's chemical makeup, she might be aggrieved by contact with the metal. Here she was, wrapped in silver, trapped by its properties, bogged down by a dose of wolfsbane not strong enough to kill her, since she wasn't true Lycan, but more than enough to make every single breath she took a further torment.

The same metal humans coveted as being second only to gold had properties treacherous to all vampires and werewolves, and maybe to every other species, if there were more. If Hope had been other than a Hunter, some alternate species closer to the earth, who was to know for sure if a metal taken from a vein in the ground could have harmed her, or whether she'd have been exempt.

But Hope James was a Hunter, all right. In the dried blood on her mouth, as well as in the tears she held back, drifted the faintest trace of a musky Were scent that was easy to miss unless you knew what to look for. A scent that whispered *Werewolf Hunter*.

The question facing Mason now was what sort of monster could attract, then inflict this much physical suffering on a pretty young thing of whatever species, visibly distorting something that was ninety percent human and shoving her into becoming a thing she might not have recognized?

This was a heinous action. Over-the-top. Aside from the issue of pain, Faith's sister couldn't talk, drink, eat. She couldn't get at the tiny threads with her trembling fingers for fear of further tearing her flesh apart, though he saw she had recently tried. Next to the crusted blood, fine trickles of fresh crimson fluid ran from both corners of her reddened mouth. There were scarlet stains on her fingers and on the backs of her hands.

Helpless, forced into starvation and tormented in the worst possible way, Hope James was fading inch by terrible inch. She was half ghost already, the life within her flickering as weakly as a sputtering candle flame. Whatever she was, whomever she served, she didn't deserve this fate or the wretched path to it. The demented bastard who had done this to her had to be stopped, taken out like the hell spawn he was.

There was no doubt about it. A sick master vampire controlled this neighboring nest, and as Guardian, Mason had waited too long to take care of the problem. There was a chance both Faith and her sister could have escaped this shockingly cruel business if he had attended to the bloodsuckers just one week before.

Can't look back. Too late to do anything about the past.

"Come with me now," he said, slipping a hand under Hope's shirt to get at the chain. "I can free you from a portion of the pain."

She drew back and held up her hands to stop him. One tear had finally escaped, slipping down her cheek. She shook it away and backed up another step. All this terrible torture, and she was flat out refusing his offer of help. As Mason groped for the reason, he heard Faith's voice calling to him again—an intrusion containing all the brilliance of a shooting star in the darkness and accompanied by the usual flush of warmth.

Facing the frigid darkness of her sister's plight, Faith's voice seemed a necessary reminder that good, decent things existed in a world that had gone wrong. Mason wanted to wrap himself in Faith's warmth, and bring Hope along. Beneath Faith's brief touch, he was chilled to the bone and sure that Hope felt colder.

"Faith is waiting," he said. "Though I can't take you to her yet, I can get you to someplace safe."

Hope took a third step back with her hands still raised.

"You can't go back to them," he said. "That must be obvious."

In trying to move her mouth, Hope's body swayed with the agony of the effort. More blood trickled from her punctured lips, dripping over her chin, running in a threadlike rivulet down her neck. Her eyes glazed over. Her blue-white lids fluttered.

Observing the trail of blood, Mason's fangs descended. Thirst beckoned at the back of his throat at the sight of the blood he had always ignored. This craving wasn't warm or personal. It wasn't in any way sexual, as the passing of blood between him and Hope's sister had been. This was hunger of a different sort—for vengeance, for justice—because he was familiar with Hope's level of pain. He had experienced it himself once, and the remembrance of that time was his own private nightmare.

Hand in hand with the descending teeth came a further sharpening of his awareness. Mason saw past Hope's waning exterior strength, as though it had been wiped away. With a startling clarity, he realized that although she had been a victim of vicious crimes, by not accepting his offer of assistance she was going to allow more of the same torture she had already endured.

She was permitting it for a reason.

"You're a Hunter," Mason said, discerning equally quickly what that reason was.

"You won't accept my offer of help," he said, struck by the irrefutable truth.

In pain, and afraid of what might happen to her next, she refused to go with him because she feared more for her sister's life than her own.

Hope was a Hunter who wasn't going to lead anyone to Faith. She had no intention of providing her sister's whereabouts to the vampires who had done these things to her. She was willing to die rather than give the vampires what they wanted. Her sister. And her sister's kind.

The sudden enlightenment must have registered on his face, Mason thought, because Hope recoiled.

Faith and Hope perhaps weren't sisters by blood, but they were connected by the particular properties of the blood in their veins. They were opposites, born to fight each other, bred to be enemies, yet they had been in denial all this time. They had been in stasis, due to a unique upbringing that had paired them up and provided a leg up on conscience.

Had their parents done this on purpose, for this very conclusion, thinking to protect each child? Thinking to halt this sort of ending?

There was no time to delve further into this. The voice in his head had grown steadily stronger in direct proportion to the distance Hope placed between them. Faith was pleading with him to help her sister, without perceiving the fact that her sister couldn't afford to be found.

It was a miracle the vampires hadn't killed Hope already.

Addressing the voice in his mind that had in it more light than all-encompassing darkness, Mason's thoughts extended further.

"By raising two sisters as strong, vibrant thinkers, your parents sufficiently tweaked a natural hatred for each other dictated by your genes. The actions of your parents might have delayed the flare of each of your natural instincts, perhaps forever, if this hadn't happened."

Although Mason didn't believe an all-out genetic truce could prove to be a clear-cut good thing, he also had to hand it to the Jameses for attempting their own experiment. He was cognizant of the fact that the bond between Faith and Hope had, even if for a short time, overruled nature.

His cold heart softened, as it had too many times lately.

"I can help you," he added, as Hope inched away from him. "Come with me."

Hope tilted her head so that her long hair covered her face. Through the dark tangle, she peered at him with wounded, defiant eyes. The blood dripping from her mouth was a macabre contrast to her paleness.

Mason's thirst bucked at his insides. When he opened his mouth to speak, he realized that Hope saw his fangs. Without any sort of gesture and no change of expression, she turned from him without looking back.

"Faith loves you," Mason said, letting her go, knowing she'd equate his fangs with those of the others who had done bad things to her. "And I know what you've done, at least in part."

He had to let her leave, though his heart ached to help her. He had to set his plan into motion, whether or not Faith's sister withstood her terrible plight for another twenty-four hours.

He would have taken her if she'd extended a hand, at the expense of his plan. Saving a soul was the best part of his vow. But it was also obvious that Hope James, reduced now to a phantomlike creation, had been the first of the sisters to find out about her heritage. This was the knowledge that had perhaps driven her away from her home.

"An honorable retreat from an inescapable fate? A kind of death wish?"

Mason watched her go with regret churning his insides, then set his shoulders. If he couldn't change the past, he bloody well would try to manipulate the future.

* * *

This time when Faith looked to the window, Andre followed her gaze as if he also knew LanVal was coming.

Andre might have seen a telling sign of the thrill running through her body. Unable to quell her anticipation, Faith used the wall to pull herself to her feet.

"He found her," she said.

Without Andre's help, she half hopped, half stumbled to the door. When the moonlight hit her face, she recoiled.

"It's your light. Let it in." Andre moved in behind her. "There's no need to be frightened. She won't hurt you."

"She?"

"The moon."

"Then why do I feel danger in my bones?"

"It's only an introduction. A different path. Marked change. You didn't know about this, and that's a shame, but you can handle it."

"What if I don't want to?"

"I'm afraid it's too late. The process has already begun."

Yes. Her leg was almost fully healed. "Your medicine…"

"Only worked if you are what you are."

"Then it's real, true," Faith whispered. "Hell, Andre, I feel so helpless."

"Those feelings will pass."

"You don't mind this, really? You've lived with it, made it work?"

"As have scores of others as far back as we can count."

"You're out here with no phone, no car and not much

unwanted company. How about me? Will I be able to do my work? Be around people? Appear—"

"Normal? Human? It's likely you can do all those things, in time."

"How much time?"

"We'll have to see. The full moon will bring about your first shift. After that, we'll assess how it's to go."

"Does it hurt, Andre? The transformation, I mean. Tell me the truth, as one healer to another." She nearly added, *As one werewolf to another.* Panic over the withheld remark forced her to steady herself.

"Yes. It will hurt," Andre admitted. "More than anything you can imagine. Not tonight though. Tonight is a first meeting. A beginning."

"I can feel it now, on my face. Light, sinking in, searching for whatever it needs. My instinct is to fight this. What if the strangeness I'm experiencing is only the power of suggestion? Your suggestion."

The fact that Andre did not reply produced a far worse outcome for her than if he had. His silence meant that the condition was inevitable, irreversible, real. And maybe it actually was the touch of the moon she was feeling. But there was also something deeper here, instinct told her, and potentially more dangerous.

Was Mason LanVal's approach causing these signals?

"He is coming, Andre," she said. "He found my sister. What will he think of me?"

"He will understand. He knows what you are. What we are."

"He isn't like me. You told me that."

"LanVal is his own creature, though he could just as easily have been like the bloodsuckers."

Faith's blood turned cold. Her legs buckled slightly

as wave after wave of panic threatened. "You're talking about vampires and identifying him with them?"

"Not exactly. I'd rather say he's more than they are. Different. Older. Stronger. On another wavelength altogether."

"More dangerous?"

"Infinitely so."

Faith's heartbeat roared. LanVal had gotten close, and she'd allowed it. She had actually been senseless enough to have believed him a potential, viable partner—someone who might be closer to a bloodsucker than merely a handsome enigmatic recluse who finds missing people.

According to Andre, vampires were the enemy.

Werewolves. Vampires...

"God help us all if there are such things," she whispered. But she was at a loss as to how to explain her sudden fascination with the dichotomies of cold and heat, touch and texture, that she was experiencing as she waited for LanVal. She was helpless to define feelings for him that had sprung into existence and refused to fade or be categorized.

Her face felt hot, while the rest of her was one continuous shiver. More symptoms of shock, maybe, over the fact of having sensed that LanVal, the man whose nearness she craved despite her reasoning, was more than he seemed.

Things were getting complicated fast, and she had the distinct feeling of lagging behind a step or two. Had it been just the leg to worry about while the search continued for her sister, her prescription would have been to get back to bed and elevate the limb. Add LanVal in, along with the alarmingly rapid rise of her feelings for him, and a better prescription for someone in her condition would be sixteen ounces of any alcoholic beverage approaching one hundred proof.

Without silver in it.

Could just as easily have been like the bloodsuckers.

She latched on to Andre's wording, seeking a way out of believing that her very strong, notably virile rescuer was a vampire. *Like* a vampire didn't mean he was one. What, then, did it mean? Enlightenment remained damnably elusive.

"Tell me who he is, Andre."

Her hands were again clutched tightly to the edge of the door. Lucas was in the yard and, beside him, another big man. Both of them looked human, as normal as any large, strapping men, and neither of them was naked at the moment. They were dressed like Andre and herself in pants and plaid shirts. They leaned against the corner of Andre's small house as casually as if they were part of the landscape; not conversing, just there—a silent, solid, commanding presence.

Faith inhaled another breath of forest-scented air and felt like choking. Her parents had shown her how to enjoy the dark, and her mother and father hadn't really been people at all. They had been werewolves, with telling birthmarks on their arms.

Mason LanVal wasn't like them. Wasn't like her.

Groping for explanations, Faith did as Andre advised and tried to allow the moonlight in. Concentrating was not only difficult, it was downright impossible. Mason LanVal's closeness caressed her skin in place of Andre's moon. He was nearly there. The air she breathed held clues of the remembrance of his breath on her face, in her mouth and lungs.

Like a woman awaiting her long-lost lover, she sent a piece of her soul greedily through the night, and past it, to meet him.

Chapter 16

Mason slowed when the cottage came into view, wary of the welcoming party.

Three Weres stood in the yard: Andre, Lucas and Gregoire. He didn't count the fourth, so ashen and expectant on the doorstep, though it was she who captured his full attention. Faith had not looked beyond him for the sister she anxiously awaited news of. Her first thought, fleeting as it may have been, and one she would never admit to out loud, was of her gladness for his return.

Her Lycan-green eyes drank him in as surely as if she had been the vampire. Her flawless skin glowed in the light. All things considered, in the world of psychopath blood-drinkers and purebred werewolf watchdogs, Faith's eyes were, for him, the weightier threat.

"Faith." Her name was torn from his lips to emerge as a whisper, and reached her long before he did. She hobbled forward, not nearly as hampered as she should have been by her injury.

You grow stronger, then.

That unspoken thought reached her, as well, by way of the link between them that refused to be severed. The blood he'd given her had dispersed completely and caused the underlying flush of heat that tinted her cheeks. His blood, in her, continued to mandate their closeness, demanding still more intimacy.

Had she heard this thought, too? Did she know the only way to appease their desires, given the ongoing intensity of their attraction, would be to let their bodies and souls have at each other? Unleash their tightly guarded passion and allow the connection to burn itself out?

She blinked slowly, as though she did understand this, perhaps without comprehending the part about a she-wolf's ability to imprint on a male, aside from his blood gift. And as though he was equally a captive.

Only then did her gaze slide past him in search of her sister. She said, "Where is she?" the question ringing in time with the last one she asked. *"What are you?"*

She and Andre had been talking, it seemed.

When Andre stepped up beside her, the Were's broad shoulder nearly touching hers, a surge of jealousy washed over Mason. She was wearing Andre's clothes. They hung loosely on her slender frame. She looked so small. She smelled like Andre.

Mason's heart kicked out a protest that carried him forward.

"How long do we have?" Andre asked in the tone of a general on the eve of an anticipated battle, his question overriding Faith's.

"Not long, I think," Mason said. Then he turned to Faith. "She wouldn't come."

Faith had been aware of that already on some level. She'd been there in his mind when he had confronted Hope. She'd heard some of his thoughts and through them must have had an inkling about what had happened.

He had to be careful, maintain some distance, though his soul cried out against it. If she surfed his thoughts so easily, how deep into his secrets would their connection take her? All the way back to Castle Broceliande, and what had happened to him there? What he had done in order to become what he now was?

Would those things repulse her?

I am sick of secrets, Faith. He was tired of living apart, and of the constancy of his attempts to maintain a balance between the humans crowding the earth and the corresponding spread of the world's darker elements.

He didn't like seeing Andre so close to Faith. Didn't like the thought of losing her, either to the secrets dictating her own fate or the secrets dictating his. His life, and how he'd lived it, hadn't prepared him for this kind of terrible sentimentality. He had a hard time remembering when this emotional disruption had begun, and how.

Well, yes, he could remember that, actually.

It was with the first scent of you, Faith.

We both did this. I placed my mouth on yours, and made the choice. You looked into my eyes and made yours.

Theirs was a forbidden liaison. He wanted her, but to be able to continue with his task, he'd have to leave behind the longings she evoked. After tonight, he'd have to forget Faith James. His vow demanded it.

He would do that—find a way to sever the tie and get on with the elimination of the nest that had distorted so much beauty, including Faith's sister. If Faith knew of his purpose, she might even understand.

"I'm going back there," he said to Andre.

"It can't wait for the others to arrive?" Andre asked.

"I don't think it can."

With difficulty, Mason stopped himself from looking at Faith. The truth was, he had never wanted anything so badly.

Andre nodded. "It's as we thought?"

"Worse."

Mason wondered how Andre would interpret that statement. Andre only knew about the vampires. The Were had no idea what controlled them or how far back this particular neighboring master vampire's existence probably went. If the chateau's vampire in residence was after werewolves, and that objective had been thwarted in any way—such as Faith's sister refusing to take direction—the creature in that chateau would show his hand in other ways sooner rather than later. Patience had never been a blood-drinker's virtue.

I ought to know, Mason thought, feeling the burn of Faith's attention without being able to do anything about it.

Out in the open now, Faith. No way around it, he silently sent to her, to prepare her for what he'd say next.

"Hope is in trouble. She may already be beyond our help, but it was she who provided the clue as to what resides in this nest. She went out of her way to do so, and at her own peril. I want to help her. I want to do as you've asked, Faith. But your sister isn't the priority here. The monsters who have harmed her are, because they can do the same to others. In order to better calculate the extent of the problem, I need a closer look."

"Alone?" Andre asked.

"Yes."

"Then this nest is more of a threat than we realized."

"By far," Mason reluctantly replied. "I know what it has to be, and I've been waiting for a hint of it. It's a moment long in the making."

"You're not like them." Faith's voice was surprisingly strong. "Will they harm you if you're enough like them, and oppose what they do?"

"They might try," Mason said. "I stand in their way, but I'm not so benign an adversary." *In spite of the fact that particles of the same blood running through my veins runs through theirs.*

"How can that be?" Faith asked aloud, causing Andre to turn his head. "How can your blood be related to a vampire's and not be the same?"

She shrugged off Andre's warning hand on her arm and rephrased her question. Audible dread lowered her tone. "Are you a vampire?"

Tired... Mason reiterated. *Weary to the bone of confidences and distances. Of ignored cravings, and differences disguised. Yet I have never lied about what I am.*

"Yes," he replied. "Close enough to them, anyway, for someone to assume so."

There. He had answered her question. He had confessed, stunned to hear himself saying aloud, and for the first time, the words linking him to an identity he had withheld for centuries. An identity necessarily kept confidential for the good of everyone.

He was telling her now because of what had brought them together. She had made him remember his differences by stumbling into a deathtrap he'd been monitoring, and then stumbling into his arms.

No one could really explain how intimate alliances happened, or what caused the mystical spark that ultimately became the uniting force between two beings. He did know that Faith felt the spark as she stood there so stoically, with his blood singeing her veins and the moonlight making her face seem not merely beautiful but extraordinary.

Maybe he had been waiting for this, at the same time longing for and dreading to embrace the concept of companionship, which in its highest form might lead to love. Yet all that was a danger for him. Look what such a thing had done to one of his brethren, and the result.

"Vampires have my sister," Faith said, the tremor of fear in her voice impossible to disguise.

"True," he said, determined not to evade the seriousness of her sister's predicament.

"They will not welcome you, no matter how many characteristics you share?" she asked.

"I am dissimilar in spirit, and the bane of their kind."

He heard her next startled thought. *Are you, then, a Vampire Slayer?*

"Something like that," he replied. "Only much, much more."

In the silence following his confession, Mason noted how Faith's chest rose and fell laboriously, as if breathing had become difficult for her. He saw goose bumps forming on her flushed neck and forearms. Her blood was up, stirred by fear for her sister's safety and anger that he wasn't like her. Although he didn't owe her more of an explanation for either his behavior or his existence, he found himself wanting to give her as much of an explanation as he could manage.

"I hold to the belief that one of my brothers might be responsible for this mess," he said, not caring who else heard. "I've been searching for him for a very long time in order to find out if this is true."

His hunger for Faith became all-encompassing when her eyes finally met his. He felt the irregular pulses beating at her, heard her subtle intake of breath, scented the strange fragrance of the mingling of their blood that had likely been sustained because of her own unique chemistry. They were able to have conversations without moving their lips.

Could she, however, see far enough into what he had *not* said? Dive deep enough to discover what he'd done, thinking to save her? The kiss. The blood gift that had helped to set this irresponsible relationship in motion?

Faith surprised him yet again by not retreating from him. She stepped closer—close enough for him to feel the warmth of her sweet, exhaled breath.

She reached out with a shaky hand. After hesitating for the time it took her to find the courage to carry on, she tentatively brushed his mouth with her fingers, all the while continuing to look into his eyes.

The effect, for Mason, was immediate. Every warring part of himself congealed with desire for her, pushing the urge to possess her, wrap himself in her, take from her all that she had to give…in turn revealing himself. Those things were, of course, impossible. Odds were against them ever coming together, with or without the Weres looking on.

With her finger, Faith pressed on his bottom lip. Her gaze lowered to study his mouth. Her heartbeat was deafening.

Mason stopped himself from commanding those wild green eyes back to his, anticipating what she was about to do and what her reaction might be. Fearing that reaction.

Not a single sound escaped her when she found the fangs that were not only lethally sharp, but an indication of his status.

She made no sound as she ran the tip of her finger across the points. Tapping that fingertip, she winced. Then she held the finger up, at eye level, for him to see the drop of bright red blood pooling on it.

Mason's thirst engaged. His focus narrowed and his pulse molded to hers, matching each thunderous stroke. Every one of her rasped breaths became his as he stared at the blood, smelling its properties—so close, so much a part of her. He barred himself from reaching out to take what he wanted, shaking with restraint.

The forest faded away into the distance, as did the protest Andre voiced. None of those things mattered. It was only Faith and himself in one suspended moment, and whatever move she'd choose to make next.

If she cowered, he'd go. If a grimace crossed her beautiful features, he'd leave her to Andre and the others and get on with things, no worse for wear for having faced temptation and lost.

"Do you want this?" she asked, alluding to the blood on her raised finger, her tone that heady mixture of fear and sultry feminine allure, the blending of those two things like catnip for a creature who had imagined himself above such earthly needs.

"I do want it," he said.

"Yet you hold back." Her eyes again found his.

"Is it not decency of purpose that sets us apart from the beasts?" he rasped.

But the blood on her finger was only an indication of the problem. He desired everything having to do with Faith James, and his willpower had already started to slip.

As if reading that, too, Faith said, "Then it seems we all are driven toward our destinies by the actions and decisions of our families."

With that remark, she retreated—perhaps afraid to turn her back to him, having discovered the fangs. Fangs equaled vampire, she'd be thinking. Of course, that's what they all thought, since the subtleties of his existence weren't within the boundaries of hasty assessments or contained within the realm of most people's imaginations. Seeing in black and white only was easy. Good on the one side, evil on the other. No gray area in the middle. No shadings at all.

The occupants of Castle Broceliande had fed from each other. He, as their successor, had fed from one of them in order to become what he was. Not from a vein, but from a golden cup.

He had died there, within the castle's walls. His heart had stopped, starting again only as the blood of his maker, as well as the purpose the castle's ancient beings had for him, took him over.

But either his maker had seen to it that his soul was preserved, as well as the spirit that had previously driven him toward the forces of good, or the Grail had done this—the chalice with dark mysteries of its own.

"No one can blame you for being afraid," he said soothingly. "You came here to find your sister, and have ended up facing your own destiny."

As a she-wolf, she wasn't supposed to care about the enemy. Were versus vampire was the information dump sealed into her genetic makeup. Two species at war. Ancient protagonists, aside from this truce.

The three werewolves surrounded her, ready to protect one of their own as she backpedaled toward the house. Fierce creatures, even in their humanlike shapes.

Nevertheless, Faith's eyes told him a different story than one of enemies and aliens. In the dilation of her pupils that had changed their color from green to a shiny black-gold, he saw an internal struggle that rivaled his own.

She still wanted him.

Sweet, sweet gods, the fragrant scent of her blood trailed her like a shadow. That shadow curled a finger in his direction as if beckoning for him to follow, daring him to break down the walls separating them and take what she was offering. What they both desired.

When she shuddered, the quakes moved through him like an infectious contagion. When her face paled further, he knew his own flesh matched hers. Her heart hammered inside his chest. The blood connecting them clung to her fingertip like a siren's song.

He was leaning toward her, his willpower further weakened by the flash of sadness in her eyes.

Of all the emotions, why sadness, Faith? For the inevitable? In honor of the things keeping us apart?

His foundation cracked. Images of Castle Broceliande and its blood-drinking occupants swirled through his mind as if they were an integral part of the chill passing over him—though his creator hadn't caused this current discomfort. Faith had dredged up the memories, and with them, regret—an emotion that could topple the strongest foundation. An emotion almost too much for him to bear.

Mason heard the sound that served to break the spell. Not words. No argument. Another kind of warning altogether. A reminder, as if he needed one, of whose front yard he stood in, and that time did not stand still for dreams and reminiscences.

The silver Were's howl split the night wide-open, allowing for the light of reality to at least temporarily shine through.

Chapter 17

The howl was like a nightmare coming to ground. Like the feel of lightning trapped in a bottle held tightly to her breast. Shocking, loud, frighteningly familiar.

Faith was taken over by an immediate need to respond, and was startled to hear the low, loose growl that bubbled up from deep inside her as if it had been torn free.

Reeling on her feet, steadied by Andre's quick reflexes, she looked first to her silver-haired host, then to the other two men beside her. Lucas growled when her gaze settled over him, his guttural sounds seeming as natural to him as any other bit of conversation would have been. But his ease sat on the top of churning waters, much like a smile that didn't reach a person's eyes.

These three men were visibly agitated. Their muscles twitched and contracted. Heat came off them in disturbed waves in reaction to what? The presence of a vampire in their midst? Surely they had known about LanVal all along.

Her eyes strayed to LanVal, whose cool, exquisite, nearly hurtfully handsome features reflected the horror she felt at the sound she'd made. In his expression she found the answer to a question she hadn't known was puzzling her.

How could she have forgotten that her father had howled, just like Andre, and that her mother had done the same? That neither parent had really attempted to fit into the world around them? They loved the night and the freedom of open spaces. The short business trips that had taken them away for a few days each month might, in hindsight, have been an ode to the lunar phases ruling their genetics. They had made soothing, loving, guttural sounds to her and to each other. Growls of pleasure, contentment and heat.

Those memories came hurtling back.

"We'd prefer to tag along on your hunt," Andre said to LanVal, easing some of the tension they all felt.

"If it comes to that, I'll return for you," LanVal replied.

He was lying, Faith knew, and thinking this fight was his.

"Morning is coming," Andre warned.

"Then it'll soon be time for all good little vampires to be in their beds."

"What about Guardians?" Faith said, drawing LanVal's attention back to her, then wishing she hadn't spoken when she found the attention disconcertingly intense, and overtly sexual. "Do they sleep?"

"About as often as werewolves do," he remarked lightly, his penetrating gaze leaving dizziness in its wake, as well as a rumble of needy vibration between her thighs.

By the time she realized that Andre and his friends were crowding around her like a muscled fence, cutting her off from the vampirelike being who possessed the ability to affect her in more ways than she cared to acknowledge, LanVal, damn his fanged, elegant hide, had gone.

His exit left a big fat hole in the fabric of the night that the three gigantic werewolves next to her couldn't begin to fill.

Transferring more weight onto her splinted leg, the ensuing ache was a welcome distraction from the fact that although she was a surgeon, she remained way too ignorant of the lesser known facts of life around her.

"What will happen to me, and when?" she asked Andre.

"In five more days, you'll start the change," Andre said.

The word *change* sent a current of fire through her.

"Like Lucas?"

"No. You won't be a wolf. Lycans are mostly half wolf and half human."

Werewolf. A terrible image. She couldn't go there.

"Will you be here when I do, Andre?"

"I won't leave your side."

"Despite the Blood Moon?"

"Especially because of it."

Faith looked beyond Andre. "What can I do like this, to help him?" She gestured to her legs.

"LanVal can take care of himself, as you've probably observed."

"You've seen his fangs?"

"Many times."

"He hasn't used them on anyone you know?"

"He helps us here, and has done so since he arrived. We have parallel goals."

"Those goals are?"

"To rid the area of rogue vampires and get on with our lives."

"Rogue vampires," Faith echoed, again searching the spot where LanVal had stood, hoping to see him reappear, while praying he wouldn't.

His closeness brought up so many feelings she'd been afraid to confront, and an equal number of old dreams. She had always known she wasn't the type for a house in suburbia with a white picket fence. She'd gone this long without being seriously attracted to the men she'd met. Remaining single was a by-product of her position and focus. She was driven, with a need to channel her energy. Work came first, while it seemed as if most men were threatened by women with un-wavering ambition.

How the hell would they have liked dating a were-wolf?

Mating with one?

She was now so far removed from what hadn't quite been a normal life to begin with, as to be totally off base. She was an injured Lycanthrope, held in a foreign country without the means to accomplish the chief ob-jective of finding her sister. And she had been waylaid by a powerful, if distracting, attraction to someone who wasn't even human.

Oh, yes, she'd been aroused by what she'd seen be-tween LanVal's talented lips. She should have been scared numb, and sent running. Instead, she desired him with a desperation she'd never known. One blister-ing look from this dark stranger, and despite everything going on, she was hungering, big-time, and riveted by thoughts of what he might do with those fangs.

The world really had been turned inside out, and she was going down for the count. According to Andre, there was a beast inside her, waiting to get out. Swear to God, she had to believe him. She imagined her beast stirring right that minute, born of that kernel of longing that began with the afterglow of moonlight on her face…and maturing when Mason LanVal had first pressed his mouth to hers.

A bond, sealed with a kiss.

She mourned LanVal's distance, with the moon looking on. The moon, a planetlike sphere so far from the earth, with the ability to rule people's personalities, as well as the fluids running through them.

Was the earth's silver satellite treacherous or desirous? Friend or foe? Nowhere in those damn medical books had she come across anything like this.

LanVal… Tall, elegant and one of the undead? What did *not exactly* being a vampire mean? Allowing for that, could she *not exactly* be a werewolf?

Her chest continued its frantic pounding.

LanVal seemed so alive, and more vibrant than anyone she had ever known. His wasn't a presence pasted onto the landscape or added by mistake from some heavenly artist's hand. LanVal was a creature created in the semblance of a man, and here on purpose. The world's protector. Its guardian. Able to rouse a host of unwieldy passions in her that had previously been inaccessible.

She would know if he was evil or immoral. She'd have been able to tell if his gorgeous exterior hid a rotten core. This wasn't the case. His nature might be dark, by its very definition, and dangerous for those who crossed his path, but Mason LanVal, whether or not he was associated with the word *vampire,* had something she wanted. It now seemed as if she had been waiting for someone like him. For this.

The nerve burn of excitement, the ongoing flood of emotion, the sudden insatiable hunger of expectation…

For the first time, she truly felt alive.

She had come back from the brink of death with a renewed enthusiasm for living, despite the possibility of harboring a beast. Or maybe because of it. Being Lycan meant that she and Mason LanVal had Otherness in common. A shared danger. A powerful bond.

With those thoughts, so personal and telling, Faith felt a flush of guilt and embarrassment color her cheeks. She was filled with desire for LanVal when the situation around her was dire. Monsters had her sister. Hope was still missing, and no outcome was certain.

And Mason LanVal had disappeared.

Andre's barking sounds, similar to tsks of leftover protest, alerted her to the fact that Andre was bent on keeping LanVal from her. Then again, maybe it was the other way around, and Andre was trying to keep her from LanVal.

Did werewolves also share a mind link, or had her recent blush of color said it all?

She faced Andre with a pinched expression, supposing his silver medicine could be behind all of these recent developments, and that, as she'd earlier supposed, she might eventually wake up. Right now, however, she wanted to tell her gracious host that she wasn't so sure she wanted to waken if a dream state could be this invigorating and physical…leaving out the part about wanting the creature he called Guardian in her bed.

"Why are there traps in the woods?" she asked, a

starting point in an attempt to make sense of everything that had happened since she had arrived in France.

"The vampires like to hunt," Andre replied. "Sometimes they hunt for food, and at other times for sport."

"Are you saying the trap that did this to my leg is part of a game?"

"An evil sort of amusement for which they appear to have an unlimited appetite," he acknowledged wearily.

In her mind, Faith saw this. She imagined the monsters chasing after their prey.

"Am I the first outsider to be caught?"

"Unfortunately, there have been several others lately, as well as animals and some of our own."

Andre didn't equate the word *animals* with *werewolves*. It was clear that he didn't count himself, or the Lucas she'd seen in his furry form, in with any other four-legged beast.

As she watched Andre, she noticed him clenching his fingers repeatedly, almost eagerly, as though he wanted to grasp hold of an object no one else could see. Faith wondered if he might have been among those caught up in vampire sport, and whether Andre's fingers bore the scars of an old wolf trap.

"Was my sister caught out there, Andre?"

"Several days ago," he said quietly, hastily adding, "She wasn't hurt."

The notation wasn't a comfort. Apprehension crawled up Faith's back, one sharp talon at a time.

"You saw her, then?"

"I found her. She was lucky. The filthy trap had caught the top of her boot. She would have worked herself free eventually, but I was close by. She ran away when I released her, and she ran in the wrong direction, appearing to know where she was going, and as though she'd come here for a reason."

Andre sighed heavily. "I suppose it's reasonable now to assume she might regret whatever that reason was."

"Vampires have her."

After a hesitation, Andre nodded again, visibly disturbed by the idea.

"Vampires are the bad guys," Faith remarked. "As are Hunters. Still, if Hope had the slightest doubt about her direction, why wouldn't she accept your help?"

"Possibly because my friends and I are the very thing she was born to hate."

Faith's pulse sputtered as she faced the term *Werewolf Hunter* dead-on.

"As a Hunter, bred to hunt werewolves, why would she turn to vampires? How would she even know of the existence of vampires?" she pressed, rushing on without pausing for a breath. "What are the chances of a vampire finding her on that tour?"

"Vampires don't run around in daylight," Andre said. "Some of them are recognizably Other, and would be spotted if they turned up in the city. We're not so close to the city, as you've noticed, which suggests to me that your sister had to have known about them, and purposefully decided to come here."

"Or else she knew about you," Faith said.

Andre's hands fisted again. "It's an option worth studying."

"Believing it would mean Hope knew she was a Hunter, and what that meant."

While I knew nothing of it and wallowed in the dark.

"*He* isn't recognizably Other, at first glance."

Her thoughts seemed inevitably to return to Mason LanVal.

"LanVal." Andre sighed the way people did when confronted with a problem they'd tried to reason out on numerous occasions, with no success.

"Guardian, you said. Of the world. I thought you were alluding to these woods, and the animals in them. Isn't he more than that, Andre? What exactly does he guard?"

"Humans," Andre said. "As I see it, he does what he can to protect humankind from the vampires."

"Not a Slayer."

"More along the lines of a Reaper. I'm not sure if he goes after them all. My sense is that he finds the bad ones and deals with them in accordance with some private agenda he holds. The growth of the neighboring nest drew him here."

An ancient vampire, protecting humans.

Going after the vampires who have my sister.

"Hope isn't a vampire, yet she has survived being around them. Is that right?"

"It's another puzzle that beckons to LanVal."

"Will he be able to help her, Andre? Will he stand against them, if it comes to that? This is the challenge you were alluding to earlier? You must be planning on helping him, even if earlier than you had planned."

"LanVal's objective benefits us all, in the end. We've pledged to assist in any way we can, and our promise is good. The rest of the pack arrives tomorrow. We'll be twelve strong."

Twelve strong and ready for action, all of these men brawny and dangerous in their own right as they awaited what was going to happen here, and their special moon. A full moon. A Blood Moon. The image of a glowing red ball of light in the sky was almost as frightening as the thought of a bunch of hungry vampires in pursuit of their next victim, chasing humans for sport and for food.

A fight was going to take place, and she was in the middle of it. Her sister's appearance here had set an inevitable event into motion, and her own presence had upped the ante. Vampires versus werewolves, with a Werewolf Hunter and a special breed of ancient slayer tossed into the mix. Tension between the two species might have been brewing for a while, but the odds were high that she and her sister had been the final straw, and that their presence here wasn't any unlikely coincidence.

Hope had to have known Faith would come after her, so how far did that plan go? All the way to killing Faith and the others of her kind?

"What LanVal does makes him more like a guardian angel than Reaper," she said earnestly, remembering his whispered words of kindness, his virulent, vital energy and the safety she'd felt in his sheltering arms. Reeling with emotion, she absorbed what Andre had told her about LanVal's goal to protect humankind from the monsters who would feed off their blood.

Dark angel...

"Guardian angel? I suppose it could seem like that," Andre replied. But Faith had caught the nuance that suggested she had gone too far in equating what essentially might have been birthed as a vampire with one of heaven's winged creatures.

Forgetting that she should have been focusing on herself and what she might change into in a few days' time, Faith tried hard to recall anything she could about vampires, and whether or not fiction might have any basis in truth.

What she came up with made her sick.

Chapter 18

Mason moved at a brisk pace, the need for urgency fueling his speed. Night filled in around him, curiously devoid of wind and sound.

"Put her out of your mind. No good can come of it," he said aloud to solidify the statement, though as was usually the way with such things, willfully attempting to avoid something invariably brought that thing closer.

Would her laughter be light, or as deep as her voice? Would the rest of her body be as flawlessly golden as the parts of it he'd already seen? When this was over, would she find it in her heart to forgive him for everything?

Mason followed the twists and turns leading to the clearing where he had first laid eyes on Faith. This time, it was more than her sweet, lingering scent that drew him. The place reeked with the fetid odor of death and decay.

Nasty things were about at this hour when they should have been secluded underground. The sun would rise in less than an hour, making vampire presence here akin to a game of Russian roulette. Nevertheless, all around him lay evidence of their having passed this way recently.

Maybe they actually were too young and ignorant to know their limitations. Conversely, these fledglings might have been clever decoys sent by an insolent master to throw adversaries off his scent.

Mason snapped his teeth together and moved on, thinking.

There were seven ways to send a vampire to its final death. Few beings knew of more than a couple of the ways to turn off forces animating the undead, or how those means had come into existence.

Then again, few people had proved beyond a doubt the true existence of vampires, though many had tried.

Mason LanVal, Blood Knight, knew all the ways to terminate life for good, because those ways had been invented for himself and his blood brothers as safety catches.

There was one path to final death for each of the original Seven. Each knight had their own specialized off switch. Seven ways to eliminate seven of the strongest creatures walking the earth…and ignorant people assumed a splash of holy water was the way to accomplish this feat.

The belief in those kinds of tricks had become so universal, in fact, with the plethora of movies and gothic novels, that new vampires had begun to believe it. Either that, or their thin, diluted blood made them weak enough for the simplest things—perhaps any trick they believed in—to be effective.

He'd seen fledglings burn away into nothingness from a cross pressed to their undead flesh. He'd ended the existence of more than a few with a sharpened stake through the place that should have housed a heart, when most vampires had no hearts.

Entering a church shouldn't harm them, since vampires weren't truly born of hell itself, but existed in a spiritual-free space of their own between the upper and lower realms. No longer the people they were, since most spirits depart after death, these new presences were free to take over bodies that hadn't been incinerated in the fires of cremation.

His knowledge of all this made him well equipped. A handy thing in theory, save for one small problem. When pitted against another Blood Knight, knowledge of the actual key to that knight's termination would be hard to utilize.

Knowing what would certainly bring about his own final end was also a lingering curse.

So, Mason considered again as he moved…which brother had caused the chaos? Was the master vampire ruling the neighboring nest close enough to this source to have scented the tapestries of Castle Broceliande itself? That kind of master would have to be quite old. Consequently, he'd also be wise enough, after Mason's run-in with the fledglings, to know Mason would be coming. There was a possibility he had known all along.

It had been such a long time since he'd found an adversary of this caliber, Mason had high hopes for this one. His blood had turned icy with anticipation for the upcoming confrontation, as it often did when the persistent question of what had happened to his brothers, and to the terrible might of the Seven, pecked at him torturously.

Which one had done this? Started this? Eventually, he'd find out, and the two of them would meet.

Which one...?

He had long ago ruled out the brother who had once gone by the name of Lance, and had been the first to visit the castle. Arthur's champion. Guinevere's lover. Undefeated in tournaments and battle after his meeting with Broceliande's occupants because of the secret fire flowing in his arteries that made him invincible. But Lance, golden and good, ever blessed, would never veer far enough from his path to create a subspecies, for good or ill. Lance had refused to turn Gwen, his love, though she had begged to join him in immortality.

That left five.

His reasoning skidded to a stop before he could get to the others, interrupted by the scent floating in the darkness of an even darker presence.

His first impulse was to attack and be done with it. However, if he jumped the gun, he'd learn nothing and prematurely display his hand.

Standing beneath the trees, blending with the night as he watched the clearing, Mason smiled grimly, thinking that if patience wasn't a universally accepted virtue in this day and age, it sometimes damn well had its uses.

"I need to go!" Faith exclaimed, suffocated by the closeness of Andre and the others gathered around her. Through LanVal's mind, she sensed danger. Her sister was as surrounded by the black wave of unfolding events as Faith had been cornered by muscle.

"Too early," Andre said. "You'll do more damage to the leg."

She'd forgotten about her leg, and looked down at it with frustration. A fine sheen of perspiration dampened her forehead and the unkempt hair hanging in her face. Her nerves were firing in white-hot flashes. She'd used far too much energy already to remain upright.

She needed fuel to use for strength and continued mental acuity, and wouldn't be able to force food down. She doubted that Hope was eating. Hope, who might be waiting to be rescued.

"I need to go after him." That sounded like a whine. She was feeling antsy and unsettled. "Something is wrong. You must feel it."

Andre followed her gaze, rolling his broad shoulders as if he also felt the urge to run and was holding himself back.

If Andre was staying here because of her, and anything else happened out there, she'd be responsible for that, too.

"Go after him, Andre," she said.

"He warned us away. I don't know LanVal well, but enough to trust in his intuition."

Faith faced the big man again. "If you can read this, as I do, you know there's something out there waiting for him."

"I do know," Andre conceded. "We all do."

"If my sister is a Hunter, and vampires have snatched her because of her talents, whatever he faces might have to do with you. With…us. He'd be taking on whatever this is for us."

How did a hundred-and-ten-pound woman move a mountain of male Lycan muscle, if pleading logically got nowhere?

"If LanVal guards the woods, who guards him?" she asked.

"You can't go out there, Faith. Even if you could do more than hobble, if I let you go, he'd come after me... after he is finished with them."

Though Andre had meant this lightly, Faith heard a ring of truth in the remark. It had become quite obvious to her, in the way these wolves had surrounded her, that they wanted no further alliance between herself and LanVal, and that they weren't aware of how deep her primal bond with him already went. She had only just permitted herself to acknowledge it, had only moments earlier become aware of the fact that there might indeed be a price to pay for whoever really tried to keep herself and the Guardian apart.

Those thoughts had crossed LanVal's mind, and she'd heard the sentiments as if he'd spoken a promise.

These werewolves might not actually fear this Guardian, but their healthy respect for him was obvious. She might not know what he was, really, but she needed him all the same. And she needed her sister to be safe and well.

If Andre wouldn't help her get to Hope, LanVal had to. Hope might listen to her over the entreaties of a stranger. Her sister might be persuaded to see reason and come back, despite what either of them might be.

Night and Day.

Suddenly, her mother's loving notation had taken on a more ominous connotation. Werewolf, and Hunter. Two opposite extremes of the same gene pool.

There had to be a reason for her parents raising someone else's child as their own, in light of the supposition of them hosting a child carefully designed to be their enemy—one who might have played a part in their death.

No! That can't be what happened. Not possible.

The image of Hope hurting her parents didn't feel right, didn't ring as the truth. Hunter or not, Hope had not had a hand in their demise. However, what if Hope thought she had? In finding out what she was becoming, there was a chance Hope might assume she was to blame.

Faith convulsed with the thought. Was this what Hope had run from? Her nature, and how it tied in to her family? How it tied in to her relationship with Faith? Had hints been there all along, in Hope's increasingly reckless behavior and the distance she'd put between them?

These suppositions were terrible. She had to find her sister, tell Hope it was all right and that she had Faith's trust, no matter how this looked to others. It was imperative, now more than ever, that she find her sister and make Hope understand that, like her, Faith had had no idea what she would grow up to be.

LanVal! Come back for me! This is my task!

Silence met her call. LanVal had closed himself to her again.

As Andre took her by the arm, she tried one last time to transmit a thought to the man, the vampire, the being in whose trust she now had to place everything.

In the process of rescuing her from her own probable death, Mason LanVal had managed to salvage not only her flickering life force, but a piece of her soul that had been lost.

An ancient vampire, long past the hunger of the others of his kind, now hungered for her.

A Guardian had gone after rogue vampires.

Vampires and werewolves. Slayers and Hunters. The world's hidden characters were about to face off beneath a bright bloody moon used to sacrifice and mayhem.

I am the mad one here.

She shifted more weight onto the splinted leg. With the werewolves eyeing her avidly, she called again.

Darkness waits, LanVal! It waits!

Heaven help me...I wait!

Darkness crept along Mason's skin, dripped down his spine, encircled his chest like a tightened tourniquet. Whatever was out here waited for movement, as if this was a devilish game of hide-and-seek.

The thing hiding up ahead had a taste of blackened dirt and unhallowed spaces. Its feel was gritty and unclean. A watchdog, Mason concluded, not the main event. Easily circumvented, unless, as in this instance, a pursuer named LanVal had a burning eagerness to find a complete list of the horrors this master vampire had up his sleeve.

To that end, he had to remain cautious, couldn't show himself too soon. He willed himself to stillness, searching a darkness that cloaked many things—some of them benign, some not. The air was thick with a superficial silence that didn't penetrate all the way to the forest floor.

He wasn't alone.

Mason tilted his head to glance at the tree beside him. Reaching out a hand, he traced the outline of several deep gouge marks crisscrossing the bark from which sap flowed like green-scented streams of blood. Knives or fangs had made these marks, a sad example of territory tagging. He was close to the chateau, and this damaged tree was a warning.

He had no fondness for desecrations. No tolerance for heartless savages of any species. Feeling the pressure of watchful eyes, he said, "Show yourself," to the venomous creature in the gloom.

At the edge of his vision, something moved beneath the branches of the towering trees. The windless night stirred with an ugly scent.

"Shy, perhaps?" Mason taunted.

A gurgled grunt of displeasure rang out, and the creature came forward with the force of a hurricane.

The ball of darkness surging forward was topped with a bone-white face ravaged by death's clutches and dark-socketed eyes demented with hunger. A vampire. Not so new, and clearly another victim of torture.

What flesh was left hung from its skeletal cheeks like shreds of torn parchment paper. Its bloody fanged mouth was open and jawing at the air. Likely it'd been starved, as Faith's sister had been. By the awful scent clinging to it, this vampire may have been locked inside its coffin, or buried in the earth until tonight, when it had been turned loose in the woods as either a sadistic final warning to trespassers…or a well-planned tease for Mason LanVal.

Feeling his anger curdle, and with his skin tingling with apprehension, Mason waited until he could stand no more of the sorry bloodsucker's stench, then he stepped forward to meet it.

The thing did not even stop to consider the power awaiting it. The stumbling blur came on with its fangs snapping and its long-fingered hands reaching, bent on its own mindless revenge.

Mason had it by the throat before it had slowed, and

quickly thrust it on the ground, flat on its back. The pathetic creature's legs continued to move, as if it couldn't quite believe it had been thwarted. Its fangs chopped at Mason's hand over and over like a rabid dog, without purchase, half the time biting itself savagely. No blood flowed from its self-inflicted wounds—only a whitish fluid carrying the odor of sickness.

"Who is he?" Mason asked calmly, kneeling down, easily collaring the struggling vampire. "Who sent you here?"

"Devil," the nasty creature spat between bites, leaving Mason to wonder if this meant the devil had sent this creature, or that Mason was a devil for capturing it.

In either case, he had been right. This was an old vampire. And a not-so-decent one, by its appalling appearance, the smells clinging to it and the clotted bits of fur between its long, sharp teeth. Decent ones wouldn't have been here in the first place. Mindful vampires tried to fit in as best they could. This creature had been at the chateau ruled by a monster, and it had resorted to snacking on rabbits while hungering for anything resembling a human.

It really should have known better.

"Does this devil have a name?" Mason asked, shaking the vampire.

"Lan…Val."

"Don't think so. Try again." Hell, the beast knew his name, which meant the monster in the nest also knew it.

"Lan…"

No, Mason thought. *Not Lance. Don't say that name. Do not let it be Arthur's champion who has done this. He was the best of us. There can't be any of us here. Must be an offspring. A mistake.*

The vampire sputtered and bit again at Mason's arm, missing by inches.

"Speak, and I will put you out of your misery once and for all," Mason said.

Any vampire worth a damn and with its soul intact, after being tortured by a monster and his minions, would have taken him up on the offer. Only with a final death could that kind of vampire be truly free of its unnatural restraints.

Of course, he knew right away that this creature wasn't one of those. His offer had been made to deceive the diminished thing beneath him into coughing up more than milky bile.

"Up," the vampire said.

"Not going to happen."

"They are…coming. Too late…for you."

Rallying whatever frantic energy was left in its artificially animated body, the bloodsucker kicked out, nearly catching Mason's left leg.

"Shall I send you out to meet them?" Mason queried soberly. "Is that what you'd like?"

The vampire hesitated, yowled, then tried again to attack. And Mason had his answer. This vampire preferred a final death to returning to the chateau. Anything was better than what had happened to him there.

A sharpened silver spike flashed in Mason's hand. One stab to the jugular, long practiced and carefully placed, and the vampire exploded in a whirlwind of dust, dirt and debris.

Before the dust had settled, Mason was on the move, his eyes glued to the path to the chateau, his mind riveted to his objective.

Chapter 19

Faith's head came up. She looked behind her from the doorway she'd almost passed through, and uttered a cry that caused Andre and the others to turn to her with tense, questioning expressions.

"He's there," she declared.

Andre's face came close. "How do you know this?"

"I don't understand how I know. I feel him at times, and hear what's in his mind."

"His blood," Andre whispered, and Lucas and Gregoire visibly stiffened.

"What about his blood?" Faith demanded in a voice weakened by the anger she felt rising from the three werewolves.

"It's in you," Andre said. "This is why you feel close to him. He gave you blood to get you safely away from the trap, and it's binding you to him. I feared this might be the case, although it maybe was, as he said, the only way to help you."

"LanVal's blood?" Her tone slipped a notch as she whispered the name, unable to grasp what Andre meant.

"Immortal blood has been mixed with yours, allowing for a thread of contact between you. It's the immortal equivalent of Lycan imprinting. A binding tie," Andre explained ruefully. "The effect wasn't supposed to last nearly this long. It seems the bond between you hasn't dissipated, as it should have by now."

LanVal had given her blood. She'd had a transfusion, after all. Of what, though? What did Andre mean by immortal blood?

Faith swayed and righted herself. In having been dosed with the blood of a vampire, would she become one? Had such an offering from an immortal caused the swift knitting of her wounds, instead of the wolf voodoo that everyone here was expecting to have done it?

"How? How did he do that?" she demanded.

Andre's eyes were shining with the brilliance of angry green fire. "As far as I know, there's only one way to get blood into another's system. He had to have punctured himself to do it, and bled into your open wound. A chivalrous, unselfish act, I must acknowledge, since vampires were on the prowl. And he brought you here, to us, which is as it should be. But a lingering blood gift in this case is also a blasphemy, you being what you are."

A kiss.

God, yes. She remembered LanVal's kiss, and the brief pinch of added pain. That had to be the way he had done it. He had passed his blood to her, from his mouth to hers.

Having remembered, she tasted that blood now, faintly, subtly. Both her fate and her desire for Mason LanVal had indeed been sealed with a kiss.

"He knew what I...what I am, Andre?"

"Only that you aren't fully human. It was a chance he took in order to help."

"Then we can't be angry with him," Lucas chimed in. "If the blood gift wears off eventually, as it should, all will be well, surely."

Faith knew this wasn't going to be true. Her prediction, if she'd dared to voice it, would have been that all would be far from well, according to the rules of these Lycans. She couldn't see how the feelings she had for Mason LanVal might lessen or fade altogether, since minute by minute, they intensified.

Something else had happened to her out there in LanVal's arms. Not just a kiss or necessary blood donation. She was feeling rightness, and the arrival of a completeness the likes of which she had never known.

Even if this wasn't his blood, they were back to the concept of animal attraction. It was too late to keep her from him, she wanted to tell these wolves. The second her eyes had met LanVal's, her life had changed—just not in the way these werewolves were anticipating.

She raised her gaze from the ground and set her jaw stubbornly. As Andre looked from her to Lucas, to Gregoire, and back to her, the blaze in his eyes dimmed.

"All right," he said. "We'll go."

Faith's heart thudded so loudly it nearly took an act of God to hear Andre's next words.

"Not you." He led her inside the cottage with a firm

hand on her elbow. "You will stay here, out of harm's way."

She said defiantly, "You mean out of your way."

"Same thing," Andre said, and the three wolves backed up, their broad shoulders jerking as if their muscles knew what was coming.

Leaning against the door frame, Faith watched them leave. With the crunching sound of footsteps on dry, loose gravel, and with seeming ease, each of them flowed into their furred-up wolf shape—one silver, one brown, one black. And then, silent as the shadows, they were gone.

"To hell with all of you," Faith shouted. Pulse racing, she reached for the splint and ripped at the tape binding it to her leg. After studying the splint, she tossed it to the floor.

With her own frantic energy pounding in her temples, she took one tentative step with the injured leg and stumbled, grabbing for the frame. Then she straightened, determined not to take any of this lying down.

LanVal was thinking about her. The Guardian was going to find her sister. Whether immortal or vampire, he was honorable. He would save her sister if he could.

And Faith James, she thought stubbornly, was her mother's daughter. Her father's daughter. She was a werewolf, as they had been, and nobody's damsel in distress. If she couldn't walk on the leg, she'd have to bite the damn thing off and crawl.

With more concentrated effort, she was able to take a decent-size step, followed by another. Grimacing, she made it outside. Grinning in triumph, she glanced up at the moon.

"Thanks for the help," she said. "Now show me what to do."

* * *

The chateau blazed with light, its unadorned windows giving the impression of foul, fevered eyes looking out.

Mason's memory hurtled back in time to that other palace, adjusting for the progress of hindsight. Castle Broceliande's occupants had been waiting for him in their restless, silent state, counting on his arrival. The vampires in this house also waited for him, and the abnormal feel of both places, in memory and in the present, were startlingly alike.

Who are you, I wonder?

Other than the dusted vamp on the path, Mason sensed no one in the open. The gatekeeper had been a tease, a mocking barrier for a Knight of the Blood. A slap in the face and also an open invitation.

Due to the closeness of sunrise, these windows should have been dark and unassuming to an onlooker, the faces behind them sunk back into their earthen crevasses. The very bones of the structure had been tainted by what lay behind its gray stone walls. Whatever resided there was a vigorous enough presence to thumb his nose at the upcoming first rays of daylight.

Mason's skin tingled with this knowledge. Small licks of fire began to lap at his cool exterior, as if his nerves were singing. *So close now...*

Another thing nagged at him from the periphery. Faith. She was misbehaving. Burning through his blood gift to her, she wanted to know about him and the things he'd done. In her attempt to rationalize the irrational, she was doing a damn fine job of breathing life into what was left of his heart.

Faith believed in him, despite what Andre, who knew so little of him or his existence, had to be telling her. She would have demanded further explanations from the silver wolf, and come up empty.

Her belief in him hurt like the penetration of an arrow point. At the same time, that trust made him feel stronger than ever, and again like the Champion he once had been.

For the first time in memory, he was needed on a personal level, and felt he had a stake in the outcome. A woman, part wolf, all determination, was close to knowing about his cause and the toll it had taken.

He appreciated her for that. Loved her for it. However this excursion ended, he would always love her for the few minutes of pleasure she brought and the poignant reminder of his mortal past.

Fortified with a new purpose that shored up foundation of the old agenda, Mason carefully walked on, certain now that the vampires knew he was coming, and therefore no longer in need of stealth.

He strode across the dried-up remnants of an old garden, and vaulted over the chateau's crumbling east wall, where he paused to glance at the rusted iron gate swinging soundlessly on its hinges.

"I'm here," he whispered, searching the outline of the chateau's great oaken door that might or might not open in a bloody, visceral greeting.

Then he walked casually up to that door, and knocked.

Darkness enveloped Faith as she limped toward the trees. Having made it a distance from the house, she increased her pace, ignoring the nearly healed leg's protests, determined to find LanVal and find Hope.

She didn't stop to consider which direction she needed to take. Scenting Andre and the others on the path, she followed their wolfishness as if it were a trail of breadcrumbs, easily separating the werewolves from their surroundings, not bothering to contemplate how she'd come by this newly honed sense of smell.

Andre had said she'd been saved by a dose of immortal blood that would eventually fade away. When LanVal's blood dissipated and the moon hit its full phase, she supposed the beast she carried inside might reign supreme. She wouldn't be like Andre and Lucas, in their animal wolf forms. In the absence of an explanation for what she would be like, she could only imagine.

Partial knowledge of a subject was hardly better than none at all, and left deep dark holes in reasonable deductions. Just one important detail or symptom left off a list could screw up a medical diagnosis. She was afraid of there being no cure for what she was about to become, and no way to turn back. A surgeon couldn't cut out a mystical entity conceived of emotion and belief. Even with a complete blood cleansing and blood bank transfusion, that mystical thing might remain untouchable.

As always, she had to make do and deal. Until her first transformation came, she'd utilize what she had to go on—feeling energized by the notion of having a piece of LanVal inside her. She felt him there, in her blood and in her mind, hot and fluid and sustaining. She would make use of the intimacy of their connection while it lasted, and mourn the closeness to him when that connection, as Andre had warned, had gone.

As she moved, the treetops thinned to make room for slender ribbons of moonlight. Limping forward, it seemed to Faith as though she was slowly leaving the discomfort of her accident behind. Outdistancing it. After going some way, she began to feel curiously fleet, noticing less of a difference between the injured leg and the good one. She couldn't afford to dwell on that, though, when the creatures who had her sister were anomalies no doubt much faster than herself. Around vampires, hesitation due to injury had to mean capture and a grisly death.

"So, why are you with them, Hope?" she whispered. "Were you afraid I'd find out about you? Did you think you'd want to hurt me?" *Or that I might hurt you?*

So intently was she concentrating on that last question, Faith swore she heard Hope's voice say, *"I'm sorry."* Imagined or not, that reply weighted her down, a sad, sorry confirmation of how fear lay at the heart of so many misunderstandings.

No longer dragging her wounded leg, she loped on with the muscles of the good one loosening. She figured she had gone a quarter of a mile, not calling on LanVal to get her bearings, but utilizing the power in the blood he had given her to discern those things.

The night that should have been black and blinding wasn't. Her surroundings were visible through a hazy gray opaqueness she remembered from when LanVal had carried her here. Out of the corners of her eye, she saw rabbits and other small animals scurrying, and birds beginning to stir.

A peculiar scent struck her, one she didn't recognize at first. With the scent came a burning sensation, skittering on the surface of her skin, and a sudden flare in temperature.

She was familiar with this smell. Blood. Somehow, she recognized it as hers.

Pausing midstep, Faith narrowed her attention, spotting in the clearing beside her what had to be the same trap that had nearly done her in. Its presence tasted like the rust corroding it. Staring at the device made her leg and heart ache.

A wolf's howl went up somewhere close by and was answered by another. The feral nature of those sounds brought a new round of chills to square off with her heat.

A passing whiteness startled her out of her motionless state. Faith wheeled. Finding nothing, she spun back with her heart pounding.

She wasn't alone.

The flash came again, to her right, closer now. Her pulse skyrocketed, jumping clear off the scale. And then she saw it again, not too far from where she stood riveted.

The trap wasn't the only disturbance now. It had been joined by a tall, angular form swathed in white fabric and outlined by a tangle of hair as dark as the night should have been.

"Hope!" Faith cried out, stumbling forward.

Chapter 20

No one answered the door.

Not a big surprise.

Mason shoved the door open with one hand and waited, listening, as the gaseous odors of wood decay and flesh decomposition rammed into him. It would have been a violent warning system for anyone other than himself. He had come across these same signals before, and knew what they hid.

Nevertheless, the illusive presence of the master vampire tucked behind those odors sent an acknowledging shiver through him as he walked forward to meet his target.

"I wonder," he said aloud, his voice echoing in the vast empty space of the elaborately tiled hallway, "if your lapsed manners at welcoming a guest mean that you have retired for the evening, or if you're suddenly admitting to cowardice?"

His words came back to him several times, routed by the high ceilings and bare, unfurnished floors. The echo brought with it another image: his arrival at Castle Broceliande, where none of its occupants had greeted him, all of them resting like the dead in the safety of their dungeon.

"You remember easily so far back?" a voice boomed from the shadows at the top of the staircase.

Mason looked up. Though the voice was familiar, he couldn't place it.

"I doubt anyone could forget their beginnings," Mason said, smelling trouble, straining to see who stood on the landing as he stopped himself from hurtling up there for the confrontation this vampire deserved.

"Just so, LanVal," the chateau's prime vampire agreed as he began to move down the stairs with the exaggerated precision of a movie star making a well-timed entrance. "I've followed your antics for years, of course, and wondered when we'd meet."

"And I have been looking forward to meeting you," Mason said, dangerously still. Going up against this prime too soon would mean the loss of valuable information. "I have, of course, met your pets," he added.

"Pets. Yes. That's a good enough term for fledglings, I suppose, and one I hadn't thought of. They were, by the way, quite impressed with you."

Mason saw the brief glitter of brocade fabric beneath the light of the dusty chandelier before he saw the vampire's face. That flashy announcement immediately threw him back to the castle that had wooed the life from him.

Three vampires had descended Castle Broceliande's great stone staircase that first evening. Powerful vampires, dressed in wealth, wielding the secret to an eternal life that went well beyond their own limitations.

Mason had had eyes for the first of them only, an unearthly beautiful female dressed in a gown the color of claret, with the graceful neck of a swan and inhumanly flawless features. That female had become his maker, his creator, his bloody muse.

"What do you want here?" this prime in his gilded coat queried, appearing in the light as if it had birthed him, stopping midway to the hall.

A sensation of latent familiarity crawled up Mason's spine as if each bone in his back was the rung of a ladder. He said, "I might ask the same thing of you," and closed his eyes briefly. Separating the dust and other horrible odors from the identifying smell of this thing on the staircase, he found the scent memory he'd been searching for that had been buried deep because it wasn't supposed to be there at all.

This creature on the stairs wasn't supposed to be here.

You! Mason thought. *How can this be?*

"I am in seclusion, minding my own business," the familiar prime said in a flat, tired drone.

"You chase people for sport," Mason said, needing time to adjust to the shock of seeing this vampire again. Not ready to accept what he was seeing. "So, I'd have to challenge the bit about minding your own business."

Lowering his tone to a threatening level, Mason continued. "You are, in fact, generating the kind of chaos you created us to stop, are you not?"

This prime was so very much more than a master vampire. His secluded presence here had been a wicked deception. The creature on the stairs was far older than the Seven, and had obviously stockpiled enough power in all that time to be able to mask his true identity. An identity that rocked Mason to his marrow.

Even to gaze upon this creature was a special kind of disrespect to Mason and his brethren, a spike to the heart of an old vow he had willingly taken.

The pale, elegant monster ruling this nest, dressed in an outfit from centuries past and wearing a heavy gold crucifix that glittered feebly beneath the shining glass crystals overhead, was not made *from* the three vampires who had sired the Blood Knights, or from any mistake made by the Blood Knights themselves. This vampire was one of the originals. One of the powerful Three from Castle Broceliande.

This vampire had been one of Mason's maker's lovers, and his presence here, in this century, above ground and on this earth, was the biggest abomination of all.

"Lord Lianour, Master of the Castle of Maidens," Mason said warily. "I believed you to have perished with your companions."

It was Hope who faced her, but something was wrong. A swift acknowledgment of that wrongness stopped Faith from reaching out.

"Hope. Honey…" she muttered, raising a hand, letting it fall, noticing the blood on Hope's shirt and the bloody mouth that stood out starkly against Hope's corpse-pale skin. "What have they done to you?" she whispered, terrified of an answer to this question that didn't seem to be forthcoming.

Hope stood silently beside the trap, shaken by a series of quakes so strong and persistent, she swayed over and over again, her body moving like white ripples in a disturbed pond.

Her sister looked too fragile, too thin, and too much like what Faith imagined the vampires housing her to be like. Hope had the haunted appearance of one who was half-dead already. In spite of that, she didn't come forward or issue a greeting. Hope didn't say or do anything at all. She just stared back with her wide, dark, dilated eyes.

"I've come to take you home." Faith knew that her voice rang with the horror and shock that roiled through her. "Nothing else matters, Hope. You will be safe."

When Hope's legs buckled, she caught herself before going down. Straightening again, Hope shook her head slowly, as if the simplest movement was torture.

Faith took another step toward her.

Hope shrank back.

"Please, Hope. Let me help. Let me take you from this place."

Hope had started to cry, and the soundless sobs shook her bony frame. Trembling hands fingered her mouth, as if her mouth was the source of her pain. Faith felt her silent scream.

Able to stand the distance no more, Faith rushed ahead and threw her arms around her sister. Biting back her own cry over the severity of Hope's state, Faith held on tightly, said adamantly, "I know what you are, and what I am. It makes no difference to me. We can figure this out later. I am so sorry, Hope. So sorry we didn't see this coming, and that I couldn't keep you from this."

Hope's hands dropped from her face.

Faith looked up, saw what Hope had been hiding from her and choked back a scream. Eyes blurred with tears, Faith let loose the cry of despair Hope would have made, had she been able to.

* * *

"Yes, well, here we are, LanVal. Meeting again after so many years, at last," Lord Lianour said.

"Though not in similar circumstances," Mason remarked, using his senses to scan the hall without taking his eyes from the nest's deadly ruler—an ancient bloodsucker with a golden gift for persuasion. A creature Mason and his brethren had long ago trusted with their lives.

All this time he'd been worried about one of those Seven starting the ball rolling on the current crush of vampires, and he hadn't been looking back far enough to see the truth.

Despite his failing and, in that moment, the unspeakable danger facing him, Mason found relief in the fact that his brethren were innocent. He withheld the sigh of a man who had at last found the answer to a particularly plaguing riddle.

"We were to perish, of course," Lord Lianour admitted. "The others took their lives, as they had sworn to do after you left Broceliande. However, in the end, I wasn't yet ready to give it all up."

"So you started creating vampires bent on destruction that put everyone on earth, including us, in jeopardy. Perhaps your aspirations were higher, still? Was playing God what you were aiming for?"

Mason sensed most of Lianour's brood underground, beneath the floors of the chateau. He also sensed a few of them upright and waiting in the rooms on either side of the great hall for their master's signal. A signal for what? To take down one of the very beings Lianour and his companions had carefully created so long ago?

Did the term *immortal* elude them?

"Why?" Mason asked. "Why have you done this?"

"I want what you took from the castle."

"What would that be?" Mason asked, knowing exactly what that thing was, and wanting to make Lianour say it.

"I want the chalice that helped to restore your life," Lianour said.

"What has that to do with all the monsters you've set loose on the world? It was you who bit so many people?"

Lord Lianour descended several more steps, his footsteps soundless, his posture dangerously languid. Mason remembered him clearly. It was a sight no one could have easily forgotten. He remembered the black hair and the ebony eyes and uncanny shine of that golden crucifix Lianour always wore. The cross was the first thing Mason had noticed when the Three had found him on the night of his arrival at the castle of the dead.

Perhaps, Mason thought, in viewing his old acquaintance's countenance with hindsight, Lianour might actually have considered the cross some kind of talisman against the final death he had eventually scammed.

Or maybe the cross was in some way Lianour's personal weak spot.

"Biting them was merely a means to an end," Lianour replied cuttingly.

"You're not after Lycans. They were never your objective."

"Werewolves are beasts, LanVal. No more than filthy, doglike beasts. If by objective you meant getting rid of a few of them, so much the better."

Fingering the cross with a tip of long, painted fingernail, Lianour added, "It took me a very long time to find you. We did our job well."

Mason frowned. "You created a world full of mindless blood-drinkers just to find me? Should I be honored?"

"Undoubtedly."

"May I ask how you knew I was here?"

Lianour had descended another two stairs, where he stopped to look down at his prey. Mason felt those black eyes on him. He felt the other bloodsuckers creeping closer. The others were no match for him, whether three or six, but adding in the dark Lord Lianour, and what the old vampire had up his sleeve, was another thing altogether.

Sharpening his focus on the vampire who'd helped to make the Seven immortals, another jab came to his mind, as unexpectedly as always. Faith had left the safety of Andre's house. She was in the woods, without the protection of the Weres. She was facing her sister.

He felt her pain, shared her heartbreak. The image was accompanied by an icy blast of bitter wind that needled at him obscenely.

Faith had found her sister, and Lord Lianour had been after an old acquaintance, not wolves. Whatever was happening here in the chateau had nothing to do with the Lycans in these parts. Faith and her sister had been accidental pawns in this monster's game.

This had been about him. About the artifact he had hidden. The Grail.

Another rush of relief hit Mason that didn't begin to cover the faux pas of having been deceptively ignorant of the chateau's real intentions. Nevertheless, with Lianour's eyes focused on him and most of the chateau's vampires underground, Faith might be all right.

She *would* be all right.

"The chalice is lost," he said to the old vampire.

The trinket he and six others had taken a blood oath to protect, and had given their mortal lives for, as well as pieces of their souls, had been removed from the world's grasp. It had been hidden from the reach of creatures like this one who might learn its secrets and pine for possession.

Only as an immortal had he, Mason LanVal, as the last of the Blood Knights, been able to carry the Grail to its final resting place. Not only had he removed that golden cup from the world, but from the other knights, as well, those who had sworn to the safety of the precious, priceless antique that had changed them.

The holy Grail had a twofold effect on those who drank from its rim. Stained with the blood of the Christ, it had the power to resurrect those whose lips it touched after that mortal had rattled a last breath. When filled with vampire blood that spilled into the mouth of the recipient at that final moment, the Grail's magic overruled the laws of the universe and of death itself.

This mystical, terribly dangerous artifact had eventually caused the dilemma the Seven had faced as time wore endlessly on. Their task had been to preserve the blood of the vampires by means of their own immortality. As immortals, however, the Seven who had sipped from that cup became its protectors for another reason—that reason being to keep others from the chore of living through years too numerous to count with an underlying thirst for blood that constantly raged. And along with that thirst, the endless, unforgiving torment of living those years in solitude.

He had been elected to take this great chalice from the castle—his first assigned task, given to him by his maker and her two male companions. One of those companions had been Lord Lianour.

Lianour had not killed himself after his part in creating the Seven, as he had pledged to his companions. He had not honored the pact he made. The Seven were meant to replace the original Three with bigger, stronger appetites. Not merely vampires, but truly immortal in their resurrections. Purified by the holiness of the Grail, the Seven were charged with keeping the Grail's dark magic with them. Removing the chalice from Castle Broceliande had been imperative, to keep the Three from a temptation that would further prolong their own weary, wavering existence. There wasn't room for so many of their kind, they had said.

And now, Lianour wanted the Grail back. Lianour desired the level of strength and immortality the Grail offered, just as the old vampire once feared he might.

Lord Lianour, who once held lofty principles for setting the world to rights, had sunk to being a monster, like the rest of his recent offspring. One of the mighty had fallen prey to his own raging thirst. Without his companions to feed from, Lianour had been freed from his confinement...and set upon the world.

Mason felt a stirring in the pit of his stomach. Disgust and a fervent mistrust of this vampire churned with a sense of vast emptiness.

He didn't fear for himself, or for the outcome of this meeting. He feared for Faith, out there in the night, comforting the sister who'd had her mouth sewn shut by this demon.

Sealed lips to keep Hope from passing on what she knew of this nest. To keep her from warning anyone. If there had been a quibble from Hope James, Lianour and his minions would have killed her outright. Because Hope had perhaps played her part too well, they hadn't bitten her.

He would have come here eventually, with or without Hope James. That had been his plan. But he was responsible for what had happened to Faith and her sister. He had to help them, and others like them, if he could. This was the vow he had taken so long ago. To protect the innocent.

"You see," the vampire called Lianour said with a cynical snap, "you search the night with eyes that should have been mine, and with a soul graced by God. While I…" Lianour waved a hand. "While I linger in this place. You have the ability to love, LanVal, and to feel, while I remain numb and lifeless. Your soul has grown, has not been diminished. Mine has been stagnated by what you took from me."

"I took nothing but what was offered," Mason said. "I accepted your challenge and have fulfilled my part of the bargain. It is you who have strayed."

"Yes. Quite so. Yet I would turn back time and start over. I would be you this time around."

"You wanted to die."

"I outgrew that longing after watching the grisly end of the others' lives, and traded that longing in for another."

"The Grail is lost to the world, Lianour. Even my brethren cannot find it. Wasn't that also in my bargain, and signed in blood? I was to ensure its removal?"

"Nevertheless, I want it back."

"In giving it to you, my existence would be a sham, with all the years from then to now amounting to nothing."

"Not for nothing, exactly, LanVal. You were blessed with the purpose we lacked. And you have found something else."

Mason's awareness of the closeness of the other

vampires intensified. They had entered the hall and were hungry. But their prime's remark further twisted Mason's stomach. The skin at the nape of his neck twitched in warning.

"She has nothing to do with this," he said, picking up on Lianour's meaning.

"On the contrary, LanVal, your she-wolf has everything to do with events, at present. I can feel your attention waver, as we speak. Do you deal with me, or go to her aid? That's what you're trying to decide, and it's all to my favor. A surprise package dropped into my lap."

"You abducted her sister."

"I merely lured her here by truthfully answering her questions. Her own genetics did the rest when the poor girl assumed she might have killed her parents," Lianour said. "Catching a Hunter was temporary icing on my game, and at first little to do with you. The wolves in these woods have gotten too headstrong and high-minded. I thought I'd teach them a lesson. As it happens, nothing is more fun than chasing a wounded Lycanthrope."

Coincidence, Mason thought abstractly. Luring Hope here, and then Faith coming after her, was nothing more than a damn coincidence. Lianour wanted bigger and better fare, and now that Mason had a stake in those coincidences, Lianour had the advantage.

"You've crossed a line," Mason said warily, afraid for Faith, needing to warn her. She was in the woods. Sensing her there, he sent a message and willed her to listen. *"Run!"*

Lianour smiled grimly with tips of his fangs showing. "Who hasn't crossed a line, Blood Knight? The one you love is a werewolf. A savage beast so far beneath our kind as to be the rubble we walk on." Lianour shook his head. "It's you, LanVal, who have both boots in the mire."

Love. Mason considered the word that suddenly seemed an accurate description for the tumultuous emotions caused by a kiss. By a gaze's fierce imprint and an ongoing blood bond.

Yes, he loved Faith, and could admit that now. He wanted to hold her, possess her, devour her. He also needed her. She alone might understand him. She also had been cursed.

And as the recipient of his love, he also had cursed her. Lianour would have seen to that.

"They have already found your wolf," Lianour said smugly. "She won't be a problem for long. When and if you see her again, you won't recognize what's left."

Although Mason's heart lurched, he didn't dare tear his attention from the demon on the stairs and his encroaching minions. He said, "The sun will disintegrate your fledglings, you heartless bastard."

The vampire shrugged. "They fear me more than daybreak, and are disposable. If these fail me, I'll make more."

"You hoped to trade? Is that it?"

"A werewolf for true immortality, LanVal? That was the general idea. And I will pity you, if you're considering those things of equal value."

"The Grail is lost."

"Then so is your lover."

The first vampire came swiftly at him from the shadows with its teeth bared. The second joined in soon after, followed by a third, while Mason's gaze remained unflinchingly fixed on their master.

Chapter 21

As Faith traced her sister's bloody mouth with her fingertip, she heard the first wolf's howl. The sound seemed to rip through the waning night, tearing from her throat a responding growl that ended in a cough of surprise.

She glanced up to see her sister's eyes widen in shock. At the same time, she felt her dark, secret love open to her.

"Run!" he directed.

She did, sensing his urgency. Savoring the vibration of his voice, she pulled Hope after her through the nightmarish woods, sprinting as fast as her legs would allow and realizing that because she was a werewolf, she had mended enough to get them out of there.

The forest seemed considerably cooler now that Mason's command had collided with an awareness of danger in the shadows, close on their heels. Rustling noises were everywhere, coming from all directions.

Faith yanked hard on her sister's hand, trying to remember how far it was to Andre's house. *Part of a mile. Maybe more.* She had to take this Hunter to her prey, hoping for safety, and to hell with genetics and whoever stood in her way.

The hard-packed earth sent shocks of pain up through her injured leg and into her hips. The echo of LanVal's urgent tone kept her going as the rustling noises grew closer. She knew something ran alongside, and refused to address what it could be until those noises closed in front of her, surrounding her and her sister.

Faith stopped abruptly, breathing hard, her senses screaming as she gripped tightly to Hope's hand.

All extraneous sound ceased.

The calm before the storm.

Then two vampires stepped toward her with their nasty fangs snapping.

"Go back to the hell that sprang you!" Faith shouted.

And as they advanced, Hope stepped in front of her with both pale hands raised.

The action broke Faith's heart. Hope, bred to hunt and kill werewolves, was honoring their parents by placing herself between Faith and the danger confronting them. Hope had been with these monsters, and after everything she had been through, Hope was standing up against her transgressors.

The vampires saw the blood on Hope's mouth. Crying out in unison, they leaped…and were hit in midair by a growling, moving wall of ferocious furred muscle and bone.

Tumbling to the ground, the vampires struggled with all their strength to get free of the giant wolves leaning on them, and their strength was considerable.

They kicked out with their legs. They struck out at the wolves with their hands, arms and teeth, to no avail. The wolves attacking them were large, quick, and had been set to motion by a strength and hatred of their own.

Silenced by a well-placed bite to their pasty necks, the vampires were rendered motionless beside Faith's feet. Dragged several steps off the path by the wolves, where the first rays of morning light penetrated the treetops, both vampires began to smolder, then went up in flames. Their white flesh roasted for a long moment, with a terrible smell. Their monstrous voices shrieked obscenities, and then they were gone.

Stunned by the suddenness of it all, horrified by what she had witnessed, Faith looked on in shock. As the wolves turned from her, she mastered the seemingly impossible effort of getting her wits back in order long enough to say through clenched teeth, "Lucas, Gregoire. I am in your debt big-time."

With Hope beside her, and tears freely flowing, Faith closed her eyes, intending a last silent call to the man who had in the past few hours become so important to her.

We are safe. But did she lust for him only because his blood had mixed with hers, or for other reasons she knew nothing about?

Had she actually found a viable partner at last, here in the kind of place she had always hated? A being that could read her mind, send her messages and win the trust of a werewolf pack?

She continued to tremble uncontrollably, uncertain how much of that was her insatiable need for Mason LanVal, and how much was the sheer terror of this night's events.

Hope also trembled, silent beside her, unable to speak, badly in need of help and comfort.

Faith's heart raced on as she searched for LanVal's matching rhythm but came up empty. Why didn't he come? Why didn't he wrap her in his arms, where she could be a damsel, just this once?

She wanted to see his face, feel his breath on her face. God, yes, she wanted that. More than anything she wanted to make that connection with him.

But in the end, there was no response from the Guardian.

Mason took a step forward with uncanny speed as a barreling tornado of silver fur came through the door and hit the tile floor with its dagger-sharp claws skating.

Two of the vampires in the hall went down beneath the momentum of the massive wolf, and Mason had the third by its neck and out of commission before it had registered surprise.

He headed for the stairs before the dust had settled—moving toward Lianour, who, with his gleaming necklace and yellowed fangs, was waiting and wearing a smile.

Hearing Andre fighting below, Mason paused inches from the demon's face, feeling Lianour's cold hands circle his neck.

"No deal," Mason said, clamping his hands to Lianour's. "No trade."

The pressure of his grip caused Lianour to stagger backward, but the old vampire was no fledgling to be bested so easily. He had once been the lord of a mighty castle, and master of a slew of men. He had been called the Black Knight, and had been feared on the battlefield, in his day. Yet his soul, though it may have flickered brightly at one time, had burned out, taking what remained of his conscience along with it. Time had been Lianour's enemy, and had worn him thin, as he'd feared so many years ago. He was, in the end, just an empty, old, angry vampire.

"I found you," he muttered, his fangs grazing Mason's wrist as he began to fight.

"I haven't been hiding," Mason replied, dropping down a step, spinning to face his lunging foe.

Out of the corner of his eye, Mason saw the silver wolf heading toward him. The room rang with Andre's howl of triumph.

"Go to her, Andre!" Mason shouted. "Keep her safe!"

"Too late." Lianour jumped in the air, landing behind Mason for a clear shot at Mason's neck. "Too late for you to have her!"

"You know better," Mason scolded, tossing the vampire back, and facing him again. "I can't be killed by your bite or your scratch."

"No. You have your own key for ending your existence, and I'm not part of it. But I tell you now that we can coexist, LanVal. I can be your comrade if you tell me where the Grail is. I can give you the companionship you've lacked."

"It's not what you think, Lianour. The Grail doesn't bring happiness."

"With its power, who needs to be happy?" Lianour said.

"I believe that I do," Mason replied. "Because what else is left?"

"You are a fool," Lianour stated coldly.

"Yes," Mason admitted. "I've often thought so."

Lianour's eyes narrowed as he rounded. "You will not give the Grail to me?"

"Not in another thousand years, Lianour, even if I'm unlucky enough to see that much more of time's passage."

"I can take care of that, you know."

"Then you should do so now, before I remember the damage you've done, and resort to wringing your pathetic neck."

"You know I can't keep you down forever, LanVal. But your lover can, and no doubt she will, now that she has seen what we've done to her sister. Now that she knows what you are." He smirked. "That's your weak spot. Your glistening key to the afterlife. A woman has to take you down. All she has to do is bite you back. One good bite to allow your blood to flow, and it won't ever stop. No one can stop it. You'd just dry up and fade away."

Lianour spun in place again to shake off Mason's grip. "Who better than a werewolf to do that, LanVal? To make that deadly final bite? Don't you realize I've been trying to do you a favor by getting rid of our enemies? By getting rid of *her*?"

Faith!

God help me, Faith! You are the beginning, and also quite possibly the end of me!

Love was the one weakness that could bring about his final demise, and the real reason, he now knew, that no women immortals had been created. It was, unconsciously perhaps, one of the reasons he'd shunned the female vampires he had found.

A woman was to be his curse, his downfall, his off button—a precaution against him losing sight of his vow not to pass along the blood or give up the Grail.

Whether in love or fear or anger, one bite from a lover or a female enemy could finish him, and ensure that the Grail remained lost forever. Only he could be affected this way. Each of the Seven Blood Knights had their own means of termination.

The Grail had been his responsibility and, in the end, his alone. He had accepted this task. And the ruthless vampire before him had seen to it that Mason would remain alone for eternity. Lianour, with his burnished golden cross, had done this.

Two more vampires had started up the staircase, though Mason could sense how weakened they had become. The sun had risen at last, and someone here had forgotten to close the shutters.

He smelled burning flesh as yellow light suddenly streamed in through the casements, and did not turn his head.

"The Grail is lost," he repeated. "So are you. I believe it is past the time to honor your own pledge. The others and I have been cleaning up your messes for far too long, Lianour. So many people have died."

"What better way to find the Seven?" Lianour said stubbornly. "What better way to find you, than to send all of the monsters out and see who appears to save the day? You always were sentimental, LanVal, and a stickler for promises."

Oh, yes, he had taken the bait, Mason thought. He had come here to fight the vampires Lianour had put in his path for this very reason.

In a blink, Lianour had jumped six stairs, heading toward the upper landing and out of the sun's reach. Mason followed, thinking that Lianour had miscalculated his power of persuasion, and also his thoughts of escape. Upward in this house, there was no hiding from the light. The chateau was practically made of glass. Ancient or not, Lianour was only a vampire, and susceptible to the sun. His demented mind couldn't be this far gone.

Mason sensed the vampire running—up, up, always up. He heard the clink of that blasted crucifix hitting Lianour's coat buttons, and each groan of the chateau's aged wood. He heard Andre's howls in the distance, ever fainter, and the breathless quiet of the vampires Lianour had made, slumbering deathlike floors below.

What he couldn't do was allow himself to go to Faith until this one part of his task was over.

There would be many vampires to chase. So many vampires. Spin-offs from each other, created with dizzying speed. Lianour didn't have to exist in order for the hordes to spread like the plague on every continent. Nevertheless, Lord Lianour was at the root of it all. There was a real possibility the old vampire had begun to take the title of *Lord* too seriously.

Mason reached the top of the third flight of stairs quickly and paused. His prey could have been behind any one of ten closed doors. Lianour's smell lingered in the hallway.

"Your time is long overdue," Mason said softly. "As is mine, no doubt. We are creatures from a forgotten age, Lianour. Not one speck of us belongs to the world as it is today. That is my burden."

He took three more steps. "Your broken oath has resulted in the spread of a disastrous infection for which there is no antidote other than extinction. It's always a good idea to start with the source of that contagion."

Mason kicked open the first two doors, and daylight flowed across his boots.

"Perhaps I would have relinquished the Grail once,

and been glad to be rid of it, if you'd asked before I left Broceliande, and in the presence of the others."

He kicked in two more doors, and motes of light and dust danced in the air.

Sheer stubborn-mindedness had seen him through all these centuries. Honor, as well, he supposed, after the crimson glow of pride had faded. He had been chosen to die in that castle, but unlike Lianour, the whole of his soul had been returned.

Now, he had to set an old wrong to rights. He had to stop the pureness of the devilry in Lianour's blood from contaminating others.

Three of the remaining doors splintered beneath the force of his boot. He felt no better. He wouldn't enjoy this. Already, he was filled with regret for the creature he had long ago supposed Lianour to be.

The ashy odor of smoke drifted to Mason as he strode to the end of the hallway. Smoke and light and dust.

Tiny orange flames reached out from beneath the door on his left like parched tongues in search of food. The aged wood of the floorboards went up like tinder. With a whooshing sound, a sea of flames ignited the walls.

"Lianour!" Mason called, backing up a pace. When he turned, the vampire was there, facing him.

"It's here," Lianour jeered. "Do you think I would have stayed, otherwise? I can feel it—I, who have held the chalice in my hands."

"Delusions," Mason returned as the fire ate away the beauty of the old house. "You must do this yourself, Lianour. Fulfill your vow, though it's late."

"Why? Because the others might be waiting in heaven to welcome their old friend?"

Mason shook his head. "Because there might be time to avoid the other place. The one you fear so badly."

When Lianour's hands went to the crucifix and held to it tightly, a sickening revelation hit Mason. This vampire was afraid to die a final death. Though weary of his existence when Mason had first met him, Lianour imagined the Grail could change everything. In pursuit of that relic, Lianour had created chaos from a purposeful bite to a human's neck.

"Where is it, LanVal?" Lianour demanded as flames whipped his pant legs and sent sparks up the sleeves of his coat.

"It's not for you," Mason whispered. "I'm sorry."

"The fire won't take me. You know that."

"Yes." Mason knew it. Lianour could regenerate his flesh.

As Lianour attacked, for whatever reason—maybe just out of frustration and rage—Mason again covered the vampire's hand with his own and yanked, snapping the chain holding Lianour's precious talisman.

Lianour's eyes opened wide. Shouting an oath, he came after Mason with his teeth bared. With even faster speed, Mason turned the golden crucifix and held it aloft, thinking to stop Lianour. When the vampire ran right into the heavy cross with the full force of his speed and unearthly strength, the crucifix penetrated his chest, sailing all the way through as though there was nothing inside to stop it.

And Lord Lianour, one of the original Three, once powerful—though in hindsight, maybe never wise—imploded in a cascade of ash.

Mason ran from the chateau with its walls crashing down behind him. Regret, excitement and anticipation filled him as he charged through the brush. The quest he'd been on for as long as he could recall had ended. He felt light, almost euphoric.

Until a silver wolf blocked his path.

At the wolf's feet was a pile of smoldering gray ash.

"Andre? Where is she?" Shaded from the morning sun by a tall oak, Mason scanned the distance with his sight and his senses, unable to find Faith or her sister, calling to Faith anyway, over and over, with no response.

His buoyant heart skidded against his ribs. He dragged his focus back to Andre.

The wolf stayed where he was, his quiet presence loudly trumpeting the phrase *"whatever it takes."*

Mason closed his eyes, refusing to believe this. When he reopened them, Andre stood there in man form, naked, sweaty and stone-cold serious. He pointed to the blazing chateau with the hand Mason had once helped him to free from a trap, then pointed to the ground. "Ashes, in return for a bloody werewolf's hand," he said. "I believe this makes us even, at least for the time being."

"No," Mason said soberly, his flare of anger tightly in check, his heart threatening to break right then and there. "No, Andre. If I can't have her, I'm afraid you win."

Chapter 22

Mason waited for the call that never came.

He walked, ran, sat, cursed, never slept. There was no rest to be had. Gone was the urge to eat, and the awareness of how many days had passed since he'd lost her. Only the thirst remained. The insatiable hunger for what lay beyond his reach.

There was nothing gentle about his need for Faith. She had become an unshakable addiction. She came to him often in his mind, like a fleeting thought or an exotic passing breeze that originated somewhere far away. She'd whisper to him things about herself and her life before coming to France, as if he could stand to know more about her when she was off-limits, for good.

He pictured her as he'd first seen her—bloody, wounded, defiant and beautiful. He pictured her standing in Andre's yard in oversize clothes smelling of wolf. He replayed the moment she had touched his mouth with her fingers to find his fangs, and the expression on her face.

Through her whispers, he began to know Faith as she was prior to arriving in France. The woman. The medical student. The doctor. She had never really been happy, he realized—a fact that may have been attributed to the secrets her body was keeping from her. Faith James hadn't had the chance to reconcile with her heritage and the beast she harbored. She had to be allowed the chance.

To fend off his own sense of isolation, Mason whispered to her in return very private things about himself. He told her about knighthood and tournaments with flying flags of red, blue, gold and green. He told her of Castle Broceliande and the Grail, of Lianour, his maker, and what his last moments of life had felt like as that life drained away. How the world feared and then had forgotten about the Seven Blood Knights after they had dispersed. How he alone had hidden the Grail.

He told her of the power he possessed that enabled him to find her, wherever she was—an ability held in check with the firmest resolve, because she obviously didn't want what he wanted. Not enough, anyway.

It would have been so easy for him to overpower her and make her change her mind. That thought occurred every other minute, quickly whisked away by the empathy he felt for her and the respect for her wishes. He refused to send that irrefutable call via her arteries, though he was sure the blood link between them remained. He felt it there. He felt *her* so very clearly.

In the end, he withheld little from her. What did divulging secrets matter if he spoke to an imagined voice, in an imagined conversation, as if they really were lovers having pillow talk? Or that in his waking dreams he made love to her every night when the sun went down. That he ceaselessly paced the pathways like a madman, in search of a closer touch that would never come.

He walked…not daring to consider the endless time behind him and the endless years ahead. Though he had already rid the woods of traps and vampires, he remained vigilant and apart from the Weres, knowing he would have to move on eventually and that he was needed elsewhere. A disheartening reminder of what he was, and of the fact that there was never going to be a short supply of monsters, despite losing a few here.

He would go on, continue on as he always had.

He walked this night, as he had on others…prowling, searching, brooding, thinking.

When he saw the moon—a full, shimmering circle casting a bloodred tint over the clouds surrounding it— he studied it with surprise. The Blood Moon had arrived, telling him that time had passed slowly, after all.

The pain of this clawed at him with a scrape of silver talons.

Tonight, someplace beneath this moon, Faith would be running with the Weres. She and Andre would be together.

Mason's pace faltered. He stopped, alerted by a scent filling the air. His heart skidded, though he knew better.

The scent was fragrant, rich, like a fine burgundy wine. There was an overlay of pepper, partly camouflaged by the heavier odor of the wolves that had recently trampled the ground, and basted with something else.

With the scent, illicit thoughts came rushing back. Moist, bronzed bare skin sliding sensuously against his. And green eyes beckoning to him to lie with her.

Movement.

Mason turned toward it with his heart racing.

The female was easy to pinpoint in the distance, with moonlight highlighting her familiar silhouette. Small-boned and slender, her fair hair seemed to be comprised of fallen moonbeams.

"Not a wolf," Mason muttered.

She stood some way ahead, staring back at him.

She didn't move.

Mason did.

A growl of anticipation rose in Faith's throat. She had sensed the Guardian with her eyes shut. She had called, hoping he would come.

Emotion ripped through her as he closed the distance separating them. Nothing had changed. She was overwhelmed by the enormous longings for him that hadn't dulled or disappeared with distance or the pull of the disk in the sky.

Nothing has changed, LanVal...

Can't you see?

Andre says it's because of you.

The Guardian heard her. He paused in the clearing, in the exact spot where she had first asked for his help. No iron-jawed trap sat there now as either a landmark or a snare for unsuspecting victims, though the faint odor of blood remained.

Mason LanVal's expression was raw and questioning, his body live with anxiousness. With her honed hearing, Faith perceived the soft sigh of his fangs descending, and knew this was in her honor. She almost ran to him then, but was holding up one hand to stop not only his advance, but hers.

Many things had been exchanged in their whispered

conversations, except for this new development, and how she could be here like this. Why she was able to hold off the shift in shape that should be taking her over now, on this night of a revered Blood Moon, and the effort it took to control what lay nestled inside her, in order to face him.

What was he going to think when he knew? The Guardian of the night hated monsters, and she had become one.

"Faith," he said in a voice so like soft, sensuous velvet that her restraining hand dipped.

"Faith and not Faith, more or less at the same time," she replied, her treacherous body already starting to fight with her resolve.

"I have done this," he said. It wasn't a question. Of course he would see the subtle changes in her, and know everything.

"Yes." She took a step forward and saw him flinch. She had forgotten she'd shed her clothes, instead of her human skin, giving in to the urge to free herself of all extraneous bonds so she could focus on just this one. She stood proud and tall in her nakedness, facing the immortal of her dreams.

"Hope is here. She's all right and recovering. The Hunter now recognizes the difference between werewolves in need of hunting, and those who don't. In that respect, she's like you."

LanVal nodded. His hands fisted the way Andre's often did, with a tenseness that mirrored her own. The excitement of being so close, without being able to take those final steps toward a complete physical connection, was hurting him as much as it hurt her.

She was naked, hot and needy. Woman, werewolf and whatever else she had become due to the blood donation provided by this special being across from her, were all working toward one singular goal from which she hadn't even tried to detour. That goal was seeing how Mason LanVal would react to his own creation. To what she was. What he had helped to make her.

"You're you," he said. "All gloriously there."

She shook her head. "I believe the word Andre used last night in regard to my new status was *abomination*."

Faith drew her lips back with her fingers, in much the same way as she had recently drawn back his. In this way, she exposed the tips of two tiny white teeth— only slightly longer and sharper than the rest—that probably wouldn't have been noticed by anyone else, but would make a difference here.

LanVal flinched again. She watched his face grow paler.

"I believe I'm what you seek, Guardian. The possible bane of the world, or at least this forest you've been watching over. No one is sure what I'll be when I grow up."

She had lifted her chin to speak because the explanations were sticking in her throat, and observed how LanVal's gaze went there—to the pulse that was thrumming beneath her ear.

"I didn't change last night," Faith rushed on. "Everyone waited for an event that did not happen. They were really surprised. The consensus is that I might be able to change, or not, at will, due to what happened to me here."

Her hand fluttered to her side. "I can almost identify with Andre and the others who are what I was supposed to be, but not completely. I'm not sure I hadn't already been suppressing the shift to a new self without even knowing it. I'm not sure if I ever would have made the transformation on my own."

LanVal said, "Andre knew you were special. He told me so."

"Did he? I heal like a Were. Andre's potion worked on my leg. My sister saw the Were in me, and distanced herself. I growl when I'm confused, frightened and angry. I'm faster than I was when I run. I don't seem to like bindings of any kind, or small spaces." She gestured to her bareness. "But maybe part of this is because—"

"I found you," he said. "And because I gave you what never should have been added to a Lycan system. I've helped to destabilize you. I'm so sorry, Faith."

"Are you? Sorry?"

"No. Not if it means the link between us remains," he said adamantly. "Not if it means that link will grow stronger, and that Andre will release his claim on your future…to me."

Faith had yearned to hear those words, and didn't know whether she might suddenly laugh with relief, or cry. Her life had changed radically in the past few days, even if her shape hadn't—though she knew the physical transition from one outline to another might eventually come, and that the immortal blood in her veins would further alter her somehow, once she had more of it.

Abomination. She had heard that word in LanVal's mind, as well, in the past. But she was part werewolf and part him.

She already had Mason LanVal inside her in one respect, and wanted him inside her in another. Was moonlight dictating the need to finish this, making her want to give in and rut with him in this place, or was it the human woman's needs desiring a final closeness? Did those remaining parts of her want to end the agony of a surgeon's former self-restraint? She seemed to always be inching toward LanVal, never quite sure of herself.

"Andre says I can stay here for as long as I like. I think he'd like that to be for a very long time, in spite of..."

"Me?"

"In spite of my messing up the Lycan gene pool," she said. "I'm not a fit companion for a Were. Hell, I might not be a fit companion for anyone. There's so much I don't know, but I do know this—that you'll need to either hunt me down or love me."

"Is there no other option?" he asked softly, almost urgently, and his voice burned through her, reaching the private places that had been hungering for him since they'd met.

"Your vow..." Faith said, feeling the electricity between them increase with each step he took toward her, until she had to look up to see his face.

"Has not been broken," LanVal said, running his fingers up her arms with alarmingly provocative feather-light strokes, and showing her the extent of his own appetite by pressing his hips to hers. "I gave no blood to a human. In truth, I didn't give much to a Were. You're no abomination, Faith. I am."

"You've created—"

"A future. At last, if that's also what you want." He added, "Hell, maybe even if you don't," then cut off her growl of acceptance by claiming her mouth savagely with his own in a full manifestation of the release of his pent-up longing.

And Faith, finding what she had come here for, finally let herself go.

* * *

Mason had her on her back, on the ground that bore the prints of the silver wolf's pack, before he realized it. Before Faith had.

He didn't let her up for a breath, devouring her with his mouth in the same way he had so often devoured her with his eyes.

Her mouth was an inferno, a slick, steamy delight. In it, Mason at last found the heat he had always craved.

She kissed him back with the greediness of a lover long kept from her mate, and as if she would have this, have all of him, or die trying. Her ripe, lush mouth, and the way her eyes had dilated to their feral green-black, told him so. Moonlight danced across her face with a fierce silver-red glow.

He had never been this aroused, never this attuned to another being. Their unique relationship pounded at them both, opening them to each other in ways no other lovers could hope to experience. His hands, beneath her silky backside, slipped over her curves to briefly rest in the hollow of her back—a place so softly erotic—while his mind probed the recesses of her mind. And though she was no longer quite so vulnerable outwardly, and now strong in her own right, she acknowledged each touch, each move, both physical and mental, with a separate shiver of pleasure that tore through him, as well.

In return for these small pleasures, she took him down...past the place of no return, knowing all there was to know about him from the whispered conversations they'd shared since last meeting face-to-face. He had told her everything, and she didn't care. They were souls in flux, finding purchase at last and digging in, needing nothing else now beyond this merging.

He wanted this. She wanted this. It was to be a healing event for themselves and a consecration of the place where Faith's blood had once been shed in the name of all that was unholy.

So be it.

She tore at his shirt with both of her hands, desperate for skin. His thirst raging, he helped her with his clothes, keeping his lips fastened to hers and their tongues dancing. When he raised himself to get at his pants, she sat up, raking his legs with her nails, scoring possessive rows of marks on his chest and his back as he lowered himself between her open thighs…where awaited a piece of the heaven he thought he'd never reach.

He entered her magnificent heat with a single thrust, unable, in spite of his unworldly powers, to hold off any longer or keep himself back. He could do this. He wasn't going to bite. He hoped she wouldn't.

She cried out just once, releasing the rumbling growls that had been building up in her chest, closing her eyes, wrapping her sleek legs around him.

She met his second thrust, lifting her hips, opening herself further, urging him on with her hands clutching his buttocks. With his third plunge, her moisture rushed to meet him, hotter than anything he could imagine and providing smooth access to the very core of Faith James, the abomination of his dreams.

He now would reach her soul, meet it, hold it in his hands.

He was so very hungry for her, his hunger could barely be appeased.

A rhythm built up between them, with him between her legs, and she open to him fully. It was an exquisite sexual give and take that proved neither of them victor. Hell, even he wanted to howl as they drove their fury for each other together, their bodies and thoughts colliding over and over again as he went insatiably deeper and all the way past any remaining defenses she might have locked away.

And then, the storm building inside him circled upward to meet and engulf hers. A final thrust into that raging storm brought the rising crescendo to a plane where the merging of pain and pleasure transformed into something new...like Faith, herself. An altogether new sensation. An altogether new place, where two beings could meet and savage each other in the name of love in a merging the likes of which might have never before been seen or felt on God's green earth.

Mason allowed Faith no leeway for a breath in this act of taking. This union had been a long time in the making. A couple of lifetimes, in fact. And it had been, Mason thought, well worth the wait.

The light of their mutual climax was blinding in intensity. The moment glowed whiter than the moon, and more like the sun. But in reaching it, suddenly, there it was. *She* was. At last. Part woman. Part animal. Part vampire, from a single droplet of immortal blood.

Faith's howl as she reached the pinnacle of her orgasm was as unique and as extraordinarily beautiful as she. The final motion of their hips and lips meeting rocked them on and on...beneath the searching light of the Blood Moon, in a darkness that finally enclosed them in its soft black fist.

And Mason knew in his bones, and by the magic of the Holy Grail buried in this very spot beneath where they lay panting, that he and his lover would fight the good fight together, uniting their forces for the protection of the Weres and upholding the vow of the Seven.

The dark magic of the Grail, which he had long despised, had in the end helped to resurrect not only a lost soul but a brighter future for this Blood Knight.

Who could have imagined such a thing was possible?

An answering howl went up in the distance, echoing Faith's wolfish shout. Two more howls came from somewhere near the clearing. Looking up at the moon, Faith smiled, then laughed with a freeing sound. She grazed his cheek with her sharp teeth and urged him to laugh along.

Mason held her by the shoulders, reading her thoughts plainly as he eyed her swollen mouth. "I didn't tell you about that. Everything else, but that. You can't bite."

"That's what comes from creating a hybrid. And from gifting blood before you know the facts," she said playfully, with only a hint of seriousness backing her tone. "I know your weakness, and how to pull the plug on your long lifetime. You think one bite from a female can do it, and both sides of me have teeth. For all you know, I could do it right now."

"Then you hold the advantage," he said.

"Not so," she argued, rolling on top of him to straddle the stiffening sign of his ongoing and unabated desire for her, sliding herself down on top of his erection. "Trust me, Blood Knight. You will always have that."

And she proved to him this was true several times over…in every way physically possible, as the calls of the werewolves encircled them with a symphony of sound.

* * * * *

COMING NEXT MONTH from Harlequin Nocturne®
AVAILABLE JUNE 19, 2012

#139 VACATION WITH A VAMPIRE
Michele Hauf, Kendra Leigh Castle, Lisa Childs

Summer nights just get a whole lot steamier...and sexy...
when vampires come out to play. Don't miss this
scintillating collection of stories from Michele Hauf,
Kendra Leigh Castle and Lisa Childs.

#140 DRAGON'S CURSE
Denise Lynn

More than just the dragon lord's twin brother,
Cameron Drake is a dragon. A beast that is almost
impossible to restrain when it falls in love with his enemy...

HNCNM0612

REQUEST YOUR FREE BOOKS!

2 FREE NOVELS FROM THE PARANORMAL ROMANCE COLLECTION PLUS 2 FREE GIFTS!

YES! Please send me 2 FREE novels from the Paranormal Romance Collection and my 2 FREE gifts (gifts are worth about $10). After receiving them, if I don't wish to receive any more books, I can return the shipping statement marked "cancel." If I don't cancel, I will receive 4 brand-new novels every month and be billed just $21.42 in the U.S. or $23.46 in Canada. That's a saving of at least 21% off the cover price of all 4 books. It's quite a bargain! Shipping and handling is just 50¢ per book in the U.S. and 75¢ per book in Canada.* I understand that accepting the 2 free books and gifts places me under no obligation to buy anything. I can always return a shipment and cancel at any time. Even if I never buy another book, the two free books and gifts are mine to keep forever.

237/337 HDN FEL2

Name	(PLEASE PRINT)	

Address		Apt. #

City	State/Prov.	Zip/Postal Code

Signature (if under 18, a parent or guardian must sign)

Mail to the **Reader Service:**
IN U.S.A.: P.O. Box 1867, Buffalo, NY 14240-1867
IN CANADA: P.O. Box 609, Fort Erie, Ontario L2A 5X3

Not valid for current subscribers to the Paranormal Romance Collection or Harlequin® Nocturne™ books.

Want to try two free books from another line?
Call 1-800-873-8635 or visit www.ReaderService.com.

* Terms and prices subject to change without notice. Prices do not include applicable taxes. Sales tax applicable in N.Y. Canadian residents will be charged applicable taxes. Offer not valid in Quebec. This offer is limited to one order per household. All orders subject to credit approval. Credit or debit balances in a customer's account(s) may be offset by any other outstanding balance owed by or to the customer. Please allow 4 to 6 weeks for delivery. Offer available while quantities last.

Your Privacy—The Reader Service is committed to protecting your privacy. Our Privacy Policy is available online at www.ReaderService.com or upon request from the Reader Service.

We make a portion of our mailing list available to reputable third parties that offer products we believe may interest you. If you prefer that we not exchange your name with third parties, or if you wish to clarify or modify your communication preferences, please visit us at www.ReaderService.com/consumerschoice or write to us at Reader Service Preference Service, P.O. Box 9062, Buffalo, NY 14269. Include your complete name and address.

*Harlequin Intrigue® presents a new installment
in* USA TODAY *bestselling author
Delores Fossen's miniseries*
THE LAWMEN OF SILVER CREEK RANCH.

Enjoy a sneak peek at KADE.

Kade saw it then. The clear bassinet on rollers, the kind
they used in the hospital nursery.

He walked closer and looked inside. There was a baby,
and it was likely a girl, since there was a pink blanket snug-
gled around her. There was also a little pink stretchy cap on
her head. She was asleep, but her mouth was puckered as if
sucking a bottle.

"What does the baby have to do with this?" Kade asked.

"Everything. Two days ago someone abandoned her in the
E.R. waiting room," the doctor explained. "The person left
her in an infant carrier next to one of the chairs. We don't
know who did that, because we don't have security cameras."

Kade was finally able to release the breath he'd been
holding. So this was job related. They'd called him in because he was an FBI agent.

But he immediately rethought that.

"An abandoned baby isn't a federal case," Kade clarified,
though Grayson already knew that. Kade reached down and
brushed his index finger over a tiny dark curl that peeked
out from beneath the cap. "You think she was kidnapped or
something?"

When neither the doctor nor Grayson answered, Kade
looked back at them. The anger began to boil through him.
"Did someone hurt her?"

"No," the doctor quickly answered. "There wasn't a
scratch on her. She's perfectly healthy as far as I can tell."

The anger went as quickly as it had come. Kade had handled the worst of cases, but the one thing he couldn't stomach was anyone harming a child.

"I called Grayson as soon as she was found," the doctor went on. "There were no Amber Alerts, no reports of missing newborns. There wasn't a note in her carrier, only a bottle that had no prints, no fibers or anything else to distinguish it."

Kade lifted his hands palms up. "That's a lot of no's. What do you know about her?" Because he was sure this was leading somewhere.

Dr. Mickelson glanced at the baby. "We know she's about three or four days old, which means she was abandoned either the day she was born or shortly after. She's slightly underweight, barely five pounds, but there was no hospital bracelet. We had no other way to identify her, so we ran a DNA test." His explanation stopped cold, and his attention came back to Kade.

So did Grayson's. "Kade, she's yours."

How does Kade react when he finds out the baby is his?

Find out in KADE.
Available this July wherever books are sold.

Harlequin®

n**o**cturne™

Take a bite out of summer!

Enjoy three tantalizing tales from
Harlequin® Nocturne™ fan-favorite authors

MICHELE HAUF,
Kendra Leigh Castle
and Lisa Childs

VACATION
WITH A VAMPIRE

Available July 2012!
Wherever books are sold.

Harlequin
Super Romance

Debut author

Kathy Altman

takes you on a moving journey
of forgiveness and second chances.

One year after losing her husband in Afghanistan,
Parker Dean finds Corporal Reid Macfarland at her
door with a heartfelt confession and a promise to save
her family business. Although Reid is the last person
Parker should trust her livelihood to, she finds herself
captivated by his silent courage. Together,
can they learn to forgive and love again?

The Other Soldier

Available July 2012 wherever books are sold.

This summer, celebrate everything Western
with Harlequin® Books!

www.Harlequin.com/Western

HSR71790